To C
My brother in Christ

A SUMMER REMEMBERED

The Lake Bradford Hotel 1947

Grace and Peace to
you this Good Friday '12

Bob Libby

BOB LIBBY

Copyright © 2011 Bob Libby
All rights reserved.

ISBN: 1461194237
ISBN-13: 9781461194231

Printed by CreateSpace
Any resemblance of characters in this book to persons living or dead is purely coincidental.

ACKNOWLEDGMENTS

I have noticed, when watching the Academy Awards, that the bedazzled recipient of an Oscar is often ushered off the stage while still reciting the names of coworkers, friends, fellow writers, parents, agents, directors, and whomever. For a writer to have a book published in today's market is in itself akin to Oscar night. While this is my fourth book, it is my first work of fiction, and there are literally dozens of good folks who have contributed to the final manuscript.

It turns out that my old friend John Ratti, who mentored me through my nonfiction works, attended Middlebury College and could check me out on the local flora and fauna, not to mention the nightlife at the local tavern. Gini Habeeb, former editor of *American Home* magazine and author of many cookbooks, advised me on recipes and matters of food preparation. Dr. Gordon Hubbell, a veterinarian and a nationally recognized expert on sharks and also an expert on the piano keyboard, researched the archives to make sure that my characters weren't singing songs in 1947 that didn't appear on the scene until the '50s. Sylvia Bennett, a professional singer, also advised me in the area of popular music.

And then there are my old friends Dr. Owene and Cmdr. Larry Weber. Owene, head of the English department at St. John's Country Day School, Orange Park, Florida, and Flagler College, St. Augustine, Florida, gave me invaluable literary criticism. Larry Weber, a retired navy pilot, did research on the prisoner of war camp at Camp Blanding, Florida. Anne Owens, owner of the *Islander News* on Key Biscayne, helped with final proofing. For railroad information, I am indebted to my old friend and train buff, Bill Fellows, who discovered an old Rutland timetable in the back of his garage. And then there was my friend Rabbi Howard Greenstein, spiritual leader of the Jewish congregation on Marco Island, Florida, and Rabbi Emeritus of Congregation Ahavath Chesed of Jacksonville. Howard, a published author in his own right, was my cohost for many years on *Viewpoint—the God Squad,* which aired on Jacksonville's Post Newsweek TV station. Then there was Sally Arteseros, book doctor extraordinary. Last but not least, in the final editing and proofing process, was my son, Robert Andrew Libby, an actor and producer in Hollywood. Who knows, the book and Andrew may end up on Broadway.

So the list grows, and there is my wife, Lynne, a professional artist, who not only encouraged me to try my hand at a novel but tolerated my getting up at 4:30 a.m. to work on it.

⁂ ⁂ ⁂

It was the summer of 1947. The war had been over for almost two years, and the shift from war to a peacetime economy had begun. New car models were pouring off the assembly lines in Detroit and South Bend. Housing developments were appearing where potatoes once had grown. You could buy a new house for less than six thousand dollars, and the minimum-wage was seventy-five cents an hour. Princess Elizabeth was betrothed to Prince Philip of Greece. Jackie Robinson broke the color barrier in major league baseball, and conventional wisdom had it that Governor Thomas E. Dewey of New York would soon replace Harry S Truman as President of the United States.

Returning GIs, later labeled the "Greatest Generation," flooded college and university campuses and the job market, not to mention receiving priority treatment from the ladies.

In the shadow of the returning veterans, their younger brothers were coming of age. Such was the case of Cooper Dawkins, who at Sixteen headed for a summer job, seeking to escape from a broken home and find a new identity as an adult male.

⁂ ⁂ ⁂

CHAPTER ONE
GRAND CENTRAL STATION

If Cooper Dawkins's parents weren't going to be living together, then Cooper figured he wasn't going to be a kid anymore.

In the spring of 1947, as Cooper finished his junior year at Manhasset High School on Long Island, he had two goals for the summer: one was to get away from home, as far away as possible—and as soon as possible; the other was to become a man, although he wasn't quite sure just what that meant.

It was the third Monday in June, and Cooper and his dad were in his father's new car, a Chrysler Town & Country, heading for New York City. As they entered the four-lane Northern State Parkway, Cooper looked at his watch.

"What time does your train leave?" queried Frank Dawkins.

Cooper didn't look at his father. "Nine twenty-nine."

"No problem. We'll be at Grand Central in plenty of time."

Getting to the station on time wasn't the concern that kept Cooper Dawkins glancing at his watch. He was counting the minutes until he was alone, apart, separated from his father and his mother, and on his own. Then he would be free. Free! Cooper busied himself with checking the contents of his sports coat. His wallet was there on the inside right. His ticket and a timetable, along with a comb, were on the left. He had five one-dollar bills and some change in his pants pocket. There was his "little black book" in his right hip pocket. Then he felt something on the right-hand side of his jacket. What was it? He pulled out an envelope, recognized his mother's handwriting, and quickly slipped it back before his father could see it.

Cooper heard his father say something about how crowded the parkway was getting, now that people were commuting into Manhattan by car, but Cooper didn't respond. Instead, he concentrated on looking out the window at the evergreens, weeping willows, and maple trees with their leaves bathed in the yellowish glow of the early morning sunlight. He rubbed the smooth leather surface of the car's upholstery and savored the new-car smell of his father's first postwar luxury automobile.

They continued in silence until they approached La Guardia Airport. A plane was taking off, and Cooper's father spoke again. "That's a DC-3 that just flew overhead. Did you see it take off?" Cooper said nothing, but Frank Dawkins continued. "During the war it was called a C-47. They flew them all over the world. It was known as the 'workhorse of the war.' Some folks believe that without the C-47, we wouldn't have won."

Cooper's father, a successful insurance executive, had a strong military background and interest. He had served in both world wars. At age seventeen he had volunteered and served in France under Douglas MacArthur's Rainbow Division. Cooper wondered if his dad's enlistment was all patriotism or an acceptable excuse to get away from home.

Cooper still didn't respond; he only thought *Oh, God, this is so boring.* He hadn't wanted to drive into the city with his father, but Frank Dawkins had insisted. His parents had separated in April. Soon after that the moving vans arrived and had taken his and his mother's stuff over to his grandfather's old place, where his mother had grown up. It was less than a mile away on Plandome Road. His sisters were off at school when it happened, so they weren't around for the move. He never worked so hard in his life.

Frank Dawkins attempted to engage his son. "That DC-3 will be in Chicago by lunchtime." But again Cooper didn't answer. *I'll be in Vermont for supper*, thought Cooper, as he tracked the take-off pattern of the plane.

Frank Dawkins changed the subject. "How are things going at your grandfather's?"

Cooper shrugged his shoulders and replied, "OK, I guess." But it wasn't OK. He missed his old room with the view of Manhasset Bay. He missed hanging out with his friends that he'd known since kindergarten days. Sure, he could get on his bike and be back in the old neighborhood in ten minutes, but it wasn't the same. It wasn't his neighborhood anymore.

"Your grandfather's home is a grand old place. It was one of the first ones built in Manhasset." Cooper said nothing, so Frank Dawkins continued. "You know, when your mother and I were first married, we lived up on the third floor."

Cooper's new room at his grandfather's was on the third floor, and he wondered if that was the room his father was talking about. His father's reference to the days of being "first married" brought back to Cooper what was now going on between his parents?

He shifted in his seat from right to left and then faced his father, blurting out, "Dad, are you and Mom getting a divorce?"

His father's hands tightened their grip on the steering wheel as he continued to look straight ahead. "Your…your…mother and I," stammered Frank Dawkins, "we haven't been getting along all that well. You've probably noticed that…" He glanced at his son. Cooper was sitting there stone-faced. "Well," Frank continued, "we thought maybe it would be better if we lived apart for a while."

He isn't answering my question, thought Cooper. Shit, he doesn't have the guts to give me a yes or a no. If they just wanted to take a break, why did Mother and I have to move? Why couldn't he have just found some place to stay in the city until he and Mother make up their minds?

Cooper stared at his father, who changed the subject again by exclaiming, "Hey! Over there on the left? That's where the United Airlines DC-4 crashed on Memorial Day weekend. Forty-four people died. There would have been more, but a man with an ax chopped a hole in the fuselage, and they hauled out ten passengers before the flames took over."

Oh, God, thought Cooper, *what a horrible way to die!* He looked at the rubble on the left and looked back at his father, he said nothing.

He consulted his watch again. Only ten minutes had passed. Cooper wondered why his father had insisted on driving him into Grand Central Station if he wasn't going to answer his questions.

Cooper had planned to take the train from Manhasset into New York, but his father had argued over the phone, "The Long Island Railroad will dump you in Pennsylvania Station at Thirty-fourth Street on the west side. Your train for Vermont pulls out of Grand Central, which is at Forty-Second Street on the east side. A cab will cost you at least a dollar, or you'll have to take the Seventh Avenue subway up to Times Square and then get the shuttle over to Grand Central." His father had an answer for everything.

"Dad, I know that," Cooper had said. "First of all, I bought my ticket from Manhasset through to Vermont. Then I checked all my big things through to Middlebury. I only have to carry a small suitcase. I can get off the Long Island Railroad at Woodside, go up the stairs, and catch the IRT-Flushing Line to Grand Central. Really, Dad, it's a very simple operation. I can handle it."

Cooper was about to end the conversation by slamming down the receiver, when his grandfather omterceeded. "Let your father take you into the city. He hasn't seen you for over a month. He's not asking that much. It will make him feel good."

Jesus, Cooper had thought, how come all of a sudden, I'm responsible for my parents' feelings?

They were well into Jackson Heights when Cooper's father said, "What do you think of my new car? It was the first Town & Country in the agency." Cooper looked over at his dad but said nothing. As far as Cooper was concerned, if his father couldn't—or wouldn't—answer his question about a divorce, then what was there to talk about?

The mention of the new Chrysler brought back memories of his dad's old 42 Hudson. Cooper remembered the morning his father brought the Hudson home all beaten up. Major Dawkins had command of the military police for Manhattan Island and had led a column into Harlem to squelch a festering riot during the hot summer of 1943. The venture was successful. The crowds were disbursed. There was no loss of life. But the Hudson looked like it had been hammered with a baseball bat. Major Dawkins received letters of commendation from President

Roosevelt, Governor Dewey and Mayor LaGuardia and was promoted to colonel.

They were on the Triborough Bridge and Frank Dawkins made one more attempt to communicate with his son and pointed down at the Hellspoint Bridge where the East River and Long Island Sound clashed in frenzy. "Remember when we tried to sail from Long Island Sound into the East River and got caught in the riptide and had to be rescued by the Coast Guard?"

Cooper looked over at his father and rolled his eyes. *Tonight,* he thought again, *I'll be in Vermont and away from all this remembering.* To be more specific, he would be part of the Lake Bradford Hotel staff, working in the kitchen. His history teacher, Dr. Martin, spent his summers as assistant manager at the hotel and had gotten Cooper the job. "Most of the summer staff will be college kids," Dr. Martin had advised, "but if you work hard and don't shoot off your mouth too much, you should have a great summer."

They entered Manhattan and headed south on the Eastside Highway. They exited at Fifty-ninth Street and headed down Lexington Avenue. As they approached Forty-Second Street, Frank said, "Help me find a parking place."

"Dad, just let me off at the next corner," Cooper insisted. "That'll be fine. You'll never find a place to park at this time of day." When the light turned red and his father pulled to a stop, Cooper opened the car door and reached into the backseat for his small suitcase. Before he could jump from the car, Frank reached out to his son and stuffed a twenty-dollar bill into the vest pocket of Cooper's jacket.

All Cooper could say was, "Thanks, Dad." He closed the door as the light turned green, took a deep breath, and waved goodbye to the father he didn't know anymore. As his father headed downtown, Cooper realized that he was now on his own. He smiled and battled his way through a parade of commuters as he headed for the information booth at the center of Grand Central Station.

"Your train will be loading on track eleven in about an hour. You change at Albany for the Rutland train, which will take you on to Middlebury."

Cooper checked out the location of track eleven and then headed for Walgreens Drugstore. He picked up a *New York Times* and a *Daily News*, went up to the clerk, and placed the twenty-dollar bill he had received from his father on the counter. Cooper stated as matter-of-factly as he could, "A pack of Chesterfields and a box of Trojans…please." The cashier brought him the cigarettes and then announced to Cooper—and everybody in the store, "You'll have to get the rubbers from the pharmacist at the back of the store. By the way, don't you have anything smaller than a twenty?"

Cooper took back the twenty, dug into his pants pocket, and found two quarters. He placed them on the counter and took his change. He stepped down a side aisle, buried his crimson face in the *Times*, and waited until the few customers who had overheard his transaction cleared out before he approached the pharmacist.

While he waited, he remembered the Saturday his father had taken him to his headquarters on Pier 90 when the *Queen Elizabeth* was in port. His father gave him the grand tour, and when they were about to leave they were caught up in an unscheduled appearance of an army doctor and several male assistants from the Surgeon General's office on Governors Island.

The doctor announced that there would be a "short arm" inspection of all the troops before they could go on liberty. This involved lining up the soldiers and telling them to drop their trousers and underwear. One of the aides took notes, while the other handed out small envelopes. Cooper's father had not anticipated this interruption, but as CO he was required to be there. He asked the doctor if he could be excused because of his son's presence, but the doctor objected. "The kid's got to learn about this sometime. Now's as good a time as any." So Cooper Dawkins stood at his father's side through the whole procedure, worrying that the doctor would want to look at him or his father after he had examined all of the men. At one point Cooper's father tried to break the silence by quipping, "Well, as you can see, all men aren't created equal." At age twelve Cooper missed his father's attempt at humor. He had no idea what his father was talking about.

On the way back home, Cooper and his father had the only talk about sex that Cooper could remember.

"Dad, what was that doctor doing?"

"Checking for VD."

"What's VD?"

"Venereal disease."

"What's venereal disease?"

"It's something really serious. It can make you blind, rot your brain, and make you insane."

"Then why was the doctor looking at their...looking at their...their peters?"

"That's because a man can get it from sex."

"What was the doctor's helper giving the men?"

"He was handing out prophylactics."

"What's a pro...pro-fill...elastic?"

"It's a rubber."

"Oh!"

Finally, when Walgreen's was almost empty, Cooper approached the bearded gentleman in the white jacket behind the prescription counter, took a deep breath, and stated his request. The pharmacist smirked as he asked, "Do you want a dozen, a half-pack, or a single?" Cooper thought a minute and then asked for the half-pack. He handed the druggist the twenty-dollar bill. "You wouldn't have something smaller, would you, son?" Cooper shook his head no, slipped the package in his pocket, and picked up his change.

Beads of perspiration were on his forehead as he headed for the door. *Boy*, he thought, *I'd rather stay a virgin than go through all that again.*

CHAPTER TWO
THE TRAIN RIDE

Cooper found his way to the club car and settled down with the papers. He carefully turned to page four of the Daily News. It almost always had at least one photograph of a babe in a bathing suit on page four. He wasn't disappointed. Three beauties—two blondes and a brunette—were posing in front of a Jones Beach concession stand, licking ice cream cones. The caption under the picture read "Beating the heat on the beach." One girl was in a two-piece bathing suit, and they all had nice legs and big boobs.

Laying aside the *News*, he scanned the *Times*. There was something about President Truman making a state visit to Canada. Cooper had been to Canada with his family in the summer of '41. The one thing he remembered was how cold the water was, and he wondered whether the lake in Vermont would be that cold.

Sugar rationing had finally ended, and Cooper wondered if that would mean more Hershey bars. Then he recalled that his doctor had told him to stay away from chocolate unless he wanted to go through life covered with pimples.

The daylight almost blinded Cooper as the train climbed out of the tunnel under Park Avenue and slid into the 125th Street Station. He looked down at the main street of Harlem and mused, "So this is the site of Dad's great World War II triumph!" *That's where it all began*, thought Cooper. After his father's promotion to colonel, things changed at home. First, there were the pictures in the newspapers and then invitations to important parties on Governors Island, Mitchel Field, and the Kings Point Merchant Marine Academy. Initially, Cooper's mother went with his father, but that didn't last too long, and Colonel Dawkins was more absent than present at home. There were always "important meetings" that kept him tied up in the city.

Then Cooper reached in his pocket for his mother's letter. He was about to open it when he noticed a shapely pair of young legs across the aisle. The upper torso of the owner was covered by the front and back pages of the *Times*. When she turned a page, Cooper held his breath. Was she Veronica Lake, or did she just look like Veronica Lake? Cooper put the envelope back in his pocket and picked up the *Times* again. He tried to look cool as he watched the lock of blonde hair flop over the girl's right eye. Her other eye looked right at him, and he ducked behind the newspaper. The United Jewish Appeal had taken a full page ad, asking for funds to resettle Jewish refugees. They expected $65 million from the New York area Jews. Cooper didn't know many Jews. The only ones he did know were the children of the merchants who lived over their stores near the railroad station. He didn't think that there were enough Jews to come up with $65 million, but then, he'd heard that most Jews lived in the Bronx, although he'd heard his father say that a lot were moving into Great Neck. There was also a full-page ad featuring a picture of Charles Boyer saying, "Chesterfields' mild, cool flavor gives me complete smoking pleasure."

This prompted Cooper to take out his own pack of Chesterfields. He fumbled around in his pockets, looking for his matches, and pulled out the letter from his mother. He lit his cigarette and was about to open the envelope when he looked across the aisle again. The Veronica Lake look-alike turned a page and brushed her hair back with her hand. She was wearing a dark skirt and a white blouse that covered two exquisite breasts encased in a brassiere that made them resemble the nose cone on the new Studebaker. No wonder all his friends called the Studebaker a sexy car!

He smiled and then went back to the *Times*, where he found the ad for the Lake Bradford Hotel, "with direct rail service to New York and Boston in the heart of Vermont's Green Mountains." Weekly rates started at forty-three dollars for a single and seventy-three dollars for a double, including meals. It boasted frontage on a ten-mile lake, with a family atmosphere and fishing, sailing, canoeing, swimming, tennis, hiking, and dancing and a golf course nearby. It sounded like a real bargain compared with hotels on Lake Placid, which started at ten dollars a day per person. But then Lake Bradford wasn't Lake Placid.

The movie page had a smorgasbord of entertainment possibilities. He skimmed it for the names of movie stars and found Perry Como, Angela Lansbury, Lawrence Olivier, Johnny Weissmuller, Ingrid Bergman, and Dana Andrews, but no Veronica Lake. He glanced over his paper to see if her look-alike was still in her seat and indeed, there she was.

As Cooper turned to the sports section, Veronica Lake caught him staring. She smiled, and Cooper smiled back and then hid behind the *Times*. Cooper's team, the Brooklyn Dodgers, had lost to Cincinnati, in spite of the fact that Jackie Robinson had his "greatest day at bat since he joined the Dodgers." He batted 1000 for the day, with a triple, a double, and two singles.

The club-car waiter came by and asked for Cooper's order. Cooper thought seriously about ordering a beer or a rum and Coke. The legal drinking age in New York State was eighteen, and even though he was sixteen, he had no trouble passing that test. Nonetheless, he thought better of it and settled for a Coke with a twist of lemon. When the waiter returned, Cooper lit up a Chesterfield and tried to focus on the Hudson River Valley that was rushing by behind Veronica Lake. It was a losing battle. As his thoughts kept returning to her long blonde hair, his head began to spin. He imagined going back with her to one of the private compartments, where the two of them would gently undress and caress each other. This was embarrassing. He tried to break the spell by turning to the crossword puzzle, placing the folded paper on his lap. He looked across the aisle where Veronica had positioned the *Times* on the cocktail table and was attacking the puzzle with one of those new ballpoint pens. *She must be really good*, he thought. He would never dare use a pen on the puzzle. Their eyes met, and Veronica broke the silence. "Are you doing what I think you're doing?"

Cooper blushed.

Veronica laughed. "No, I mean, are you trying to work the crossword puzzle?"

Cooper, still a bright pink, nodded his head.

"Well, then, what's a four-letter word"—she paused—"for National Socialist?"

"Oh, that's easy. It's Nazi. I just did that one."

They called words back and forth to each other until the conductor announced, "Albany, Albany. Change here for the Vermont Special to Rutland, Middlebury, and Burlington."

Cooper followed his dream girl off the train. He offered to carry her suitcase, but she insisted, "I'm a big girl, and I can take care of myself."

They walked across the platform together, and he heard the vendor cry out, "Sandwiches, ice cream, soda pop, candy bars, and cigarettes! No dining car or club car service on the Vermont Special."

Cooper blurted, "Sounds like there's nothing special about the Vermont Special."

"You can say that again," retorted Veronica, and as they stopped to buy their lunch, she was standing less than a foot away from him. She was what his sisters called "petite" and probably weighed no more than a hundred pounds. He was a full head taller and imagined that he could rest his chin on the top of her blonde head.

"Are you going to Vermont, too?" he asked.

"All the way to Middlebury."

"Wow! This is incredible...and...and ... we were sitting across from each other all morning, doing the *Times* crossword puzzle in the club car, and we're both going to Middlebury. Are you going to summer school at the college, or what?"

"I'm a student at Sarah Lawrence. No, I'm taking a break from the books. I'm going to work as a waitress at the Lake Bradford Hotel. Have you ever heard of it?"

"Wow! That's where I'm going. This really is a coincidence. What a small world. What a small world." And then he thought *what a piece of luck! This is really going to be a great summer.*

When they boarded the Vermont Special, they placed their small suitcases next to each other on the overhead rack and slipped into a seat on the right-hand side of the car. They ate their sandwiches and shared their histories, oblivious to the sounds and smells of the old steam train. When they pulled into the Rutland terminal, the train from Boston was standing across the platform. A handsome young couple wearing sweaters that declared Harvard and Radcliff as their schools of choice were among the dozen or so passengers who boarded the train.

"I'll bet they're heading for a summer at Lake Bradford. What do you think?" said Cooper.

"We'll find out when we pull into Middlebury."

The train chugged along a stream bordered by acres of grazing cows. The passenger car was suddenly plunged into semi-darkness as the train entered a deep cut in the bedrock of a hill before sliding into the Middlebury station. By the time it came to a complete stop, Cooper had discovered that his traveling companion was Madeleine Stillwell, from Montclair, New Jersey, but that her friends at Sarah Lawrence had nicknamed her "Ronnie," which was short for Veronica, because she reminded everybody of the movie star. She preferred Lucky Strikes to Camels or Chesterfields. In addition its being a break from her studies, she had signed on at Lake Bradford to earn a little money for clothes in the fall. She also confessed that she had taken the job because she wanted to get away from her parents, who were fighting all the time.

"Do you think they will get a divorce?" asked Cooper.

"I certainly hope so," stated Ronnie. "At least we'd have some peace and quiet around the house. What about your parents?"

"Oh, they don't fight. But they don't live together anymore." Cooper went on to explain about the move to his grandfather's house.

"Are they getting a divorce?" asked Ronnie.

"I hope not, but it certainly looks that way," said Cooper. "No one will tell me anything."

By the time the train pulled into the station, they'd discovered a lot about each other.

They shared a love for swimming, sailing, bridge, and crossword puzzles. They both liked Winston Churchill and Frank Sinatra and admitted to being Episcopalians. But Cooper didn't want to admit his age or have anyone know that he was still in high school. He allowed that he was heading for a career in architecture via the University of Michigan.

The Middlebury station reminded Cooper of a dozen similar depots on Long Island that had been built before the turn of the century. Its walls were painted a yellowish-cream color, and it was trimmed in brown and dark green. Its massive roof overhung the platform by a good twelve feet, giving shelter to the oak benches that lined the outer walls of the stationhouse. The roof was topped with what looked like a small cottage, which served as the stationmaster's quarters.

There was a real station wagon waiting at the Middlebury platform. Quite unlike his father's Town & Country, it was an eight-passenger paneled box, mounted on a 1939 Ford chassis. The side panels had been freshly varnished, and new lettering proclaimed "Lake Bradford Hotel." In charge of this was a dapper young man with blue eyes and wavy brown hair that was combed straight back and glistened with Brylcreem. He wore white flannel trousers, two-tone saddle oxfords, a blue blazer with a Lake Bradford Hotel crest on his breast pocket, and a tie that revealed his Yale connection. He reached out his hand to Ronnie. "Hi, I'm Standish...er...Stan Phillips. I'm sort of in charge of the staff this summer." After Ronnie introduced herself, Stan turned to Cooper. "You must be Cooper Dawkins, Dr. Martin's student from Manhasset High School."

Oh, shit! thought Cooper. *So much for the University of Michigan.* Ronnie glanced at Cooper as he nodded to Stan, and then she moved one step closer to Stan. They were soon joined by two basketball types from Seton Hall. It said so on their jackets. Cooper's instincts had been right. The couple from Harvard and Radcliff did join the group. The last to arrive was a short, plump girl who wore her long, dark, reddish hair in a ponytail. She was clutching a large suitcase and dragging a duffel bag. "Hi, I'm Rosalind Morris. Everybody calls me Rosie. I'm from the Bronx, and I'm Jewish."

There was a sudden silence that Stan broke with an announcement. "Well, it looks like everybody's here who's supposed to be here. We have a full wagon, and we'll be off to the hotel as soon as we tie down all of this luggage." This took a bit of maneuvering, as a summer's supply of clothing for seven young adults was something of a bundle. With all of the equipment piled high on the roof of the Ford and then tied down with a spider web of rope, and with the eight passengers piled inside, Cooper thought the old wagon must look like a scene from the *Grapes of Wrath*. It listed to starboard as it crept away from the depot and wound its way past a series of red brick factories, which a sign said specialized in marble products. They then entered the lower reaches of the village green, which was dominated by the stately First Congregational Church. Its tall, white clock tower stood at the high end of the green and presided over the life of the community. There was also a stone Episcopal church on the green and a Methodist sanctuary on the southern edge. The Middlebury Inn shared the high ground with the Congregational church and was flanked by an elaborate Civil War memorial. When the wagon finally managed to creep through the commons in first gear, it passed a row of old houses that looked as though they had been there for a century or two. Eventually, they reached the open road of Route 7 and could see the gray outline of the Adirondack Mountains to the west and the more clearly defined Green Mountains on the eastern horizon. Stan shifted into third gear and actually reached a speed of twenty-five miles an hour. Cooper looked out the window and saw green fields filled with grazing cows, which gave the fresh air a slightly pungent country scent. This definitely wasn't New York or even eastern Long Island, for that matter.

The wagon came upon a small white roadside store and a sign that announced "Bradford Farms, dairy products and Vermont white Cheddar cheese our specialty." Behind the store there were barns, silos, and a long white building, where a number of delivery trucks were parked. Just south of the store was a sign pointing east to the Lake Bradford Hotel.

Stan, who the newcomers would soon discover was known at the hotel as the "Blue Bird of Preppie-ness," crept up a constant line of chatter as he navigated his vehicle along the narrow, winding road to Lake Bradford. "We're now on land that's belonged to the Bradford family since right after the American Revolution. Ever hear of the Green Mountain Boys? One of them was a Bradford, and a grateful Continental Congress handed out land grants to just about everyone who survived the war. They returned from the Revolution, cleared the land, built their homes, farmed the land, cut granite out of the hills, and then after the Civil War, they discovered that the people they used to call the 'down landers' liked to come up here in the summer.

"The hotel was built in 1886, and folks came up by train from Boston, Albany, and New York City. It was Ethan Bradford's grandfather who put the thing together. He thought he could compete with Lake Placid and Lake Champlain, but he never did. Some people call us the poor man's Lake Champlain. I don't think that's fair. It's a good family place, with lots to do if you like the outdoors. We even have a few great-grandchildren of the original guests coming up for a big family reunion on the Fourth of July. The hotel will hold about 150 guests, and then there are six family cottages. We're usually full from the Fourth through Labor Day. The war almost put us out of business. The summer of '42 was a disaster, what with gas rationing, food rationing, and good help hard to find. Then the army tried to use it to house their 'Sixty Day Wonder' officer training program. Everyone nearly froze to death, this is a summer hotel. The gas heaters in the rooms barely take away the chill in July, much less heat the place in a Vermont winter."

Cooper thought Stan's speech sounded scripted, like the ones given by tourist guides at the Museum of Natural History. Obviously, he had perfected his presentation and saw it as his responsibility to inform every one of the glories of the Green Mountains in general and the Bradford domain in particular. Stan slowed the wagon as they approached an old covered bridge—Cooper had never actually seen one before. *I really am in Vermont*, he reflected. *I'm not on Long Island anymore.*

"Everybody hold your breath and make a wish," Stan instructed. "There's an old Vermont saying that if you can hold your breath for the length of the covered bridge, you'll get your wish."

Cooper thought he would turn blue as the wagon clank-clanked through the dim light and across the loose boards at what seemed to be a mere five miles an hour. There was a great burst of expelled air and then a collective gasp when the wagon finally broke out into the sunlight.

"Everybody get their wish?" asked Stan. His passengers looked at each other. Some laughed. The Seton Hall boys smirked. Ronnie looked over at Cooper, and Cooper blushed.

The stream they had just crossed eventually made its way into Otter Creek, which divided pasture from forest and Bradford Farms from the territory of the Lake Bradford Hotel. The narrow road began to level out, and the solid green forest on the left side of the wagon was broken with patches of blue water. But Cooper wasn't taking in the scenery as much as he was enjoying being wedged in the seat next to Ronnie. The warmth of her thigh pressed against his leg was beginning to get to him—and to trigger his newly expanding fantasy life.

Cooper came back to reality when Stan announced, "Well, here we are." And there she was—four stories of cream-colored, fading Victorian elegance, with a wrap-around porch trimmed in dark green gingerbread. The wagon crunched over the bluestone pebbled driveway and paused briefly at the covered entrance, which was flanked by two barrels of newly planted red, white, and blue petunias. Like week-old kittens whose eyes had just opened, the tiny blossoms were barely peeking over the edge of the barrel. The front steps led to great oak doors with thick beveled glass, which allowed the arriving guests a view through the entrance hall and out to the lake and the Green Mountains beyond. Stan announced his arrival with three toots on the horn and then drove his passengers around to the south side of the hotel, where they would unload at the kitchen platform.

"You're the last staff to arrive," he told them. "Dr. Martin will give you your room assignments. We're all going to have a meeting at five and then a buffet supper in the main dining room. It's the only time the staff will eat in the dining room. And of course, you know that the guests start arriving in the morning."

Cooper smiled when he saw Dr. Martin, his old history teacher at Manhasset High. Dr. Martin introduced himself to each new staff member and repeated their names several times. It was the same technique he used at Manhasset High. Once he had your name right, he never forgot it. Cooper was the last in line. Whatever he expected by way of a special welcome, he didn't get. As the assistant manager, Dr. Martin was a thorough professional. "Dawkins. Cooper Dawkins. D-a-w-k-i-n-s. From Manhasset, Long Island. Here's your key. You're in room 412. That's on the fourth floor." Dr. Martin paused for a minute, and again Cooper hoped for a note of personal recognition. All he got was a nod and a half-smile. "Welcome to Lake Bradford, Cooper. We have a long summer ahead of us. I hope you're up to it. By the way, the luggage you checked through on your ticket from Manhasset arrived this morning. You'll find it over there behind the kitchen door."

CHAPTER THREE
INTRODUCTIONS

It took Cooper three trips to the fourth floor to get all of his luggage up to his room. It reminded him of the day he had moved all his things into Grandfather Goetz's house. His mother, in an effort to save money, had hired the services of a local truck farmer and his son, rather than get a regular moving company. This meant that Cooper had to do all his own packing. For weeks he collected boxes from the local grocery and liquor stores. His sisters came home from school one weekend and packed their stuff in the boxes he had collected, so Cooper had to make the rounds a second time for a second set of cartons. The farmer and his son made three trips with the furniture and placed it all in the proper rooms, but they just stacked the boxes with their possessions on the front and back porch, leaving Cooper the task of sorting them out and carrying them up to the bedrooms on the third floor.

Now, as Cooper stumbled up the back stairs of the Lake Bradford Hotel he recalled that miserable and exhausting day at his grandfather's, and he became more and more convinced that his parents' marriage was over. Why didn't they have the guts to just tell him and be done with it? Then the thought struck him that his parents were in New York, and he was in Vermont. He dropped his last piece of luggage on the floor and collapsed on the bed. "I'm in Vermont, and they're on Long Island!" he repeated over and over again with a smile on his face. "They're not my problem anymore, and I'm not a kid anymore."

Cooper bounced off the bed and started to unpack but got only as far as taking out the Silvertone radio that he had bought with his birthday money just before the war. It was a Sears basic model with four vacuum tubes. He discovered that he could improve its reception if he had a long enough antenna, so he had brought along a spool of bare copper wire, which he attached to the radio on the dresser and then sent it spiraling out his fourth-floor dormer window onto the branches of a nearby maple tree. With a little luck, maybe he would be able to pick up more than just the local stations.

Then he checked his watch and realized that he had just enough time for a shower before going down to the staff meeting. He put his hand in his coat pocket, felt the letter from his mother, took it out, and looked at it for a moment. He wondered what was in it and if he had time to read it. He looked at his watch again, shook his head, and placed the letter, unopened, on the dresser and grabbed a towel.

He could have arrived in the dining room at five on the dot, but he purposely held back ten minutes and took a seat at an empty table over to the side of the massive stone fireplace. This was all part of a strategy he and his friends from high school had adopted in the ninth grade when they went to their first dance at the Knickerbocker Yacht Club in Port Washington. They stayed on the fringe, were as inconspicuous as possible, acted cool, and took mental notes on how the seniors and their dates behaved.

One look around the room, and Cooper knew he was outclassed. Every male was older and in most cases taller than he was. While he had mentally prepared himself for the company of college students, one glance at the assembled group told him that most of the guys were returning veterans, as much as four to six years his senior.

Back at Manhasset High, he and his buddies had come to resent the war heroes who started appearing in their classrooms in the fall of '45. They had money. Even the guys who didn't have jobs had money. They were members of the 52-20 Club: twenty dollars a week for fifty-two weeks, a gift from a grateful nation. They had cars, and they had the girls. It was difficult enough competing with seventeen- and eighteen-year-old males, but the vets had whatever they wanted. A year earlier, Cooper had given his soccer sweater to Debbie Watts, a girl he had known since the third grade. Giving her the sweater had meant they were going steady. For six months they showed up at the sock hops together, and sailed in Manhasset Bay, and rode the train to Flushing, where they would go to the RKO Keith Theater, a high school favorite because of its dimly lighted balcony. Cooper dreamed of the day when he could get his driver's license so he and Debbie could really have a date. But before Cooper passed his driver's test, Debbie had been discovered by a former navy lieutenant with a 1941 Buick convertible.

Tonight, Cooper was wearing brown corduroy trousers, an L. L. Bean black and red lumber shirt, matching socks, and penny loafers. But the uniform of the day appeared to be khaki GI trousers, white socks, sneakers, and a sweatshirt with either a college emblem or a service logo across the chest. For the first time he was grateful for the two pairs of his father's old army slacks, packed at his mother's insistence. He made a mental note to write his uncle in Detroit and ask him to send a University of Michigan sweatshirt.

The girls all looked like cheerleaders with the "new look"— pleated flannel skirts, way below their knees, white socks, penny loafers, and sweaters in an assortment of school colors. Just about everybody lit up a cigarette. Camels seemed to be the favorite. Whoever thought up the line "I'd walk a mile for a Camel" had done a great job. Lucky Strikes were in second place. Some of the girls were going for Kools. Cooper seemed to be the only one smoking a Chesterfield. He made a mental note to switch to Camels.

Ronnie walked into the dining room and did a 360-degree turn, twirling her skirt and hair simultaneously as she checked out the seating arrangements. She smiled at Cooper but chose a chair next to a six-foot-two crew cut with "Property of the US Marines" stenciled on his chest. The Seton Hall boys, Kevin and Danny, nodded to Cooper but started a new table down front. Cooper opened a fresh pack of Chesterfields in a deliberate manner, tapped one on the side of the pack, and proceeded to light up. He used a match and realized that everyone else was using a lighter. He inhaled deeply and started to blow smoke rings. The first one did just fine, but the second went down the wrong way, and he started to cough. It felt like every eye in the room turned to him. Rosalind Morris bounced over, with her ponytail swishing from side to side, handed him a glass of water, and then pulled out the chair next to Cooper. "Is this table reserved, or can anybody sit here?" Cooper stammered a welcome, but she cut

INTRODUCTIONS

him off. "Remember me? I'm Rosie from the Bronx and Columbia. We met this afternoon in the station wagon, or were you too busy ogling Veronica Lake? You know, the one over there talking to the marine."

Rosie's comment reminded Cooper of his losing Debbie to the sailor. He took a gulp of water. It went down the wrong way, and he almost choked on it. Rosie slapped him on the back, and he slumped into his chair.

Dr. Martin entered the dining room with Stan Phillips, the "Blue Bird of Preppiness," They stood before the group. Without a sign or signal the room became quiet. It was the same technique that Dr. Martin used in the classroom back at school. Without raising his voice, he announced, "I'm Dr. Aaron Martin, the assistant manager, and this is Stan Phillips, my associate and chief of staff. Welcome to the Lake Bradford Inn." There was a pause but no applause. "It is now our great honor and privilege to present the owner and general manager, Ethan Bradford the fifth. He is the grandson of the founder and builder of the Lake Bradford Hotel. Let's welcome Mr. Bradford."

Dr. Martin and Stan led a brief round of applause, and an authoritative military voice shouted, "Ten-shun!" Half the room was on its feet before the laughter started. Mr. Bradford, a tall, slender, graying man in a brown tweed suit and a maroon bow tie, walked to the center of the dining room. "At ease…at ease… please take your seats," he said in all seriousness. "No need for formalities." A second round of laughter rippled across the room. Mr. Bradford limited his remarks to a general welcome and concluded with a royal wave and a jolly "Cheer-re-O." I know we're all going to have a pleasant summer and that you will all do splendidly."

It was obvious that Dr. Martin was the man in charge and that Stan and everybody else operated in the shadow of that power. Dr. Martin made it perfectly clear that the girls' dormitory was off limits to the boys, and vice versa. Both sleeping areas were located on the fourth floor, but the connecting hallway was sealed off. "I expect everyone to be professional in his or her relationships with the guests. As they said in the Army of Occupation, there is to be no 'fraternization' with the guests. Girls, watch out for old Mr. Grumbacher. He's a groper and a pincher. Humor him, but don't turn your back on him or go into his room." A buzz of side comments went through the room, and Kevin pinched one of the waitresses. She squealed and jumped out of her seat, and everybody laughed. Dr. Martin didn't crack a smile. The room quieted down, and Dr. Martin continued. "Gentlemen, there are a couple of dowagers on the guest list with whom you'll need to be on guard. You'll know them when they get here." It was now Danny's turn to play it for laughs. "Did you say rich dowagers or just dowagers?"

Dr. Martin just stood there and looked bored. Danny slouched into his chair. Then Stan took over. He read a long list of dos and don'ts and then had everybody stand up and introduce themselves. Cooper discovered that his legs were cramping, and he wondered if they would go totally wobbly when it was his turn to stand up. He put his hand on the table's edge to steady himself and said, "I'm Cooper Dawkins from Long Island. I like to swim, sail, play tennis and soccer, and I plan to graduate from the University of Michigan with a degree in architecture." The staff responded with "Hi, Cooper," and he sat down. He thought he had made his relationship to the University of Michigan vague enough to get by, but someone from the other side of the fireplace shouted, "When are you going to Michigan? '50? Or will it be '51?" There was laughter, and Cooper slumped in his chair. With luck, the chimney would collapse on him. Wasn't

INTRODUCTIONS

that the way they buried the dead in the Old Testament? Pile rocks on top of the body and walk away? Cooper looked over at Rosie, and she shrugged her shoulders. Dr. Martin got out of his chair and stood next to Stan. The crowd settled down and the introductions continued. Now it was Rosie's turn. "I'm Rosalind Morris...call me Rosie." And they did. "Hi, Rosie!"

"I'm from the Bronx, and I go to Columbia University. I'm Jewish, and I took piano lessons for six years." Again the gang chanted, "Hi, Rosie!" Then someone called out, "The Catskills are west of the Hudson, not east." Rosie stood her ground. Her maroon ponytail swished as she aimed a finger in the general direction of the voice.

Brief announcements followed. Cooper took note of a tall, lanky, athletic young man with sun bleached hair. "I'm Graham Morgan." The group chanted back, "Hi, Graham", and then he continued. "I'm in charge of the waterfront. If anyone, male or female, boy or girl, man or woman, who knows Red Cross lifesaving, I could use some help in the afternoon. Also, if anyone has had any experience with sailboats, speak to me during or after supper."

"Speaking of supper," interjected Dr. Martin, "it's about time to introduce our featured attraction. We are very fortunate to have a distinguished international chef heading our kitchen staff this summer. Rudolph Hoffman and his lovely wife, Gretchen, come to us from Palm Beach, Florida, where they preside over the kitchen—or should I say 'cuisine'—at the Breakwater Club. Rudy and Gretchen please come up front and take a bow."

There was polite applause as the couple came forward, and then someone began to whistle "Rudolph the Red-Nosed Reindeer." Dr. Martin faced the whistler with his "Oh, why don't you grow up" look, and the tune aborted in mid-stanza.

Cooper almost laughed out loud because Rudolph-the-chef did in fact have a red nose, a very large W. C. Fields-type red nose.

Rudolph and Gretchen presented themselves in crisp, starched white uniforms topped with the high headgear of their profession. Speaking in a thick German accent, he began. "We are very happy to be here and will be offering our guests a great variety of specialties. There is a staff table in the kitchen, and a schedule of staff servings has been posted on the chef's bulletin board. You will also find the staff mailboxes next to the bulletin board. Please check your box and the bulletin board before every meal. Consider anything you see on the board as an order, and do not ask me or Gretchen for an explanation. I do not have the time to explain or repeat things two dozen times for every waitress, busboy or kitchen worker." He paused for effect and then smiled. "But for tonight, we all eat in the dining room like the guests." There was a cheer, and then Rudy continued, "We have prepared lovely smorgasbord, which is laid out on a table in the kitchen. So help yourself and when you have finished, please take your dishes into the kitchen, scrape them clean and place them the wooden racks for the washing machine."

Everyone applauded and headed for the kitchen, where Rudy had prepared a magnificent spread of food, elegantly presented on a great round table. There were cheeses, salads, celery, black olives, relishes, baked potatoes, and corn on the cob, all crowned with an arrangement of fresh fruit. The first stop, however, was at the chef's serving table, where Rudy had prepared three choices of meat: roast beef, ham, or broiled chicken.

Cooper hesitated for a moment before filling his plate and then realized that he was waiting for someone to say grace. He was poised to hear "Bless O Lord this food to our use and us to

Thy service..." But he wasn't at home, nor was he at church camp out in Sayville, Long Island, where he had spent part of the last two summers. It was at Camp DeWolfe that he first heard the news that America had dropped the atomic bomb on Hiroshima. Canon Gillette had taken all the campers into the chapel and explained that (1) the world would never be the same again; (2) the war would probably be over very soon, and (3) we should pray for all of the Japanese people who had lost their lives.

Rosie brought him back to reality. "Are you going to eat, or are you just going to stand there and dream about Veronica Lake?"

Cooper sidestepped the invitation. "You go ahead and get in line. I want to catch Graham Morgan and put my name in the pot for the sailboats." Cooper approached Graham, who was surrounded by a cluster of waitresses. To Cooper's relief, they were all interested in swimming, not sailing. Graham extended a firm hand to Cooper. "Hi, I'm Graham Morgan. Aren't you Dr. Martin's protégé, the high school kid from Long Island?"

Cooper blushed. Once again his plan to pass himself off as a college student was a flop. Nevertheless, he took a deep breath, reached out for Graham's hand, and shot back, "That's me! Or should I say, 'It is I'? I've been around boats all my life and have done a lot of sailing in Manhasset Bay on Long Island. Maybe I can help during my time off in the afternoon."

"How about fresh-water sailing? There is a difference, you know."

"I sailed on a lake north of Boston last summer. The wind shifted a lot. It practically bounced off the hills. It took a little bit of getting used to, but the basics are the same, once you find out which way the wind is blowing."

Graham grinned. "That's true of a lot of things," as he ushered Cooper along as they moved toward the food. "What kind of boats did you sail on Long Island?" Graham asked.

"My first one was a plywood dinghy with a centerboard and a gaff rig. My dad made it for me when I was ten. That was before the war. Then we had a Cape Cod Nimlet. It's a round bottom sixteen-foot Marconi rig with a wide cockpit. It will hold a lot of people. It's more of a family boat than a racer, but before the hurricane in '44, the yacht club had a fleet of twenty-four of them in the bay, and I raced mine every weekend. Last summer I crewed for a friend on his eighteen-foot Lightning. It was a really fast boat. We even sailed it in the regatta up at Larchmont, where Arthur Godfrey was the master of ceremonies at the awards banquet."

Graham told Cooper that he had raced a Lightning the previous summer down on the Cape. By this time they had filled their plates and were seated at a table by the lakefront window, also occupied by the Harvard/Radcliff duo who had boarded the train at Rutland. They appeared to be totally absorbed in each other as they ate quietly, exchanged glances, smiled, and blushed. After two unsuccessful attempts to engage them in conversation, Graham turned back to Cooper. "I've heard Arthur Godfrey on the radio. I kind of like him. Did you get to meet him? What was he like in person?"

That was just the opening Cooper was hoping he'd get, and he related in great detail his encounters with the radio celebrity.

"That's impressive," stated Graham.

Cooper smiled.

The dinner conversation was interrupted by the sound of a fork tapping against a water glass. Stan loudly cleared his throat, saying, "Don't let me interrupt your conversations." Then someone shouted, "But you just did." Stan ignored the wisecrack and

INTRODUCTIONS

continued. "Remember, the guests start arriving in the morning, but for tonight, the lounge is yours. There will be a log burning on the hearth, a phonograph on the table, and a keg out on the porch." This announcement was greeted with loud cheers and applause. Everyone stampeded toward the kitchen with their dirty dishes and then outside in search of the beer.

Stan unpacked the phonograph that United Parcel had delivered the previous day. "It's the new kind," he announced. "It's got two speeds. It can take the new long-playing records that spin at thirty-three and a third revolutions per minute, as well as the standard seventy-eights. Unfortunately, we don't have any new records to play tonight." He was interrupted with a storm of boos and hisses, which he tried to ignore. "We've ordered them. Maybe they'll be here soon. Anyway, we'll start with a slow number, 'To Each His Own' with the Ink Spots."

This was followed by Frank Sinatra singing "Give Me Five Minutes More" and then Perry Como doing "They Say It's Wonderful." Harvard and Radcliff had the dance floor to themselves for about fifteen seconds, and then everyone joined them, except for Cooper, who stood in the shadow of the fireplace to observe, as he had done so many times at the Knickerbocker Yacht Club. The marine was holding Ronnie really close, and they hardly moved. But he didn't have her for long. The Seton Hall boys broke in, one after the other, and then Graham, the waterfront man, took over. Ronnie laughed and giggled with the arrival of each new partner. Once when they glided by the fireplace, she spotted Cooper and gave him a wink and a faint wave over her partner's shoulder. Rosie contented herself with sorting through the pile of 78s until she found "A String of Pearls."

"How about a fast one?" she asked, and the tempo went from mild to frantic. The room went wild, but Cooper still watched.

Graham Morgan was doing some fancy footwork when the lights dimmed and then began to flicker. The music slowed...and then died. The room was dark except for the yellow light from the burning logs in the fireplace. There was a collective moan, and everyone stood in silence. Then the music started up, but the lights did not follow suit. It was "String of Pearls" again, but the music wasn't coming from the phonograph—it was coming from the grand piano. Rosie had taken charge and was knocking out the familiar tune while the jitterbug dancers resumed their exercise. A cheer went up, reinforced by applause and shouts of "Yea, Rosie!" Her repertoire appeared to be endless. From "String of Pearls" she slid effortlessly into "Jersey Bounce" and then to some Andrew Sisters' favorites. When she hit "Don't Sit Under the Apple Tree," the crowd accompanied her by singing the lyrics. One wartime favorite led to another. "The White Cliffs of Dover" was followed by "When the Lights Come on Again All over the World," and predictably as they ran out of words, the power was restored to the hotel and the lights came on all over the room. They went back to the phonograph, but Rosie-the-miracle-worker had become the bright star of the opening night at the Lake Bradford Hotel.

All this time Cooper stood by the fireplace, slowly sipping a beer and smoking an occasional Chesterfield. His foot tapped along with the fast tunes. He liked to jitterbug. Debbie and the girls at Manhasset said he was good at it, but tonight he felt more secure standing on the sidelines, just watching. He really wanted to join in, but he could almost hear Grandmother Dawkins advising, "Stop, look, and listen before you cross the tracks."

"Gamma" Dawkins had a special place in Cooper's life. She was a mixture of Victorian propriety and a reassuring hug. She had lived with her son's family since the beginning of the depression and always had a ready supply of Band-Aids and kisses for her grandson. She also took it upon herself to help him with his table manners and other matters of etiquette. Thus, she had indelibly inscribed a multitude of phrases into his subconscious.

It was close to midnight when they ran out of beer and shut down the phonograph. Cooper was returning from the shower, clad in pajamas, slippers, and an L. L. Bean plaid bathrobe, when he passed a room packed with the male staff. A few still had on their khakis, but most were in their skivvies. There was not one bathrobe or pair of pajamas in the room. Cooper slipped by the open door, returned to his room, and changed into a clean pair of Fruit of the Loom briefs and a T-shirt. Then he returned to the room where the male staff had gathered and took a place quietly on the edge of the bull session.

Kevin had the floor. "These two New England farmers met on a Monday morning. One was complaining that he spent over an hour in the morning picking up the rubbers left in the pasture by the city slickers who drove up from Boston for the weekend. 'I must have picked up a bushel of them before I was through.' The other farmer replied, 'That's nothing. Up along the road a piece, I had forty acres of corn fucked flat.'"

Not to be outdone, Danny offered, "Do you know why a bride on her wedding night and a linoleum rug are alike?" He looked around at a room of blank faces. "Give up?" They all nodded. "Well," said Danny, "Lay 'em right the first time, and you can walk all over them for the rest of your life."

One story followed another. A bottle of Old Overholt rye whiskey made the rounds. Cooper feigned a slug and passed the bottle along as he mentally took attendance. Everyone was there except Stan, who had his own quarters down on the third floor.

But someone else was missing—Forrest, the Harvard guy. One of the others realized it, too, and called out, "Hey, where's Forrest?" An answer came back, "He's probably giving it to Miss Radcliff right now."

"Man, that's a fine-looking piece of ass. How come he's getting into it so soon?"

"Oh, come on, use your brain. Harvard and Radcliff? Aren't they right next door to each other? Those two probably had something going long before they got here."

"You don't suppose they're married."

"They wouldn't be working here if they were. The only married workers besides Dr. Martin are Rudolph and Gretchen Hoffman. Don't you remember the employment application? 'Due to the lack of adequate facilities for married couples, only single persons can be considered for employment this summer.'"

The conversation switched to Madeleine Stillwell, alias Veronica Lake. "Now there's some fine pussy," stated Danny. "I wonder who's going to get a taste of that." Danny continued, "who didn't get the hots for her on the dance floor tonight? I mean, she really snuggled up close, nose to nose, toes to toes, and belly button to belly button. Is there anyone in this room who didn't dance with her at least twice?"

"Cooper didn't dance with anybody," declared Kevin. Suddenly, Cooper realized, all the eyes in the room were on him. "He just stood on around, watching. What were you doing, kid? Taking notes? Were you trying to figure out how to do it?"

Cooper's face turned crimson, but the marine came to Cooper's defense. "Lay off the kid," he said. Had he stopped there, it would have been OK with Cooper. Then the marine ruined it. "He's still in high school. He's probably still a virgin." Cooper wanted to die.

INTRODUCTIONS

At the same time a similar meeting was taking place at the other end of the fourth floor. Beyond the sealed hallway door in room 428, the female staff had gathered. "Rosie, you were fabulous," said one of the waitresses. "You saved the evening. Where did you learn to play the piano, and how did you ever find time to learn all of those popular tunes?"

"I owe it all to Mrs. Feldman, my piano teacher, and to my father. I didn't want to take piano lessons, but my father said that music ran in the family. My grandfather was a cantor. My father used to pick up extra money playing the piano on weekends down at the neighborhood bar and grill. Mrs. Feldman said I had a good ear for music and that I must have inherited it from my father. She took me straight through the classics—Bach, Brahms, and Chopin."

"What about Beethoven?" asked Ronnie.

"Oh, yeah, him, too. But once Mrs. Feldman had taught me the basics, I found that I could play the popular tunes by ear. Last year my father won a bet by sending me down to Broadway to see *Finian's Rainbow* and then, after the show, I went directly to the bar, sat down at the piano, and played 'How Are Things in Glocca Morra' and all the other tunes from the show. I did it without the score or the words in front of me."

The girls let out a collective "Wow!"

Then Sheila said, "Did you take a look at some of the cool guys who are working here this summer?"

Rosie stood up and turned toward the door. "Listen, girls, I'm going to my room and hit the sack. We've got all summer to talk about the boys." Rosie left, but the others weren't ready to turn in; after all, they wouldn't be waiting on any tables until lunchtime.

"How about that marine?" said Sheila. "He looks like he won the war single-handedly. What a body! I'll bet he lifts weights. I'd like to see him with his shirt off."

"You'd like to see him with his pants off, too," said Audrey, a petite blonde from Smith College.

"Wouldn't we all?" countered Sheila, who added, "What about you, Ronnie? You and he were snuggling up to each other on the dance floor."

"Ronnie was snuggling up to just about everybody on the dance floor," chirped Audrey. "Just about everybody except that kid Dr. Martin brought along from Long Island."

"I thought everyone here was in college or a veteran," said Sheila. "I mean who the hell let him in?"

"Oh, that's easy. Dr. Martin did," offered Ronnie. "He is kinda cute, and he could pass for eighteen or nineteen and he's not dumb, either. I rode up on the train with him. He did the whole *New York Times* crossword puzzle. He must be one of Dr. Martin's better students." Ronnie was silent for a minute and then added, "Oh, I've got it. He told me that his parents were about to get a divorce. I'll bet Dr. Martin offered him the job to give him a break from the home scene. I've been through the same thing, and let me tell you, it's no fun at all. My parents are still at each other's throats. First they battle it out in court, and then they try to pull in the kids. That's what's happening to my younger brother and sister. I've learned the game by keeping my distance and playing one off against the other."

"Well, you're right," said Audrey. "He is kinda cute with that wavy blond hair and those innocent blue eyes."

"Speaking of innocent," observed Sheila, "I wonder just how innocent he is."

"Why don't you try and find out," Ronnie suggested. "I'll bet you could teach him a thing or two."

Sheila smirked. "That sounds like a challenge and an interesting summer project."

CHAPTER FOUR
WORK BEGINS

First light came early in Vermont. Cooper lay on his lumpy mattress and reached for his watch. It was only ten minutes to five, but even if it had been six-thirty, he wouldn't have wanted to get up. He didn't ever want to get up again. Everything he had anticipated when he got off the train with Ronnie only fourteen hours before had turned sour. Cooper looked at the shadows on his wall and wondered whatever happened to "rosy-fingered dawn." The light was blue and gray and cold. He wanted to stay in bed, but the beer he had consumed the night before was begging for a trip down the hall. As he put his feet on the floor, the calf muscles of his right leg reacted to the cold and knotted themselves into an agonizing cramp. He fell back on his bed and massaged his lower leg. Finally, Cooper was able to straighten his leg. He took a deep breath and put his feet on the floor again—and this time his left leg went through the same process. It was another painful three minutes before he could limp toward the door and head down to the bathroom. The hall was freezing. At this point he didn't care about being like the other guys who ran around in their skivvies. It was too damn cold; and he returned for his slippers and bathrobe.

When Cooper had completed his bathroom chores, it was only twenty minutes after five. Slivers of sunlight had found an opening in the mountains to the east, and the light reflecting on his wall was turning yellow, with the promise of at least some warmth. Cooper reminded himself that people came to the Green Mountains in the summer because it was cool. He sat on the edge of his bed and stared at his luggage. He had only opened one suitcase. Maybe he should repack rather than unpack. Nothing was going as planned. Everyone knew that he was still in high school. All the guys were a lot older than he was, and many of them were returning veterans with lots of experience, especially with girls. And what about Ronnie? When he got off the train in Middlebury, he thought he had a great summer romance going, for sure. But then the marine stepped in, and it was all over even before it had started. Why stay now? He could probably hitch a ride with one of the delivery trucks into Middlebury. He could leave a note for Dr. Martin, sneak out in the bakery truck, and nobody would miss him. He could hang out on Long Island at the North Hills or Soundview Golf Club and pick up some change as a caddie. *That's it*, he thought. That was the plan of the day. As he took a step toward his open suitcase, his eye caught the pink envelope on the oak dresser—the letter his mother had slipped in his coat pocket. He picked it up and studied his mother's delicate handwriting. He put it down again but then changed his mind and opened the letter. It read:

WORK BEGINS

Dear Cooper,

I decided to write this letter and put it in your pocket, hoping you will find it and read it when you get on the train for Vermont.

As you know, your father and I haven't been getting along for some time, and we have decided that it would be best for all concerned if we got a divorce. That's why we went ahead and moved into your grandfather's old house and why I have gone to work in the city.

I should have told you this before you left but it's now official. Your father and I met with the attorneys last Monday and signed all the papers.

The divorce should be final by the end of the summer.

Cooper took a deep breath and sat down on his bed. He felt like someone had just kicked him in the balls. He wanted to scream but couldn't. It was like when Grandmother Goetz died. She had had a stroke and had been in a coma for a week. He knew she was going to die—the doctor and everyone in the family said that it was just a matter of time—but when the doctor said, "She's gone," it was like being hit with a baseball bat. He had that same feeling now, after reading his mother's letter.

At the movies, Cooper always knew ahead of time when there was going to be an unhappy ending, because there was the sad music started before "The End" appeared on the screen. Now, there was no sad music, but he still wanted to cry, but couldn't. Was it Gamma Dawkins's voice he heard that kept saying, "Men don't cry?"

Cooper took slow, deep breaths until his breathing returned to normal. He started to crumple the letter and throw it in the wastebasket, but realized he hadn't finished reading it. It went on:

I am also writing this letter because in spite of all that has been going on, I want you to know that you are missed and that you are loved. It's so important in this life to know that you are loved by someone.

I know that this past year has been very difficult for you, as it has been for all of us. I also know this is a difficult time for any young man, and I am sure you are no exception.

We're all looking forward to a big Fourth of July weekend with your grandfather at the beach cottage. But of course, it won't be the same without you.

I know that you will enjoy the challenge of your first summer away from home. I guess that's all part of growing up. Have a good summer. I know you'll do well.

Love,
Mother

Cooper sat back down on the bed. Why was he so angry? He knew the divorce was coming, and he was angry about that. He was angry that neither his mother nor father had the guts to tell him to his face. But he didn't like the rest of his mother's letter, either. Was it her assertion that she knew how he felt? How did she know how he felt? She had always used that phrase. When he was a little kid, he was convinced that she could read his mind and because sometimes when she said she knew how he felt, she was right on target. The first time he heard the prayer that said God was somebody "unto whom all hearts are open, all desires known, and from whom no secrets are hid," he thought that God must be just like his mother. But how did his mother know what he was feeling or what the divorce was doing to him? He didn't know himself, so how could she know? But one thing he did know was that he wanted to stay as far away as he could from his mother and father, with all their pain and all their tension. He had no idea if he could handle the Lake Bradford crowd, but his mother's letter pretty well convinced him that staying in Vermont would be better than going back to Long Island.

※ ※ ※

Day one was a blur of orientation and instruction. It didn't take Cooper long to figure out that he was the littlest chicken in the Lake Bradford barnyard. He was going to be a dishwasher, a pot-and-pan washer, a potato peeler, a coffee maker, and anything else Dr. Martin or Rudolph wanted him to be—nothing special, nothing special at all.

On day two, his first full day, Cooper had to be in the kitchen at 6:30 a.m. He stumbled into the big empty room to fire up the copper coffee urn and then he sat down alone at the staff table with a glass of milk, some orange juice, and a bowl of Wheaties. If he wanted oatmeal or eggs, he would have to wait for Rudy or Gretchen. When Rudy did arrive, groggy and in a bad mood, he gave Cooper his vegetable assignment. The hotel prided itself on serving fresh country vegetables, so there were potatoes to be peeled, carrots to be scraped, corn to be shucked, peas to be shelled, and beans to be snapped. By 7:30 the dirty dishes were piling up from the first wave of early birds in the dining room, so Cooper dashed across the kitchen and cranked up the washer— the breakfast and lunch dishes were his full responsibility. For the evening meal, he was told that Benson, a slightly retarded local, would come in to help out with the dishes in exchange for the scrapings, which he would take home to feed the pigs.

Rudy warned Cooper not to fall behind with his work. "If you let those egg yolks sit for even five minutes, they won't come off in the washer." Cooper moved back and forth from the dishwasher to the vegetable bin. It reminded him of the time he set pins in a bowling alley, because after a while, his brain shut down and his body switched to automatic, just as it had in the bowling alley. He took on the rhythm of the kitchen, and it began to feel like a ballet, one in which the waitresses also had a part. Ronnie and Rosie and the others glided through the swinging doors, dropped off orders—eggs and bacon, pancakes and sausage, French toast, omelets, kippered herring—and then slid back into the dining room, took a deep breath, and reappeared with new orders, refilled their coffee pots, and finally dumped the dirty dishes on the counter by the washer.

At 7:45 in the morning on his first full day, Cooper faced his first failure. An irate guest stormed into the kitchen, yelling, "What did you do with the coffee? Wash your socks in it?" Ronnie, wearing her starched uniform and carrying a pewter coffee pot, followed the man and grinned sheepishly. Fortunately, Dr. Martin was on hand and asked Ronnie to pour him a cup of black coffee. He tasted it, smacked his lips thoughtfully as if sampling a vintage wine, and then gave the order to Cooper. "Put two of those twelve-cup percolators on the stove. Use the spring water from the cooler." Then he sipped the coffee again and turned to the irate guest. "It's a little on the tart side. Do you use cream and sugar, or do you drink it black?" Dr. Martin wasn't going to let the guest beat up on one of his summer workers, and the guest knew it. He allowed that he took his coffee black. "Don't worry about a thing," Dr. Martin assured him. "We'll have a fresh pot of coffee perked with our own mountain spring water on your table in less than five minutes." After the man returned to his table, Dr. Martin took Cooper aside, "Did you scrub the coffee urn before filling it with water?"

Cooper was about to lose his composure. "Nobody told me to wash the pot or showed me how to do it. How was I supposed—"

"That's my fault," Dr. Martin cut in, putting his hand on Cooper's shoulder. "We'll drain it after breakfast and scrub it down before lunch. Actually, the coffee you made wasn't all that bad. It may take another day or two before the old pipes start delivering our own crystal-clear mountain water. Put a pinch of salt and a slice of butter and an egg shell in the coffee urn. The butter and salt will take the bitterness out of the coffee, and the egg shell will settle the coffee grounds. Just to be on the safe side, we'll keep the percolators going for the folks who take it black."

Dr. Martin was a real prince, Cooper realized, but Mrs. Martin was something else. She came into the kitchen after the breakfast guests had left the dining room. There was something fragile, something sad, that lurked just below the surface of her outward gaiety. She was a good-looking brunette, a little on the pudgy side, but she covered this with loose-fitting, flowing, lightweight summer dresses. The new fashion, in reaction to the short skirts of the war years, had sent hemlines down to the ankle. It also went in for padded hips. The style was made for Elizabeth "Libby" Martin. What didn't fit her well, however, was the abundance of wine that was available at the inn. This morning, after her first champagne party to greet the arriving guests, she had walked quite normally into the kitchen and headed for the ice chest and the water cooler to quench her thirst. For some reason, the cold water reactivated the effects of the champagne, and within three minutes her speech began to slur and her legs to wobble. The staff at first thought she was putting on some sort of comedy act, but then Dr. Martin put his arm around her and led her gently but firmly out of the kitchen.

The waitresses were off duty after they'd cleared all of their tables and reset them for lunch, but it was a long morning for Cooper—he still had lots of vegetables to prepare and a floor to sweep. Then he discovered that he apparently was there to cater to Rudolph Hoffman's every whim. As chef, Rudy considered it beneath his dignity to concern himself with anything but the meats, fowl, and seafood and their appropriate sauces. Gretchen managed the vegetables and soups and presided over the salad counter. She kept a huge cauldron of soup stock simmering on the back of the stove, and into the pot went celery leaves, carrot tops, cabbage leaves, and chicken and turkey bones. When Cooper brought her his offering of vegetable peelings, she said she particularly liked the carrot tops and celery leaves. "It gives the soup stock a bit of a zing," she explained.

By the time Cooper had finished preparing the vegetables, it was time for lunch, which passed as a big blur. By the time he had completed his post-luncheon chores, he discovered it was already three o'clock. He went back to his room with the intent of putting on his bathing trunks and joining the staff on the beach, but he never made it. He lay down on his bed, and the next thing he knew, Dr. Martin was gently nudging his shoulder. "Time to get back to the kitchen, Cooper."

Rudy was in a nasty mood. "Here have you been? I needed you thirty minutes ago to scrub these potatoes so that I can put them in the oven for baking. But before you do that, come follow me. There is someone I want you to meet." When they reached the dishwashing equipment at the other side of the kitchen, Rudy pointed to a short man. His hair was graying hairing, but he had the face and gestures of a child. "Cooper, this is Benson," Rudy said. "Benson this is Cooper." Cooper put out his hand.

"Hel...lo Coop...err," stammered Benson. "I help with the dish...es at din...ner time and...Dr. Martin lets me take the slops home to feed...the pigs."

A few minutes later, Dr. Martin's wife glided back into the kitchen with an empty wine glass in her hand. "I see you've met Benson," she said brightly. "He's a strange one, but he really does do a good job with the dishes."

"Where's he from?" asked Cooper.

"He's a local boy…but he isn't a boy anymore. He has a man's body—although not a very good one—but a child's mind. He can barely read, just simple words like cat and of course, pig."

"Do we just call him Benson, or does he have a last name?"

"He has one," said Libby, "but I'm not allowed to say. Maybe Dr. Martin will tell you his name when you get back to school this fall." Libby waved her hand as if to shoo him away and laughed as she headed for the water cooler.

Libby Martin was not the only one at the hotel who had a drinking problem, Cooper realized. Rudy seemed to begin the day with a hangover, even though Gretchen did her best to cover for him. She was in the kitchen at 6:30 in the morning to start the breakfast bacon, which she baked in the oven, and the eggs, which she scrambled, and the pancake batter, which she mixed. Then there were the hash browns, corned beef hash, grapefruit, melons, and juices. Rudolph was supposed to do the short-order items, but he seldom arrived before eight o'clock and when he did, he was in a bad mood. "Please don't do anything to upset him," Gretchen would beg the waitresses, and they did their best to tiptoe around and not make any noise. Rudy kept several cases of beer in the walk-in cooler, and he began to imbibe as soon as he arrived. By noon, he had moved from sullen to jolly. He laughed, sang songs in German, and flirted with all of the waitresses—except Rosie. But by the evening meal, his mood had returned to downright nasty. The general consensus was

"Gretchen's OK, but watch out for Rudy. He's a drunk and a real Nazi."

Cooper did his best to stay on Rudy's good side, mainly by asking questions like, "What is the difference between a chef and a cook?"

"All the difference in the world!" Rudolph retorted. "A cook is nothing! A nobody. You can hire a cook for forty dollars a week. A chef is an artist. All a cook knows how to do is boil water and throw meat in a frying pan. Fry or boil—that's all a cook knows how to do. A chef can broil, bake, braise, poach, steam, singe, sauté, baste, and smoke. But the real difference is in the sauces. It is the sauces that make the difference between a truck stop and a five-star restaurant. Follow me around, and I will teach you about sauces and a few other things you need to know. Maybe you will be a chef someday yourself, yah? A good chef in New York or Palm Beach can make twenty-five thousand dollars a year. That's a lot of money."

Cooper wasn't sure he was ready to sign on for life, but he certainly preferred Rudy in a mentor role than when he was barking orders like a prison camp guard. He asked Rudy another question. "Do you know how to fix sauerbraten?"

"Do I know how to fix sauerbraten? Is the Pope a Catholic? Of course I know how to cook sauerbraten. Every German hausfrau, not to mention every German chef, knows how to cook sauerbraten. But how do you know about sauerbraten? Dawkins isn't a German name."

"Well," said Cooper, "my Grandfather Goetz is German. I mean, way back his family was German. His great-great-grandfather was a Hessian mercenary with the British army during the American Revolution. When the Americans won, he decided to stay here. Grandfather Goetz prides himself in being thoroughly American, but he had a second cousin who moved to New York from Cincinnati. She spoke German, and once a year she had the whole family over for sauerbraten and potato dumplings."

"Sauerbraten *mit kartoffelklosse*," corrected Rudy. "Did you like it?"

"Oh, yes, did I ever!"

"Then I will make it for you sometime. I will make it for all the guests in the hotel. I will teach you how to make it for yourself."

Cooper was pleased with Rudy's offer of sauerbraten, but he wished he hadn't shared his Germanic heritage with Rudy. Hadn't his father fought in two wars against the Germans? And hadn't he turned the pages of *Life* magazine and viewed with horror the pictures of Hitler's death camps? Even Grandfather Goetz had turned his back on his ancestral culture and decreed that German would not be spoken in his home. "We are Americans. This has been our country since 1787. Adolf Hitler and his gang of criminals have twisted and sullied the honor of the German people. This is an American home, and we will speak English here." Once, Grandfather Goetz had chewed out the rector of St. Philip's for allowing the choir to sing "Glorious Things of Thee Are Spoken," the German national anthem. "Don't you know that we are at war with Nazi Germany?" his grandfather had said.

Cooper tried to sort out his feelings about Rudy and decided that as long as the chef kept his conversation to the secrets of being a chef, they could get along.

"I will teach you how to be a chef, yah?" offered Rudy. "I will start with breakfast. As soon as you have made the coffee, you will come over here to the stove and help Gretchen. She will show you how to fry the eggs and all that sort of thing. If nothing else, when you go off to college you will be able to get a job as a short-order cook in some hash joint near the campus." Cooper was wondering how he was going to add this assignment to his already crowded morning schedule. Rudy seemed to read his mind, "I will ask Dr. Martin if he can get Benson to come in and do the breakfast dishes. In the meantime, we will start right now, yah? You see all those little frying pans hanging over the stove? We don't call them frying pans. They are skillets, and we only use them for breakfast. You never put a skillet in the water. Soap and water will ruin an iron skillet. They are kept oiled, and they are kept hot. When the breakfast is finished, you wipe out the skillet with newspaper and then sprinkle some salt in the skillet and wipe it out again. They are for eggs only. See those two with the red paint on their handles? Don't ever use them for eggs. They are special for kippered herring. We have a Jew boy and his wife from Boston who always want kippered herring. The herring is in a tin in the walk-in cooler. At the Breakwater Club in Palm Beach, we don't have to worry about kippered herring because they don't let the Jews stay at the hotel." Rudy broke into a big grin and laughed, "You know what I mean?" Cooper could only stare at Rudy.

"You see that shiny surface over there at the end of the stove?" continued Rudy. "That's the grill. We use it at breakfast for the pancakes, except Mr. Bradford likes to call them Vermont flapjacks. They look like pancakes and they taste like pancakes, but Mr. Bradford says they are special because they are made with flour that is ground at the mill in Middlebury. He uses a lot of heavy cream from the family dairy and says that the flapjacks can only be served with lots of Vermont maple syrup or maple butter. He has his own little maple syrup factory and when the guests go home, he insists that they buy a small case of the syrup or a box of Bradford's genuine Vermont maple leaf candy."

CHAPTER FIVE
SETTLING IN

Beneath the kitchen was the laundry, which contained a thousand-gallon heater that supplied the hot water. The washing was done in an enormous copper barrel that sloshed in a trough of soapy water. It was the prototype for every washing machine that was being built for the postwar home market. The contraption was bulky and noisy, but it represented state-of-the-art commercial equipment from the late 1920s. In the spring of 1946, a Corps of Engineers captain, who was just home from the Pacific, spent three months, with the help of a local plumber and garage mechanic, putting it in working order so that it would be ready for the hotel's grand reopening.

The laundry was the domain of Mercy and Dorcas, who washed, dried, and pressed the sheets, pillow cases, and table linen each day. They also processed the waitresses' uniforms, which were handed out freshly starched and ironed before the evening meal.

In the morning when they arrived, they followed a ritual that varied little from day to day. Dorcas was always the first to take off her coat and hang it up in a rusty old school locker. She always wore a cloth coat, even in the summer, as there was often a chill in the air as she drove her '37 Chevy out from Middlebury, first depositing her husband at the stone quarry and then taking a shortcut down a dirt road from the quarry to the lake. Her coat covered her standard uniform, a blue sweater over a pink cotton print dress, which didn't quite cover her slip. Her legs were clothed in light brown surgical stockings, which were rolled down to a position just above her knees. Her feet were firmly planted in high-top sneakers. She wore no makeup, and her graying hair was tucked under a turban made from a genuine silk paisley shawl that her husband had given her on their fortieth anniversary. As the day warmed up her sweater was often discarded and sometimes, when the thermometer topped eighty, both laundry ladies took off their sneakers and long socks and wiggled their toes as they worked.

Dorcas' first duty of the day was to turn up the gas under the boiler. Meanwhile, Mercy hung up her coat and carefully spread a linen napkin on top of an apple crate. Then she removed a thermos of tea from her tote bag and went to her locker for a sugar bowl, cups, saucers, and two spoons. When the table was set she uncorked the thermos and addressed Dorcas. "You didn't forget to bring the cinnamon toast, did you?"

"I never forget the cinnamon toast," retorted Dorcas. "Have I ever forgotten the cinnamon toast?"

"Well, once last summer you brought the toast, but it didn't have any cinnamon sugar on it. Don't you remember?" said Mercy. "We had to ask Standish to bring us some jam from the kitchen. As I recall, he brought us a jar of blackberry preserves, the kind they make up at Bradford Farms."

"Well, that was an exception."

"It was also a treat."

Dorcas and Mercy pulled their chairs up to their makeshift tea table. Mercy's outfit was almost identical to Dorcas', except Mercy wore a hairnet and covered her head with a baseball cap. It had belonged to her late husband, who had been a fan of the Boston Red Sox.

This morning they sipped and savored their hot tea, quietly stirring their spoons and adding more sugar.

"Did you hear all that thunder last night?" Dorcas asked.

"Ay-ah. Went on for over an hour. Sounded like the Normandy Invasion all over again."

"The folks over in York State used to say the angels were playing ten pins on the heavenly green," offered Dorcas.

York State? Thought Cooper. *What are they talking about?* Then he realized that the old ladies were talking about New York State. Living on Long Island, he rarely heard either term. To Cooper's family, anything north of Westchester County was called "Upstate."

"Angels playing ten pins! That's not what my Jonathan used to say," objected Mercy.

"What did your Jonathan used to say?"

"When the noise woke him up, the first thing he'd do was to measure the time between the lightning flash and the thunder. He'd count out 'one thousand and one, one thousand and two, one thousand and three' to mark the seconds. For every five seconds, he said the storm was a mile away. When he didn't get past two seconds, he'd say it was time to say our prayers."

"Mercy, you've gotten off the subject. You started to tell me what your Jonathan thought the thunder sounded like."

"He said it sounded like the angel Gabriel breaking wind."

Before Dorcas could respond, the sound of steam coming out of the boiler signaled Mercy and Dorcas to begin the day's work.

Each day, in addition to the hotel laundry, Mercy and Dorcas handled the guests' laundry, and on Tuesdays and Thursdays, the staff could bring in their clothing, which Mercy and Dorcas would wash and dry but not iron. There were two ironing boards available to the staff, and they were in use most of the time. Cooper had never done his own laundry, much less iron his shirts or trousers. On his first visit to the laundry, the ladies instructed him to sort out the colored items from the whites. "If you put that red shirt in with your underwear, you're going to end up with a drawer full of pink panties," advised Dorcas. "In fact, you better wash that red shirt by hand in cold water in that tub over there, and then we can put it in the dryer with your other things. When you come back later this afternoon, I'll show you how to use the iron."

Cooper enjoyed the laundry room and especially liked Dorcas and Mercy, who kept up a constant chatter about the local doings, the habits of the guests, and the personalities of the staff. Mercy and Dorcas had been "helping out" at the Lake Bradford Inn since they were young girls at the turn of the century. From Labor Day until Memorial Day they helped out in Middlebury, such as at the mayor's Christmas reception or a special weekend at the college. They helped the Smiths with their blackberry preserves and the Stoddards with their pickles and green tomato relish. They helped their neighbors with Thanksgiving, Easter, and Mother's Day, but come Memorial Day they were back at Mr. Bradford's place on the lake. Cooper was impressed by the fact that they never spoke of "working" for someone; they were always just "helping out."

Much of the chatter between Mercy and Dorcas had to do with the returning veterans. The week after Pearl Harbor, about a dozen of the county's young men rode the train to Rutland and volunteered for the army. Mercy and Dorcas had practically raised. Those boys, who called themselves the "Green Mountain Boys," in honor of their ancestors who had marched off with Ethan Allen to Saratoga in the War of Independence. The laundry ladies sent V-mail letters to all of the boys at Christmas and Easter and on two occasions, when dead bodies were returned from Guadalcanal and Normandy, Mercy and Dorcas were in church to mourn with family and community.

"I hear tell that they had four christenings at First Congregational Church last Sunday," observed Mercy. "Those Green Mountain Boys had a lot of catching up to do when they got home. The chaplain must have read them the Scripture on all of the begats before he sent them home."

"That's about all they've been doing," added Dorcas, "begetting little Green Mountain boys and girls."

"They're getting caught up, all right. I saw the Stoddard woman in the market last week, and she had one in the baby carriage and another one in the oven. It looked like she was due any day now. They're about caught up, I'd say. There's a boom in babies, that's for sure."

"Just about everybody's gotten caught up, except for Paul and Stephanie McKay. He came home from the Pacific in time for Christmas in '45 but only stayed a month, and then he took a job over in York State. They say he only comes home on holidays to see his older children, and there aren't any new ones coming along."

"Maybe the two older children are all they want or can afford to have. Maybe the job over in York State is the only one he could get."

"Rhubarb!" scoffed Dorcas. "If that's the case, why doesn't she move over to York State and live there? It's just not right for a married couple to sleep apart. Joseph and I have been married for forty-six years, and we have never slept apart, not even for one night."

"Does that count nights you made him sleep on the couch?" Mercy teased.

"Oh, I'm counting them, too. Joseph never spent a full night on the couch. He may have started there, but he usually came back to our marital bed to make up, and he was usually back by midnight." She raised her eyebrows and added with a smile, "If you receive my meaning! Like I say, it's just not healthy for a married couple to sleep apart. It was one thing during the war, but now that the war is over, married people ought to be under one roof and one blanket," declared Dorcas.

"Speaking of being under one blanket," sighed Mercy, "I sure do miss my Jonathan."

"How long has it been?"

"It'll be five years in October."

"Five years?"

"It was the second Monday of October. There was a bit of frost on the ground and the leaves had all turned red and brown and yellow. I packed his lunch, like I always did. meat loaf sandwiches. He liked meat loaf sandwiches with lots of ketchup and maybe a small baked potato. The carpool picked him, and off he went to the quarry, just like every other working day since we were married back in 1905, when he was twenty, and I was seventeen. We were married as soon as he finished his apprenticeship as a stone cutter. It was a lot of hard work. He had to lift a lot of stones, but it built up his muscles. He was a beautiful man." Mercy paused and took a deep breath. "There hadn't been much work to do at the quarry because of the war. But then they had a big order from the government. That's kind of sad, isn't it? They needed grave markers for the cemeteries! They were going to make a big cut in the rock wall that morning. They had been working on it all week, drilling holes in the granite and placing sticks of dynamite. It was supposed to be a controlled blast, and nobody was supposed to get hurt." Mercy stopped to wipe her eyes and blow her nose. For a minute it looked like she was going to continue, but she was finished. "Enough of that!" she declared.

Dorcas finally broke the silence with, "Back to what we were saying about one blanket—the maids tell me that couple from Harvard and Radcliff must be married, or something is going on."

"How's that?"

"Well, the maid on the fourth floor went into the staff rooms to change the linens yesterday, and neither of their beds had been slept in. The linens were as fresh and clean as they had been last week when the staff arrived."

"Where do you suppose they're sleeping? I mean, last year half the summer staff were using the boathouse and the icehouse for romancing, but that would be a weird place to spend a whole night, especially every night since they got here."

"You don't suppose they're married, do you? If they are, Mr. Bradford won't let them stay. He's very emphatic about that. No married couples except Rudolph and Gretchen and Dr. and Mrs. Martin."

"That's a dumb rule, a lot of rhubarb, if you receive my meaning," said Dorcas. "I mean, if they're married, then they have a license to be romantic. It's all very legal and very moral. Says so right in the Bible! It isn't as if Mr. Bradford has issued chastity belts to the summer staff."

"Well, if he did issue chastity belts, it would just be a matter of time before one of the veterans would find the key."

About that time, Mercy and Dorcas noticed that Cooper seemed to be taking in every word they were saying. With a glance in his direction and a knowing nod to each other, they went back to work. But as soon as Cooper left, they started chirping again. "That's the young high school fellow Dr. Martin brought up from Long Island," noted Mercy. "He's only just finished his junior year. It will be another summer before he goes off to college."

"Well, he looks older than that," observed Dorcas. "He could easily pass for a college student, except I guess everybody knows that he's still in high school, and they're giving him a hard time. They'd probably be really cruel, except I've heard he's Dr. Martin's pet, and he will only let things go just so far."

"I also understand that the chef has taken a liking to him and is going to teach him how to cook."

"I hope that's all he teaches him. They say that Rudy's a real Nazi and has already started giving that Jewish girl from the Bronx a hard time."

"I thought we just fought a war to stop people like him."

"I hope that Cooper fellow is smart enough to figure Rudy out."

"Well, right now, I hope he's smart enough to figure out what the girls are up to."

"How so?"

"Well, to put it bluntly, according to Standish, the general opinion is that he's not very experienced in the boy-girl department, and the college ladies are taking bets on who will further his education … if you receive my meaning."

⁂

When Cooper returned to the kitchen, he found a letter in his box. He could tell from the handwriting that it was from his cousin "Guts," John Charles Goetz III. Pops—Cooper's Grandpa Goetz—begat John Charles Goetz Jr., and John Charles Goetz JCG, Jr. begat John Charles Goetz III, also known as Guts. Guts and Cooper, whom Guts called "Coop," were first cousins. Guts was older by about twenty months, but they had been best friends for as long as either one could remember. The family album was filled with pictures of them. One was the picture of a smiling Guts, still in diapers, offering his milk bottle to his newborn cousin. More recently, another picture showed two very serious young males holding a tape measure, out on an appraisal assignment with Pops. Weekends at Pops's summer cottage overlooking Long Island Sound forged an unbreakable bond between the two cousins. All the relatives said they were more like twin brothers than first cousins. On the mantel of the stone fireplace at Pops's cottage was a framed enlargement of Pops with his two tow-headed grandsons, proudly displaying their first catch of blowfish. In the photo, Guts was six and Coop, four and a half. As the two grew older they discovered the joy of climbing the sandy cliffs that defined the entrance to Port Jefferson. From Pops's place they would row a dinghy down the beach, climb the cliffs, start sand slides, and roll and romp. In the winter they transferred that activity to the sand pits in Port Washington.

Cooper opened the letter from Guts and read it eagerly.

A SUMMER REMEMBERED

Hey, Coop,

How's it going up there on the lake with all those college broads?

Have you gotten any XXX yet? I want a full report by return mail.

Going to summer school is no picnic, but it's something I've gotta do before they let me enroll in the construction course at Long Island Tech. One good thing came out of it—Dad bought me an old jalopy so I don't have to spend three and a half hours every day riding the bus and the Long Island Railroad to get to class.

It's a 1936 Humpmobile. What a name for a car! XXX...hump...hump. It needs some work on the valves, but who doesn't? XXX!

Pops says that when you get out of architecture school and I finish the construction classes, we'll be a winning business combo. Levittown, get out of the way! Speaking of Pops, he took me out to the Belle Terre Golf Club last Sunday after church. Pops shot a 95 and I got an 82. Pops says I'm a natural golfer and that with a few lessons and a lot of practice I could be another Bobby Jones. He even hinted that he might drop a line to Santa Claus and suggest that he replace my old clubs, the ones with the wooden shafts, with the modern ones with shafts of steel.

Pops says the bluefish should start running any day now, and he wishes that you were here so that we could crank up the old Evinrude and put our rods (fishing, that is) in the water.

Have a great XXX summer. Don't do anything I wouldn't do.

Your cousin and friend for life,
Guts

CHAPTER SIX
JULY 4, 1947

Dr. Martin entered the kitchen, followed by Mr. Bradford. Dr. Martin grabbed an empty pot and proceeded to beat on it with a wooden spoon. All work stopped. Then Mr. Bradford announced, "We have a full house for the Fourth of July! Every room is booked. We even have three families on the waiting list. Isn't that splendid?"

A shout of joy and a dutiful handful of applause greeted the announcement.

"We're going to have a splendid old-fashioned Independence Day at Lake Bradford," added Mr. Bradford, "just like in the old days before the war."

"I've just arranged for three barrels of Cape Cod clams, packed in ice, to be shipped up here on the morning train on the Fourth of July," added Dr. Martin, "and we'll send the truck over to Lake George and get a big kettle of fish."

Again, the staff offered appropriate sounds of approval, which were halted by Rudy's loud voice behind the serving counter. "What is this with the clams and the fish orders? I already have made plans for the Fourth of July!" Rudy's face was red, and it looked like steam was starting to come out of his nostrils.

Eyes shifted from Rudy to Dr. Martin and back again. Rudy was holding his two-edged carving knife as Dr. Martin walked across the kitchen. The tension rose.

"Mr. Hoffman," whispered Dr. Martin, "why don't we go out on the loading platform and see what we can do to work this out."

"The chef's place is by the stove and behind the serving counter. If you want to talk, we do it here," declared Rudy. The color of his face had changed from red to maroon.

"There is nothing happening on July the Fourth that the two of us can't handle," Dr. Martin said calmly. "I'm going to pick up a cup of coffee and go out on the loading dock for a cigarette. Gretchen and Cooper can handle the breakfast orders for ten minutes. Rudy, I'll see you outside." Then he turned to the waitresses and kitchen crew, "OK, everybody, let's get back to work."

Rudy busied himself around the stove for at least five minutes before his color returned to normal. He took off his chef's cap and apron and walked casually out the kitchen door, where he found Dr. Martin, with coffee in one hand and a cigarette in the other, sitting on an old cracker barrel. Dr. Martin stood up. "Rudy, can I offer you a cigarette?"

Rudy shook his head.

"Well, why don't you pull up an old cracker barrel and have a seat?"

"I would rather be still standing."

"OK, then, tell me what the problem is, and we'll figure out how to fix it."

Rudy folded his arms across his chest, "I am the chef. Right?"

"Right!"

"And the chef is in charge of the kitchen. Right?"

"Right."

"And I make the decisions about what to serve, and I place the orders, and I buy the food. Right?"

"Rudy, I see where you're going with this, and you're 95 percent correct."

"No! I am 100 percent correct. ... Right?"

"Rudy, I'm afraid that's not the case here. The Fourth of July at Lake Bradford has traditions that go back several generations. Some of our older guests came here as children, and they want their grandchildren to experience what they had fun doing back at the turn of the century. I thought I covered all of that when we interviewed, and I hired you to be our chef for the summer."

"I am the chef," insisted Rudy. "I am not a cook. I have my own plans for good food that you will like and the guests will like. I fix what I fix at Palm Beach, and they all applaud."

"And the guests at the Lake Bradford Inn are also applauding your excellent cuisine. You have received many compliments from our guests this summer. But I believe it's my fault that I didn't spell out how we celebrate Independence Day and what the guests will expect. It's a tradition, like the Octoberfest in Munich or turkey and sweet potatoes at Thanksgiving. Yes, you are the chef of the Lake Bradford Inn, and you are in charge of the kitchen. But we all work for Mr. Bradford, and Mr. Bradford is accountable to his guests and the traditions they expect to be honored." Dr. Martin held out his hand. Rudy accepted the gesture with some hesitation, but eventually the two men shook hands.

"Now," said Rudy, "I will accept one of your cigarettes."

The two men stood side by side and gazed at the evergreens, the lake, and the mountains beyond. Dr. Martin broke the silence. "I really love this place. I first came here with my parents before the First World War. Then, when I was sixteen, Mr. Bradford's father gave me a summer job as a busboy. I learned how to swim here. I learned how to sail a boat. I learned how to cook, and I learned how to dance. This is where I met Elizabeth. She came up with her parents from New Haven. The help weren't supposed to mingle socially with the guests, but we couldn't keep our eyes off each other. I was a lifeguard that year, and Libby spent most of her time down at the dock."

"Then you worked here when you were in high school, just like Cooper?"

"That's right. Almost the same age, too. By the way, how's Cooper doing?"

"He is coming along," allowed Rudy. "He is a smart young man, and he is learning very fast. I am teaching him how to do the breakfast. This morning I showed him how to flip the eggs and the potatoes in the frying pan. The first time, it was eggs and potatoes all over everything else. Ha! But now he is doing OK, and when the guest orders his eggs over lightly, Cooper can do it without spilling the eggs or smashing the yolk."

❖ ❖ ❖

At daybreak on the Fourth of July, an early-bird continental breakfast was laid out in the dining room for the golfers and the fishermen. By seven o'clock, Stan Phillips was on the road

JULY 4, 1947

in the station wagon, delivering the first two foursomes to the golf course, while Graham Morgan was shoving off four boats equipped with tackle, bait, and would-be anglers. Flags with forty-eight stars, and red-white-and-blue banners were everywhere. The old folks carried their second cups of coffee outside and sat in the rocking chairs on the porch and reminisced about holidays past. The younger generations plunged into the activities of the day. There were contests in horseshoes, archery, croquet, badminton, and tennis. A softball game was scheduled for mid-afternoon, as well as relay races, three-legged races, and a variety of water sports. Stan had bought out the trophy store in Middlebury and had a bushel basket of ribbons: tri-color, blue, and red for the top prizes, and even yellow for honorable mention so that "everybody would be a winner, and everybody would get a prize."

Cooper had wanted to work with Graham Morgan on the waterfront, but his assignment was changed at the last minute. The kitchen was closed down after breakfast and most of the cooking operation was moved outside. Cooper had been put in charge of cooking the hot dogs and hamburgers and serving them for lunch, along with Boston baked beans, coleslaw, and potato chips. Then, in the afternoon, he was to help Dr. Martin and Mr. Bradford with the evening meal down by the lake. Rudy and Gretchen had been given the day off. He couldn't imagine why, on this day of all days? Little by little, however, Cooper was learning to keep his mouth shut and not ask too many questions. Nevertheless, half of his desire to work the waterfront had to do with boats; the other half had to do with the girls in bathing suits. At the hot dog stand, he realized at least half his wish. A small gaggle of thirteen- to fourteen-year-old girls, all guests at the hotel, gathered around his grill and began to flirt.

"Can we help you with the hot dogs?" one asked.

"No, thank you. I'm doing just fine."

Most of them were clad in bright-colored bare-midriff bathing suits with the double torpedo top. He suspected that they had been padded to simulate the Varga Girls in *Esquire* magazine. The one who caught his attention, though, was a tall brunette who was wearing a one-piece navy blue wool suit, of a kind issued to girls in high school swimming class. It was still wet and although he couldn't see through it, it clung to every curve of her body. There was no question that her breasts were real and rather large for someone so young. If he had been back in Manhasset, he would have asked her for a date or at least offered to walk her home from school, but Dr. Martin had made it perfectly clear that "fraternization" between staff and guests was definitely "verboten." Cooper did have one idea of how to circumvent the hotel edict. He smiled at the girls and said, "If you ladies really want to help, why don't you come back around five this afternoon? I have five bushels of corn that I have to shuck. Have you ever shucked corn?"

"Oh, yes," said the one-piece bathing suit, "we've all had lots of experience."

Cooper thought that Dr. Martin's chat with Rudy on the kitchen porch had smoothed things over and that all would go well on the Fourth. But everything fell apart when later that morning, Cooper noticed a delivery truck pull up to the kitchen door and unload twenty bushels of tomatoes. Cooper didn't realize that Dr. Martin was standing on the porch, smoking a cigarette, until he heard him address the delivery man. "That's an awful lot of tomatoes. Are you sure you got the order right?"

JULY 4, 1947

"Oh, yes, it says right here: 'Twenty bushels of ripe tomatoes for Lake Bradford Hotel. Deliver before ten in the morning on July 4.'"

"Who gave the order?" Dr. Martin demanded.

"It says right here—Rudolph Hoffman, executive chef."

"There must be some mistake," muttered Dr. Martin as he opened the kitchen door and looked for Rudy.

"No, no," answered Rudy, coming out of the kitchen, "There's no mistake. I ordered twenty bushels of tomatoes."

"How are you ever going to use twenty bushels of tomatoes in the salad?"

Rudy put his hands on his hips. "The tomatoes are for the clam chowder. Didn't you say you wanted a big pot of clam chowder? I get the tomatoes for the chowder, yah?

"We don't put tomatoes in the clam chowder," retorted Dr. Martin.

"That's the way we always make clam chowder in Palm Beach and in all of the good hotels in New York."

"Oh, no!" exclaimed Dr. Martin. "You're talking about Manhattan clam chowder. It's made with lots of tomatoes and is sort of like a vegetable soup with a lot of clams in it. Our guests are looking forward to New England clam chowder. It's made with milk and cream."

Rudy folded his arms over his chest. "I have never heard of such a thing. All the good chefs I know make clam chowder with lots of fresh tomatoes. I will show you how we do it, and the guests will like it very much."

"Oh, dear," replied Dr. Martin. "I'm afraid our guests will be very disappointed if they don't find New England clam chowder in their soup bowls."

"It is better with tomatoes. You will see."

"I'll tell you what, Rudy, you can make a small pot of the Manhattan clam chowder, but I'll be in charge of making the large cauldron of the New England chowder. That will settle the problem."

Dr. Martin turned and started through the kitchen door. Cooper heard Rudy mutter in German, "Indieser kuche bin ich der chef. Der idioit Martin denkt er kann mich herum kommandieren. Er weiss nichts, ist nur ein koch und blode." Roughly translated, it came to, "I am the chef, and I am in charge of the kitchen. That idiot Martin thinks he can boss me around. What does he know about preparing meals anyway? He is not a chef; he is a cook and a stupid one at that!"

Dr. Martin did an abrupt about-face. In perfect German, he addressed a startled Rudy. "Come here and say that to my face!" Rudy flushed to purple as Dr. Martin continued—and again, his German was flawless. "If you say anything like that again in German, English, French, or Italian, you can pack your bags and leave Lake Bradford!"

The two men stared at each other, and then Dr. Martin took a deep breath and spoke in English. "Rudy, you are an excellent chef, but you have much to learn about the Fourth of July and its celebration in Vermont. You are the chef, but I'm the manager, and I'm afraid I have done a poor job in orienting you to the way we do things at the Lake Bradford Hotel. I think it would be better if you and Gretchen took the day off. You have been working very hard. The Fourth of July is a holiday. Go up to Middlebury or over to Lake George and spend the night. I'll pay the bill. We'll just forget that we ever had this conversation, and we'll start all over again in the morning."

Rudy started to sputter a response, but Dr. Martin cut him off. "Mr. Bradford knows how to prepare the clam chowder. And since you've done such a good job training Cooper Dawkins, we'll take him off the waterfront and put an apron on him. As for me, I may not be a chef, but I'm a damn good cook!"

Oh, shit! thought Cooper. There goes my big plans for an afternoon on the dock.

※ ※ ※

Cooper reported for duty, and he and Mr. Bradford spent a good part of the afternoon working on the chowder. There was an outside cooking area behind a clump of bushes by the lake, which was made up of several large open fireplaces for grilling and the two old cast-iron wood stoves that had once served the hotel kitchen. They checked the clams and put them in large cauldrons, along with their liquid. "The brine is an important ingredient in New England clam 'chow-da,'" declared Mr. Bradford. "It's the basis for the broth, and you have to strain it through the cheesecloth to get rid of the sand and other impurities. Then we want to refill the clam barrels with fresh spring water and let them sit for twenty or thirty minutes. The clams are still alive, and they will suck in the fresh water and then spit out their juices, along with any more sand that is inside the shell. We'll run that through the cheesecloth, and then we'll put the big pots on the stove. We don't want the chowder to boil; it's just supposed to simmer."

Cooper remembered the many times that he and Guts had followed their grandfather through the clamming process in Mt. Sinai Harbor and then were given the job of hauling the buckets of clams down to Long Island Sound to keep them fresh. He wondered if Guts was doing that very task as Pops prepared for his own Fourth of July celebration.

"Now, Cooper," Mr. Bradford instructed, "you take that wheelbarrow, go back into the kitchen, and get the potatoes and onions. I'll start preparing the clams for the chowder. It's the little things like the clam chowder that keeps bringing the guests back year after year. Guests need to go home with good photographs, good memories, and a good taste in their mouths. If you're going to run a successful a summer hotel, you have to make sure that they get all three, or they won't come back."

When Cooper returned with the potatoes and onions, Mr. Bradford was busy doing surgery on the clams. He had cut off the hard necks of the clams into one pile and was filling a bucket with the softer portion. He put a skillet on the hot end of the stove and filled it with assorted scraps of bacon rind, and while it was being rendered, he chopped the clam necks into small pieces. Next, he strained the crisp pork scraps out of the skillet and stirred in the clam necks, along with a bowl of chopped onions. "This is a very important part of fixing the chowder," stated Mr. Bradford, "A lot of people throw the necks away, and then they wonder why the chowder doesn't have any flavor. Now, put the potatoes into the broth and when they have simmered about twenty minutes, we'll add the chopped necks. In the meantime, take the wheelbarrow up to the kitchen and fetch two of those big metal milk containers that come from the dairy. Make sure the cream hasn't been skimmed off the top. You know, the milk and cream is what makes New England clam chowder so good and so famous all over the world. It's not at all like that vegetable soup they serve down in the New York City hotels. Just because they throw a few clams into the kettle doesn't make it clam chowder!"

It occurred to Cooper that Mr. Bradford was presiding over the final ritual of mixing milk, soft clams, and broth with the devotion of a priest at an Easter celebration. Cooper stood by as a dutiful acolyte. The only difference between this and St. Phil's-on-the-Hill was that there were no bells to ring and no prayer book pages to turn, and instead of a final amen, Mr. Bradford ended his liturgy with an emphatic "*Splendid!*" Then, obviously pleased with his production, he turned to Cooper and directed, "Now all you need to do is stir the pots every ten minutes or so, and keep a low fire going under the kettles."

Mr. Bradford took off his apron, like a clerical vestment, and said, "While we're waiting for the first stir, why don't you push the wheelbarrow over to the icehouse and bring back about four blocks so that we can ice down the cola and the bottles of tonic?"

The icehouse was huddled in a grove of trees on a small incline close to the lake. All Cooper could see was a roof. The rest of the structure was underground. One of the staff members had told him that every winter, when the temperature stayed below freezing for three weeks and the ice was about a foot thick, the Thompson brothers, known locally as "the ice men," would make the rounds of the local lakes and ponds and refill the icehouses with crystal-clear blocks, which they then covered with sawdust. As Cooper headed in that direction, he realized he was whistling the Pepsi jingle he'd heard on the radio:

"Pepsi-Cola hits the spot, twelve full ounces, that's a lot / Twice as much for a nickel, too / Pepsi-Cola is the drink for you! Nickel…nickel…nickel…nickel…" The commercial worked its magic—Cooper wished he had one.

The door to the icehouse opened with a creak, reminding him of the opening and closing sound on one of his favorite radio programs, *Inner Sanctum*, which every week brought programs of mystery, terror, and suspense. The cool air was a welcome contrast to the eighty-degree weather, not to mention the heat from the old iron stove in Mr. Bradford's outdoor kitchen. Cooper took a shovel and began to clear away the blanket of sawdust until he heard the clink of the shovel against the ice. He also heard something else. This was beginning to remind him even more of *Inner Sanctum*. He called out, "Hello...hello... is anybody in here?" Then he heard the sound again. More than a little spooked, Cooper stepped back to the door, opened it as wide as he could, and stood at the entrance. The sound was definitely coming from the far corner of the icehouse, somewhere behind a mound of sawdust. And then, from behind that mound, two heads appeared. "Cooper? Cooper? Is that you?"

"That's me...er...it is I. Who are you?" There was no answer, but as Cooper's eyes adjusted to the dim light, he made out bare shoulders and the faces of Harvard/Radcliff. Cooper took the tongs off the wall, then loaded four blocks of ice in the wheelbarrow. When he closed the icehouse door, he considered putting a stick through the latch to seal the couple in the icehouse for the evening. He smiled at his thought but realized that it would be a mean thing to do. If he had a chance to bring a girl into the icehouse, he wouldn't want anyone to do that to him. He smiled again at this strange application of the Golden Rule. As he headed back to the outside kitchen, images of the two lovers rolling around in the sawdust ran through his mind. He unloaded the ice and chiseled it into small pieces but said nothing to anyone about what he had just seen, heard, or imagined.

※ ※ ※

In addition to the permanent picnic tables on the lawn by the lake, temporary tables had been improvised by placing planks over carpenter's sawhorses. Old tablecloths had been put over the planks to produce an outside dining room under the trees for more than 150 guests from the hotel and cottages. A small platform in front of the flag-pole, decked with red-white-and-blue bunting, had been set up at the water's edge, and at five o'clock a brass band from Middlebury High School set up shop and began a medley of patriotic songs. Their repertoire only lasted for fifteen minutes, and then they started all over again, but no one seemed to notice. During round two there was a burst of applause as eighteen children—toddlers up to twelve-year-olds—marched by the reviewing stand to the tune of "Stars and Stripes Forever." The three leaders were dressed in Revolutionary War costumes. One beat a drum, one carried a flag with thirteen stars, and one pretended to play a flute. Cameras clicked and flashbulbs (on the more expensive cameras) went wild. Two grandmothers brought up the rear, clutching a pair of infants who were keeping time to the music by waving American flags with forty-eight stars.

When the parade ended, the young bathing beauties, now attired in white summer dresses, reported to Cooper for duty at the corn-on-the cob counter. "Here we are," said the tall one who had worn the one-piece wool bathing suit. "Well, except for Marge, who met the trombone player and was over there, sitting on the edge of the bandstand." Cooper was in his element in the center of four adoring females. He had suddenly gone from low man to high man on the totem pole and took charge of the conversation. "Where do you ladies come from?" They giggled and identified their homes as New York City, Hartford, Albany, and Rutland. Cooper nodded. "I see, but I meant, where are you in school?" And then with a smile, he added, "I mean, what college do you attend?"

That brought a peal of laughter, and the tall one responded, "Well, actually, we're still in high school, but we're all going to go to college. My mother went to Smith, and that's where I'm going."

"That's interesting. My mother went to Smith," Cooper said. "It's supposed to be a very good school." Then it crossed Cooper's mind that she hadn't said when she was going to go to Smith and that the girls were playing the same game that he had tried when he arrived in Vermont. He smiled, and they smiled back, and then he decided it was time to get down to work before they asked him the name of his college. He took an ear of corn and demonstrated the art of what one of the girls called "peeling the corn." The operation lasted for one bushel and six minutes, and then Mr. Bradford came by to see how he was doing and shooed the girls away. They quickly regrouped and headed for the bandstand.

At six o'clock Mr. Bradford, megaphone in hand, stood before the assembled guests and began: "This is a splendid day in the life of Lake Bradford, in the life of Vermont, and the life of the United States of America..." Most of the guests had heard his speech many times; some had even memorized it. It would last approximately ten minutes, but nobody seemed to mind. It was like the parade, the chowder, and the fireworks—all part of the tradition of Lake Bradford; that was why they were all there. He wound up his address by saying, "From the Green Mountain Boys at Ticonderoga and Saratoga, to the men and women who served under Eisenhower and MacArthur, Vermonters have always been proud to answer the call to serve their country." He then asked all those among the guests and staff who were veterans to stand. Next he asked the wives and mothers of veterans to stand. They were all given a round of applause. After the

JULY 4, 1947

ladies had been seated, he added, "I especially want to recognize the Gold Star families. Mrs. Wilford, whose son was killed on Omaha Beach, and Mrs. Adams, whose husband gave his life for his country on Iwo Jima—will you ladies please stand so that we can thank you for the sacrifices that have kept this a free nation? The women stood with tears in their eyes and the gathering rose with them in sustained appreciation of their sacrifice.

"Please join me in the Pledge of Allegiance and then we will sing our national anthem."

I pledge allegiance to the flag of the United States of America and to the Republic for which it stands, one nation, indivisible, with liberty and justice for all.

When the pledge was finished, Mr. Bradford turned expectantly to the band. The leader threw up his hands and shrugged his shoulders as he moved closer to Mr. Bradford. "We don't have the music for the 'Star Spangled Banner.'"

"How about 'God Bless America'?" came a voice from the crowd.

"Yeah, we can do that one," said the band leader.

"Can I help you?" asked the same voice.

"Oh, please, we need all the help we can get," responded one of the boys in the band.

Rosie stepped on to the stage and took the megaphone from Mr. Bradford. The band had the tune but not the tempo, and even Rosie had trouble singing along.

"Let's do that again," she said, loud and clear through the cardboard funnel, "and this time around, will everybody please sing along with me?" The crowd joined her in singing. "God bless America, land that I love..."

The crowd stamped their feet, clapped their hands, and whistled. Then someone shouted, "Let's do it again!"

A SUMMER REMEMBERED

❖ ❖ ❖

"Kate Smith couldn't have done it better," said Cooper as he sat down next to Rosie to watch the fireworks over the lake. "You really were terrific, and you saved the day for Mr. Bradford."

"Thanks," said Rosie. "It was the least I could do. You wouldn't have a cigarette would you?"

"No problem," Cooper said, reaching for a pack in his shirt pocket. "Here, have a Camel."

"I thought you smoked Chesterfields."

Cooper shrugged nonchalantly. "I used to, but it seems like just about everybody is smoking Camels or Lucky Strikes."

Rosie took a cigarette from his pack and then leveled her gaze at him, asking, "Do you really want to be like everybody else?"

Cooper didn't answer, because he didn't know the answer. Yes, he had always wanted to be like the big guys. When he was in the third grade, he would watch the guys in the fourth grade to figure out what was the cool thing to do.

He remembered the first time he picked up a baseball bat in a game with the big kids, swung at the ball—and struck out. Everybody laughed, and he ran into the woods and hid until it was getting dark and the street lights came on. When he got home, he told his mother that he didn't feel good and wasn't hungry, and he ran up the stairs to his room and shut the door. His sister Vicki eagerly brought home the story of her little brother's humiliation, and Cooper's father came up to his son's room after supper with a dish of rice pudding with raisins. He placed it on the bedside table and then sat down at the foot of the bed. After five minutes, Frank Dawkins cleared his throat and said, "I understand you're learning how to play softball." Cooper turned over and pulled his pillow over his head. His father patted Cooper's leg and continued. "It took me a long time to learn how to swing that bat so that I could hit the ball." There was no verbal response, but Cooper had taken his head out of the pillow and was staring out the window. "What would you say if I told you that I could get a box seat at Ebbets Field on Saturday for the double-header with the Boston Braves?"

Cooper looked at his father for the first time, his eyes wide. "A box seat?"

"That's right, son, a box seat. I have a friend who has a box seat right near home plate. If he'll let us use it on Saturday, we can watch the pros up close."

Father and son took off early on Saturday morning, drove into Brooklyn, and watched the Dodgers beat the Braves 3–2 and 5–1. Then on Sunday afternoon Frank took his son into the backyard for his first lesson. Frank had driven a bamboo stake from an old fishing pole into the ground. On the top of the pole he had impaled a twelve-inch section of garden hose, which provided a perfect platform for a softball. Frank demonstrated the proper grip and swing before he handed the bat to his son, with the advice, "Take it easy. Don't try to murder the ball. Easy does it."

Cooper missed the ball completely with his first four swings. Then he hit the bamboo shaft several times. But finally, he connected and drove the ball over the back hedge.

"Looks like a home run to me!" yelled Frank as his young son clapped his hands and jumped up and down. Cooper's mother and two sisters, Vicki and Evelyn, watched from the kitchen window as the practice continued. Eventually, Cooper was connecting three out of four swings. "Nobody hits the ball every time," Frank assured him. "Even Babe Ruth strikes out more times than he gets a hit, much less a home run."

That weekend was probably the best one that Cooper ever had with his father, and it set a pattern for him of finding a "box seat"—watching and taking note of what the big guys were doing before trying to play the game. Cooper also realized, though, that there was a part of him that didn't want to be forced into a mold, just because everybody else was doing it. Yes, he had switched from Chesterfields to Camels because everyone was smoking Camels, but maybe what he really wanted to smoke was a cigar.

"You're being awfully quiet," said Rosie, "and you seem like a million miles away. You're not getting homesick, are you? I always get homesick on the Fourth of July. When I was a little girl, my mother would pack a picnic lunch, and we would leave our apartment really early to walk over to the Grand Concourse. We'd put a nickel in the slot and catch the subway for Battery Park, where we would board the Staten Island Ferry. It would go right by the big, green Statue of Liberty, and my *abba* would point and say, 'There she is! There's the great Lady of Freedom.' I was eleven when I first saw her. We all stood on the deck of the ferryboat and cheered, and Momma cried. Then Abba would point over to Ellis Island and say, 'That was my first home in America. It was like a prison, but we didn't mind because we knew that we were going to get to be Americans.'"

"Who is Abba?" asked Cooper.

"Abba is father in both Hebrew and Yiddish. Maybe it should be translated as daddy. You really are a goy."

"What's a goy?"

"It's Yiddish for Gentile—a non-Jew."

"Oh?"

"I think I'll start calling you goy-boy."

JULY 4, 1947

After the fireworks the crowd left the shoreline and moved into the grand lounge of the hotel, where there was dancing for the guests but not the staff. For a while Cooper and others stood on the porch at the window and watched. They were not allowed to mix or fraternize with the guests. Then they realized that the music could be heard outside on the porch, they began to pair off for dancing. Cooper watched as Ronnie and the marine did a number to the "Jersey Bounce." He lifted her off the floor, bounced her on his right knee and then his left knee, slipped her through his legs, and then tossed her over his shoulder. The guests heard the staff cheering for the dancers on the porch and had gathered at the windows; they were clapping their hands in time with the music.

When "A String of Pearls" dropped onto the turntable, Rosie bounced over to Cooper, her ponytail swishing from side to side. "Hey, goy-boy, I understand you like to jitterbug. How about the next dance?" Before Cooper could respond, Rosie had a firm grip on his left hand and started dancing, even though Cooper stood completely still. "You can't be a spectator all your life," she said. "Let's dance!" Almost against his will, Cooper's feet began to move with the music. "There you go goy,-boy. I knew you could do it." This time, the other dancers formed a circle around Rosie and Cooper and clapped their hands in time with the record. "Can you do that fancy stuff like the marine and Ronnie?" asked Rosie.

"I've done it once or twice."

"Let's see if you can bounce me on your knee. We'll take it slow and easy."

The audience picked up on their conversation and chanted, "Do it! Do it! Do it!"

Cooper nodded his head and then performed a flawless maneuver to the applause and cheers of staff and guests alike.

"Now, how about slipping me between your legs?" challenged Rosie. "Let's try that first and then when we get that down, you can throw me over your back." Cooper guided Rosie between his legs and back on her feet to more applause. "OK, now for the grand finale: first the right knee, then the left, between the legs, and then over your back. And a one, and a two, and a three."

It started as an award-winning number, but when Rosie slid between his legs, she emitted a primal scream. Cooper let go of her hands and looked down at his partner.

"My tush! My tush!" Rosie cried. "There's a splinter in my tush!"

CHAPTER SEVEN
JULY 5+

In spite of the fact that Cooper dropped into his bed totally exhausted after the Fourth of July festivities, he awoke at first light to the sound of the roosters crowing. He started to reach for his watch but changed his mind—he didn't really want to know what time it was. Then he tried to hide his head under the pillow and go back to sleep, but that didn't work. Reluctantly, he sat up and placed his feet in the slippers at the side of the bed. *No more leg cramps from the cold floor, thank you!* Almost by rote he reached into the drawer in the bedside table and pulled out his copy of the summer issue of "Forward Day by Day." It had come in the mail a week after he arrived. There was no note, just the wallet-sized booklet with daily Bible passages and brief thoughts for the day. The postmark was Mt. Sinai, New York, which meant that it had come from his grandfather Goetz. Pops always began his day with a reading from "Forward." Cooper remembered the first time that he and his cousin Guts had spent a Friday night at Pops' house so that on Saturday they could help him in his garden and, if they were lucky, go out with him in his old Buick to measure a building for appraisal purposes. The two boys had sat at the old oak kitchen table, and before Grandma Goetz poured milk for them and coffee for Pops, Pops would take out the pamphlet and read quietly. Then he would reach in his pocket, take out a coin or two, and place it in a mason jar marked "For the Missionaries."

"What ya reading, Pops?" Guts had inquired.

"It's about the prodigal son," said Pops. "I'm sure you heard about him in Sunday School." The two boys tried to look knowledgeable, but their grandfather read their expressions correctly and added, "You know, the story of the younger brother who left home and, after he had lost all his money, didn't know whether he could go home again."

Pops' description was faintly familiar to them, so the boys nodded their blond heads and assured their grandfather, "Oh, yeah."

"Well, it says here that God loves us so much, that even if we run away from the Lord, he will always welcome us back."

Now, Cooper heard a distant rooster announce the new day. He wondered how Pops would feel if he left Vermont and showed up on the doorstep of the beach cottage. Cooper shook his head, opened the booklet, and turned to July 5, hoping that in about an hour, Pops would be doing the same thing. The reading was from the nineteenth chapter of Luke's Gospel, the story of Zacchaeus. That was one of his favorites. He remembered that in Sunday School he had colored a picture of Zacchaeus sitting up in a tree, and he remembered learning a silly song: that went, "Zacchaeus was a wee little man and a wee little man was he." Cooper liked Zacchaeus because the wee little man had found a safe place up in a tree, where he could watch what was going on and see Jesus, and at the same time no one could get to him. Cooper read on:

Sooner or later all the Zacchaeuses of this world have to leave the safety of the tree branches and enter into the real world. Nothing happened to Zacchaeus until he joined the crowd and met Jesus face-to-face.

"No, thank you," said Cooper to himself. "Maybe when I get to college, maybe when I figure everything out, but for right now, if you'll excuse me, I'll stay up in the tree where it's safe."

For some reason the old lullaby "Rock-a-Bye Baby" drifted through his head. *When the bough breaks, the cradle will fall, and down will come baby, cradle and all.* He threw the booklet into the drawer and closed it with a bang.

Cooper was in the kitchen at 6:30 to fix the morning coffee. Having done that, he went out on the back porch to smoke a cigarette. He was alone, and he liked it that way. It gave him time to think about all that had happened during yesterday's big celebration. He was wondering about Rosie when he heard her voice from inside the screen door. "Hey goy-boy, is that you, Cooper?"

"Yes, it is," he called back. "It's me ... er ... I mean, it is I."

"Do you have another Camel, or do I have to walk a mile to the general store to get one?"

Cooper was on his feet. "Rosie, are you all right? Are you OK? I am so sorry. It was stupid of me to try to do all that fancy stuff that Ronnie and the marine were doing."

"Listen, kid, it was my idea, and it was my fault. I had to drag you out on the dance floor. It was like prying one of those clams loose from its shell to get you to dance, and you're a good dancer, too, even better than the marine. How were you to know that there was a splinter loose on that old porch floor just waiting to stab this little Jewish princess in the tush?"

"How do you feel? I mean, how is your...your..."

"If the truth be known, it's a pain in the ass. You notice I'm not sitting down. The splinter went in pretty deep, and it had jagged edges, so they couldn't pull it out. Dr. Martin called in Dr. Schuller—you know, the old guy down in the cottages. He did what he could and then packed me in his car and drove me into Middlebury, where they had to cut open my tush, take out the splinter, and then stitch it back up. They gave me a shot of penicillin and then some painkiller so that I could sleep."

"Does it hurt?"

Rosie broke into a broad smile. "Only when I laugh." Then she paused and "Only when I laugh or fart."

Cooper wasn't sure whether he was supposed to laugh at her comment. He thought that it was rather clever, but at the same time, he had never heard a female use the word fart. The guys used it all the time in the locker room and out on the ball field. His grandfather used it, but only in male company. Once, Cooper had used it at the dinner table when he didn't know what it meant, and he was dispatched into the kitchen to finish his meal. "The use of such vulgar language is not civilized," admonished Grandmother "Gamma" Dawkins, who was the self-appointed guardian of dining room etiquette. "It's definitely NTT—not table talk—and definitely not to be used in the presence of ladies." Pops had used the word once when he broke wind unexpectedly and told his grandsons, "That's why some people call us old farts." Cooper and Goetz doubled up with laughter until Pops instructed them, "Now don't tell your mothers or your grandmother that I said that. This is men talk. The ladies are offended by it."

JULY 5 +

Rosie's smile disappeared when a prewar Packard convertible with a Florida license plate came down the driveway. In the car were Rudy and Gretchen. Rosie stamped out her cigarette and headed for the dining room. The chef and his wife emerged from the car carrying a small overnight bag. Rudy had his usual early morning hangover look, and Gretchen just looked plain tired. "Is the coffee ready?" Rudy queried.

"It should be ready just about now," answered Cooper. "Can I fix you and Mrs. Hoffman a cup?"

"*Nein*, we will have one when we have changed our clothes and are ready to open the kitchen for breakfast. Have you started the bacon?"

"No, but I will get it in the oven in just a minute."

Cooper had learned how to prepare the bacon so that every strip came out flat and crisp. The secret was in baking rather than frying. Rudy had shown Cooper how to powder the bottom of a shallow pan with flour, and then place the strips of uncooked bacon in the pans, powder them again, and stick them in a 425-degree oven until they were crisp and brown. Rudy advised that the grease needed to be spooned off as soon as it accumulated and should be saved in a large coffee can, to be used for frying the eggs and the breakfast potatoes. "It is the bacon grease that gives the eggs and the potatoes their flavor," declared Rudy to his apprentice. "Oh, by the way," he added almost matter-of-factly, "I would stay away from that Jew girl if I were you. She is nothing but trouble. You will see."

Rudy and Gretchen returned twenty minutes later in crisp, fresh culinary uniforms and got down to business. Cooper and the waitresses wondered where the chef and his lady had been, but no one had the courage to ask, and Rudy wasn't about to give an explanation.

A SUMMER REMEMBERED

✣ ✣ ✣

Twelve feet below in the laundry, Dorcas and Mercy were sorting out the wash and the events of the previous day. Dorcas allowed that she had been "helping out" at a party in town. She had seen the parade in Middlebury and brought her colleague up-to-date on all of the town gossip. Mercy had signed on to help set up the picnic tables and had then helped with the children's games. But she had been at her duty post near the laundry room door when Rudy and Dr. Martin had had their now-famous confrontation on the kitchen porch. "I never heard such a thing. They were arguing over the chowder. Rudy claimed that there was only one way to make a proper chowder and that was with tomatoes. Dr. Martin said that they might do it that way over in York State or down in Palm Beach, but that at the Lake Bradford Hotel, they had been making the chowder with milk and cream for some sixty years, and they weren't about to change now. Then Rudy started saying something nasty in German. He didn't know that Dr. Martin spoke German and understood every word of it, and then Dr. Martin told Rudy and Gretchen to take the day off and to mind his tongue or he would lose his job."

"Well, what I want to know is, what did they ever do with all those tomatoes?" said Dorcas.

"You always did have a practical mind," said Mercy. "I heard that Dr. Martin and Libby started cutting them up for the salad. They did about two bushels when they saw that it would take all day, so rather than let all those tomatoes go to waste, they called Benson and told him to feed them to his pigs."

Dorcas chuckled. "Imagine all those happy pigs rolling around, squashing all those tomatoes."

Mercy added, "I wouldn't be too surprised if Benson got in there and rolled around in the tomatoes with the pigs." The two ladies giggled. Then Mercy became somber and interjected, "It really is sad about Benson, if you receive my meaning. His family had such great hopes for him."

"He always was a queer one, wasn't he?" Dorcas said.

"You never hear anybody call him by his full name, do you?"

"That's because nobody is supposed to know that he's a Bradford."

"Everybody knows, but nobody says. He's Mr. Bradford's nephew."

"I remember when he was born," said Dorcas. "Just about everybody in town was invited to the christening at First Church, and then Mr. Bradford's brother invited everybody over to the inn, next door, for a big party. They predicted a great future for the boy and toasted the heir to Bradford Farms."

"From the time he could walk, he couldn't stay away from the pigs. When he was three he broke loose from his mother and ran right down to the sty and jumped into the mud."

"They thought it was just a phase he was going through, that he'd outgrow it. He was a happy boy, but a queer one. They sent him off to boarding school, and they sent him right back home in less than a week."

"Enough of that," demanded Dorcas. "Everybody in these parts knows the story and nobody is supposed to talk about it. What I want to know is, where did Rudy and Gretchen go?"

"Nobody seems to know, but he and Gretchen came back this morning. They're upstairs in the kitchen, as busy as a couple of bees in an apple orchard. But they say that Gretchen looks like she spent the night crying her eyes out. I'll tell you something, Dorcas. I wouldn't want to be married to that man. She puts up with a lot, poor creature. He's a Nazi—and a drunk on top of that."

"It's none of my business, but if I were a wagering woman, I'd be willing to bet that the two of them don't make it through the summer."

Mercy's eyebrows rose. "You mean their job or their marriage?"

"Either way, but let's change the subject. I agree; it's none of our business. How on earth did they manage all the cooking yesterday without Rudy and Gretchen?"

"Actually," said Mercy, "it all went rather smoothly. Dr. Martin put on an apron and took over getting ready for the picnic. Mr. Bradford fixed the chowder, and that nice kid Cooper did the hamburgers and hot dogs and a dozen other chores. He really is a lot of help, even if he is still in high school. Everybody said that it was the best Fourth of July picnic ever, and the waitresses and kitchen staff said they didn't have to tiptoe around, trying not to upset that red-faced chef."

Mercy nodded her head in agreement and started folding a bunch of towels and then asked, "What's this I hear about that couple from Boston. You know, the guy is from Harvard and the girl wears a Radcliff sweater?"

"My, how news travels," said Dorcas. "They must be in some sort of trouble. Dr. Martin sent Stan out to find them this morning, and they're supposed to report to Mr. Bradford's office right after lunch."

CHAPTER EIGHT
OFF TO THE MOVIES

As the staff gathered for supper, Stan posted a notice on the bulletin board. "It's good news," he said and then disappeared through the dining room door. Everyone clustered around as Graham Morgan read the notice:

Mr. Bradford is happy to announce that in appreciation for the splendid work done by all the staff on the Fourth of July, he has secured a block of tickets at half-price for the showing on Wednesday and Thursday of the Academy Award-winning picture, The Best Years of Our Lives.

Those wishing to avail themselves of this opportunity should sign up below. Please indicate your evening of preference. Transportation will be provided in the hotel station wagon.

"You'd think he could just give us the tickets," said Sheila. "I mean, after all the work we did yesterday."

"Half-price is better than nothing," said the marine.

"So, it will cost everybody a quarter," said Rosie. "Big deal!"

"Let's go for Thursday," added Ronnie. "Then I'll have time to shampoo my hair tomorrow."

"Why don't you just cut it all off?" Sheila sneered. "Then you'll be able to see the movie with both eyes."

"Hey, girls, break it up." It was Blue Bird Stan. "I have an announcement to make. I'm sorry to have to report that Forrest Lowell and Abigail Danvers, from Boston, are no longer in the employ of the Lake Bradford Hotel. Forrest was on the grounds crew, and Dr. Martin believes that it will not be a problem to cover his duties."

Kevin punched Danny and said, "You know what that means? That means you and I will have more work to do."

Stan ignored the interruption. "Abigail, as you know, had responsibility for four tables, and we will have to redistribute that responsibility until we can find a replacement."

"That means more work," said Sheila.

"And more tips," countered Stan.

"Why are they leaving?" was the question that came out of a dozen mouths. Everybody knew the answer, but they wanted to hear what Stan would say.

Stan paused and then, in his most officious voice, replied, "I'm afraid that I am not at liberty to divulge that information."

❧ ❧ ❧

The wagon was definitely overloaded with ten people crammed into the small space. In deference to Rosie's "delicate condition" from the splinter, she had the front seat all to herself, next to Stan, and even then, she sat at an angle and shifted her position every three minutes. In the back three rows, Ronnie, Sheila, and Audrey sat on male laps or bounced on knees. Ronnie was with the marine. Each one of the Seton Hall boys contributed a knee to support Audrey, and Sheila was wiggling on the lap of Graham Morgan. Cooper was pressed up against the door with half his rear end barely clinging to the edge of the seat.

"They found out that they were married," declared Sheila.

"Well, it was pretty obvious that something serious was going on between them," observed Ronnie. "I mean, did anybody ever see her in *her* bedroom?" After a long silence she added, "Well, there's your answer. How about it? Did Harvard—I mean, Forrest—ever show up in the men's end of the fourth floor?"

"He never joined our bull sessions," offered Kevin, "but I did see him shaving in the morning. He was something of a loner. Nice guy. He did his job, but he didn't go out of his way to make friends. On the Fourth he worked like a Trojan, setting up the picnic tables, but then he disappeared. He didn't help out with the games or hang around for any of the ceremonies."

Cooper blushed at the memory of seeing Harvard and Radcliff in the icehouse and thought Kevin's reference to Trojans was rather funny. He considered reporting on his icehouse meeting with the pair but thought better of it. Rosie, perched precariously on the front seat, was facing the rear of the van and noticed the change in Cooper's expression. "Hey, Cooper." She snapped her fingers in front of his nose. "Are you daydreaming again? Come on snap out of it. A penny for your thoughts." The pink in Cooper's cheeks turned scarlet as she added, "I'll bet you were trying to imagine them doing it." Everybody laughed except Cooper, who wished he hadn't signed up for a night at the movies.

"Well, there she is," declared Stan. "There's the theater, and look at that line at the box office."

The marquee boldly declared:

A SUMMER REMEMBERED

1946 Academy Award **Winner**
THE BEST YEARS OF OUR LIVES
Starring
Dana Andrews, Myrna Loy, Fredric March, Teresa Wright

"It's a good thing we already have our tickets," said Stan. "But I doubt if we'll be able to sit together." Like a line of ducks, they filed out of the wagon and into the theater.

"Who said we want to sit together?" said Graham Morgan as he grabbed Sheila's hand and disappeared up the balcony stairs, followed by Ronnie and the marine, Audrey took the arms of both Kevin and Danny and marched them down the side aisle toward the stage. That left Stan, Rosie, and Cooper standing in the lobby. "I've either got to get a seat on the aisle or stand at the back," said Rosie, "There's no way I'm going to put my sore tush in one of those folding seats."

"Does it still hurt?" Stan asked.

Cooper cringed; he knew what was coming next.

"Only when…only when…" Rosie looked at Cooper and smiled. "Only when I smile or…or when I sit on it."

Cooper expelled his breath and smiled back at Rosie.

"Why don't we stand at the back and keep Rosie company?" Stan suggested as he staked out a spot on the barricade that divided the orchestra seats from the lobby and the refreshment stand. "Besides, we can smoke in the lobby whenever we want. Otherwise, we would have to go up in the balcony to light up."

✤ ✤ ✤

There was wild applause when Dana Andrews kissed Teresa Wright and "The End" appeared on the screen. Afterward, the hotel gang gathered on the sidewalk outside the theater. When Ronnie brushed the lock of golden hair off her face to light up a cigarette, Cooper noted sadly that her lips were a pale pink, rather than their usual bright Chinese red, and the Marine had traces of the lipstick on his earlobe and his shirt. Graham was adjusting his brass belt buckle and Sheila was adjusting her sweater. It had already been agreed that they would drop in at the Pine Room in the basement of the Middlebury Inn for a beer before returning to the lake.

As the station wagon chugged up the hill in first gear on the south side of the village green, Stan pointed to the massive Civil War statue across from the hotel. "Take a look at that statue! Do you see the sailor with the spy glass?"

The wagon tilted to the left as everyone tried to see what Stan was talking about. "OK," said the marine, "what about it?"

"Middlebury students," continued Stan, "say that it's not a statue at all but the dean of men with a telescope, taking down the names of the students going into the tavern."

"Do they really say that?" countered Rosie. "Or are you just making that up?"

"I think he just made that up," said Ronnie as Stan pulled the hotel wagon into the one remaining parking space in front of the hotel. "Did anybody really like the movie? I don't care if it did get an Academy Award. It wasn't the best movie I've ever seen," she continued. "I mean, Fredric March looked too old to be a sergeant. He looked ancient. I mean, he looked over fifty. He was too old to be drafted, and wasn't there an age limit on volunteers?"

Cooper thought about his own father coming home after the war. He was forty-one when the Japanese bombed Pearl Harbor and only forty-five when they surrendered. He came out a colonel and not a sergeant, and he looked a lot younger than Fredric March.

Rosie chimed in, "How about Teresa Wright? She was supposed to be his daughter, which meant she couldn't have been more than nineteen, but she looked more like thirty-five. And then she was supposed to be a nice girl, but she went after Dana Andrews when she knew he was a married man."

"That was very touching about the sailor who had lost his hands," said Sheila, "but he really gave me the creeps. I mean, how would they…what would it be like to…you know. I mean, having a man touch your body with those claws or with those stumps where his hands are supposed to be?"

"Well," added Ronnie, "Dana Andrews was really a gorgeous guy, a great physique and all that, but if he wakes up in the middle of the night, sweating and having nightmares, I don't think I would like to be married to him and have to put up with those bad dreams. I don't think I would like to have to deal with that for the rest of my life. I mean, really!"

Audrey finally jumped in with her opinion. "I don't think that the Academy Award had anything to do with the acting or with the plot. I'll bet they gave it an Academy Award simply because it was about all the returning veterans, and how they are having difficulty getting jobs and adjusting to civilian life, and how we're supposed to be grateful for their sacrifices on the battlefield."

"What's wrong with that?" yelled the marine, who had been doing a slow boil as he listened to the running commentary. "Let me tell you, when you've spent the longest night of your life lying on the wet sand of a beach in the Pacific, with bullets zinging over your head and the dead bodies of your buddies all around you, you're entitled to a few bad dreams! And if your hands just happened to have been blown off while you were fighting for your country and for the people back home, and if it hadn't been for a few men like Roosevelt and Churchill and Eisenhower and MacArthur, and yes, Fredric March and Dana Andrews and that guy Homer with the claws, we would be living in quite a different kind of world, one that was being run by the likes of Hitler and Tojo. Thank God for Homer, claws and all. He was a real-life veteran, by the way. I hope he made a lot of money in the movie and gets to marry the prettiest, sexiest girl in the world—one with a big heart who will appreciate what he did for his country."

As the wagon pulled into the parking lot, the Seton Hall boys chimed in, "We'll say amen to that."

※ ※ ※

Luckily, there was one empty table available in the Pine Room. It was set up for eight, but they squeezed in another two chairs.

"I don't really need a whole chair; just a half will do," declared Rosie, "if you folks know what I mean."

"What are you saying, Rosie?" teased Kevin. "Are you telling us that you're half-assed?" He looked at Danny for approval, and the others grinned.

"Something like that, cowboy. But if you don't put a bit in that big mouth of yours, I know an old nun in Hoboken, New Jersey, who'll come up here and wash your mouth out with brown laundry soap and rap your knuckles with a ruler so you'll never play basketball again!"

"What language are you guys doing tonight?" asked the waitress who was standing behind Ronnie.

"What do you mean, 'language'? What language? We just came in to have a beer," stated said Stan, who still thought of himself as the leader of the group.

"Aren't you from the college?" asked the waitress. "Everyone in summer school is taking a language full time. They eat, sleep, and drink in French, German, Italian, Spanish, or Russian."

"Well, we drink in English," said Rosie.

"Aren't you from the college?"

"No, we're from the Lake Bradford Hotel."

"Oh," said the waitress. She chewed her lip nervously and quickly disappeared.

She was replaced by the bartender, who asked, "Did you say you're from the Lake Bradford Hotel?" They all nodded, and the bartender narrowed his eyes. "If you brought that big fat German with you, you'll have to leave."

"Are you talking about our chef, Rudolph Hoffman?" Stan asked. "How do you know Rudy?"

The bartender explained that Rudy and his wife had checked into the inn on the Fourth of July. "They came down to the Pine Room for supper, ordering pitchers of beer. They kept pretty much to themselves until the college kids started coming in. By that time your chef was pretty mellow and started singing along with the kids, especially the ones at the German table. Next thing you know, he stands up and starts singing the German national anthem '*Deutschland, Deutschland über alles.*' Some of the veterans in the tavern started yelling for him to sit down.

Then there was a table of Lutheran missionaries who were here for the summer crash course in Spanish. They stood up and tried to drown him out with the words from the old hymn 'Glorious Things of Thee Are Spoken,' which has the same tune as 'Deutschland.' Then your chef started yelling stuff in German, and the students at the German table understood what he was saying. Next thing you know, the students were squirting bottles of beer at your chef. We almost had a riot on our hands. Eventually, the Vermont state troopers came in and took him and his wife out to their squad car. Boy, that man must have been in the Gestapo. It must be hell to work for him down at Lake Bradford. Does he act that way at the hotel?"

The bartender left without waiting for an answer, and the waitress came back to the table. "Before I take your orders I'm going to have to check a few IDs. This is Vermont, not New York State. You can drink in New York at age eighteen. The legal age over here is twenty-one, not eighteen."

Cooper almost blurted out "Oh, shit!" but caught himself; in his head he heard Gamma Dawkins admonishing, "NTT." He considered making a dash for the men's room, but the waitress only pointed to Rosie, Audrey, and Kevin, saying, "I need to see yours and yours and yours."

"I'll show you mine if you'll show me yours," Kevin wisecracked.

"Maybe later, big guy, but right now, all I need to see is your driver's license."

Kevin and Rosie were twenty-one, but Audrey was barely nineteen.

"Just order a Coke," whispered Stan. "The rest of us will ask for pitchers of beer and then you can drink whatever you want."

"OK, that's six pitchers of beer, one Coke, and three bowls of pretzels. Is it all right if I put this on one check?" the waitress asked.

"One check will be fine," said Stan and then as she left, all eyes were on Cooper, who had a silly grin on his face.

"Twenty-one!" was the quiet hiss of the whole table. This was Cooper's unexpected moment of glory. At least someone thought that he was a grown man and not just a kid from Manhasset High.

"We'll have to treat him with a little more respect," offered Rosie as the Spanish table broke into song with "La Cucaracha" The Germans followed with a Heidelberg drinking song, and the French countered with "Chevalier de la Table Ronde."

Their beer had arrived and so Stan stood up with a pitcher in his hand and led his group in "To the Tables Down at Mory's." Before another table could offer a song, the marine stood up and thundered, "Let's sing a real man's song!

> From the halls of Montezuma,
> To the shores of Tripoli,
> We will fight our country's battles,
> On the land as on the sea."

He was joined by a few other marine vets, who broke ranks with their language tables and joined in.

> "First to fight for right and freedom
> and to keep our honor clean.
> We are proud to claim the title of
> United States Marines."

There was a round of thunderous applause as the gaggle of marines sat down, and then Ronnie leaned over and said, "Well,

I'm glad you got that out of your system. Now, maybe we can forget about the war and get down to some really important things."

"Forget about the war? I hope we never forget about the war!" declared the Marine. "God help us if we ever forget about the war!"

"Cigarette, anybody?" Cooper broke in as he aimed his fresh pack of Camels in an arc around the table.

"I'll take one of your Camels," said Ronnie. Cooper handed her one, and she brushed back her hair as he offered her a light. At the same time, the marine got up and walked to the bar, where he was joined by the four other Marines who had accompanied him in the hymn.

"Those veterans really think they're something special," stated Ronnie. "I mean they expect everybody to bow and scrape just because they were out in the Pacific. They think they're the greatest generation that ever lived."

"Why don't we change the subject?" said Cooper. Ronnie's nose was no more than six inches from his, and she was gently blowing smoke in his face. He turned to face her. "So, how are you doing with the crossword puzzles in the *Times*?" asked Cooper. Ronnie commented that the New York and Boston papers arrived at the hotel a day late and that Dr. Martin and all the guests who got them also worked the puzzles.

"My first week here," she said, "I saw a big stack of newspapers out by the trash cans and I went through every one of them, and either the puzzle had been completed or someone had torn it out. I tried the puzzle in the *Addison County Independent*, but that only comes out once a week and is not even close to being as tough as the *Times*, so I put in a collect call to my mother in New Jersey. She agreed to cut out the puzzles and send me a batch each week." As she spoke, Ronnie's free hand rested on Cooper's knee under the table. He shifted his legs and adjusted his trousers, but the hand remained. "When I get the next batch," she told him, "I'll bring them to the staff table, and we can work on them together, if you like."

Cooper nodded and reached for a fresh pitcher of beer. He refilled their glasses and held his up to Ronnie. "You've got a deal!" Ronnie blew another stream of smoke in his face, most of which, unfortunately, went down Cooper's throat the wrong way. He started to cough and struggle for air. Ronnie jumped up and banged him on the back, and in regaining his breath, he spilled his beer, much of which landed in his lap. Cooper grabbed a napkin, but Ronnie took it out of his hands and knelt before him, blotting his shirt and his crotch, and said, "Let me help you with that." Cooper nearly fainted.

"Hey, what's going on over there?" yelled Stan, who had assumed the role of chaperone, if not for the whole group then at least for Cooper.

"I spilled my beer," sputtered Cooper, who had turned the color of rare roast beef.

"Well, have some more," offered Danny as he took on the task of replenishing everyone's glass. Cooper nodded in agreement.

"We were discussing the next presidential race, if you two care to join us," said Stan as he stared directly at Cooper and Ronnie.

"Nobody seems to think Truman stands a chance," Rosie put in. "After all, he's an accidental president, and the only nice thing anyone can say about him is that he's better than former Vice President Henry Wallace."

"I overheard a discussion in the lobby," said Stan, "that Jim Farley and some other leaders of the Democratic Party are planning to dump Truman and draft General Eisenhower."

As the discussion ran its course, the consensus seemed to be that Governor Dewey of New York would be the next president. Cooper kept quiet, but he wasn't thinking about politics anyway. He was thinking about what had been going on with Ronnie—and then he felt her hand on his leg again. There was no question about it; she was flirting and doing it in high gear. When the marine came back to the table, she hardly noticed, and he made no attempt to communicate with her. Cooper poured himself another glass of beer, and his mind went back to his fantasies during the train ride.

Meanwhile, the tavern was back into competitive singing. Even though it was July, the Germans offered "O Tannenbaum," and the French countered with "Jeanette Isabella." When it was Lake Bradford's turn, Rosie hobbled over to the piano, sat gingerly on the stool, and belted out "Who owns New York? Oh, who owns New York? Oh, who owns New York? The people say, Oh, we own New York. Oh, we own New York. C-O-L-U-M-B-I-A!" Once at the piano, she was stuck for the rest of the evening, concluding with "God Bless America."

It was well after midnight when the old Ford wagon inched its way along to Route 7 and headed toward the lake. When they turned off the main highway at Bradford Farms, it seemed to Cooper that the road was bumpier and had more curves than on the way into town, and the collective beer breath of the wagon's ten passengers was less than invigorating. They swerved once to avoid a dog chasing a fox and then came to a jolting stop—a startled deer stared back at the headlights. Someone started singing the "Whiffenpoof Song" and about the time they came to the line, "We're little black sheep who have gone astray," Cooper interrupted with the request, "Mind if I roll down the window and get some fresh air?" He didn't wait for an answer and proceeded to stick his head out of the car and gulp for air. He might have made it back to the hotel if it hadn't been for the covered bridge.

"Everybody make a wish!" shouted Stan.

Cooper didn't hold his breath or make a wish. His hope that he not throw up was thwarted by the musty air inside the bridge and the clanking of the loose planks under the weight of the wagon. "Let me out!" he yelled as he threw open the car door.

The plea to stop the car was seconded by a half-dozen voices. Fortunately, the wagon had crept across the bridge and was doing only five miles an hour when Stan slammed on the brakes. Cooper fell onto the soft shoulder and stumbled to a nearby fence, leaned over, and let it flow. He was joined by the Seton Hall boys, who had also consumed more than their fair share of the fruit of the hops. The marine found a place behind a bush and sounded like someone had opened a fire hose.

CHAPTER NINE
THE MORNING AFTER

If there's one thing Rudy ought to understand, it's a hangover. Cooper repeated this thought over and over in his head as he sat at the staff table and waited for his boss to come down for breakfast. Cooper had fixed the coffee, but he couldn't drink it. He tried some weak tea but gave up after a small sip. He held his head in his hands, as if that would stop the pounding, but the worst pain was in his ego—the ego that had soared when the waitress didn't ask him for an ID and when Ronnie put her hand on his knee, only to crash as he puked over the fence at the side of the road. He was trying to figure out what he was supposed to do next to get breakfast started, but was having trouble holding on to any coherent thought.

"Well, goy-boy, you really tied one on last night," declared Rosie as she drew a cup of coffee and took up half a chair on the other side of the table. "I'd make you some chicken soup, but I doubt if you could handle it at this tender point in your newfound adult life."

Cooper shifted his eyes in Rosie's direction, but that hurt so he closed them and bowed his head. A casual observer might have guessed that he was saying grace, but he felt nothing to give thanks for.

"Welcome to the wild world of college life," chuckled Rosie, who was trying to be funny but realized that she wasn't helping a bit. Then she tried another tack. "My uncle Morris used to say that a raw egg and some Worcestershire sauce was good for a hangover."

Hearing that suggestion, Cooper made a mad dash for the staff toilet. Rosie was going to add that there were others who recommended tomato juice and Worcestershire sauce, but Cooper was already behind the bathroom door making morning-after noises.

When Cooper returned, Ronnie was seated at the end of the table. He was embarrassed to see her and was certain that he had ruined all of his chances with her, which had seemed so promising when they first started connecting at the tavern. "Oh, Cooper," she said, "are you OK? Do you feel all right?" She slid behind him and offered, "Let me rub the back of your neck. Maybe that will help."

Cooper, feeling as though his pale face qualified him for a role in a Frankenstein movie, sat quietly as Ronnie began her ministrations. She brushed her hair to one side as he put his elbows on the table and cradled his head in his hands. Ronnie gently stroked his head and then placed her hand on the cords at the back of his neck. It was soothing and stimulating. Cooper was cookie dough in her hands. Gradually, he forgot about the throbbing and began to consider other possibilities. Ronnie broke into his fantasy when she lowered her voice and purred, "Cooper, when you were a little kid and had a tummy ache, what did your mother do for you to make you feel better?"

The first image that crossed Cooper's mind was a vaporizer hissing at his bedside, but that was for a bad cough and a stuffed-up nose, not an upset stomach. Then he remembered the ginger ale. "My mom always got me a glass of Canada Dry ginger ale," he told Ronnie. "It would go down and stay down when nothing else would work."

Ronnie excused herself and ran into the dining room and brought back a bottle of Canada Dry. She stopped at the old ice box, chipped off a chunk of ice, and brought it to her patient. "Here—sip this slowly." By this time the movie crowd, minus Stan, had all gathered at the staff table. Except for Ronnie and Rosie everyone looked like they had spent the night on a twenty-mile hike. Only the marine was drinking coffee; the rest had opted for hot tea or were eyeing Cooper's ginger ale. Ronnie continued massaging Cooper's neck, and his moans of agony were turning to sighs of contentment.

"Can anyone get a neck rub?" asked the marine, but Ronnie ignored him.

Suddenly the misery-loves-company meeting was jolted out of its doldrums when Rudy shouted, "What is going on here? Why is everybody still sitting around when there is much work to be done? Cooper, have you started the bacon? Ladies, are there any guests in the dining room? Let us not be still standing. Everybody up und be busy, yah?"

The kitchen morning ballet proceeded in slow motion. Cooper powdered a rasher of bacon with flour and placed it in the oven. The big double-boiler was fired up and the oatmeal flakes stirred into the hot water, but Rudy noticed that Cooper was moving like a reluctant turtle. "Do you feel all right?" Rudy inquired. "Are you sick or just daydreaming, thinking about that blonde who was rubbing your neck?"

Cooper again thought that if anybody knew what to do for a hangover, it was Rudy, so with some embarrassment he shared the previous night's adventure.

"I have just the remedy to fix you up as good as new," said Rudy. "Come and follow me into the big meat locker." Under a blanket, behind several hanging sides of beef, were three cases of beer and one case of Canadian Club. "We will do what the Americans call 'taking a bite of the hair of the dog that bit you,'" said Rudy. He poured a generous portion of Canadian Club into a coffee cup and handed it to his apprentice. Cooper looked in the cup and then back at Rudy. He had never drunk Canadian Club, although there was always a bottle of it in his father's liquor cabinet. In fact, the only hard liquor he had ever had was a Tom Collins at a sorority dance at the Knickerbocker Yacht Club and some rum punch at a wedding reception. Rudy tried to overcome the boy's hesitation. In a very paternal voice he urged, "Here, drink this. It will make you feel better." Cooper wanted to please Rudy, and at the same time he wanted to feel better. He took a sip from the cup; it burned his throat and he started to cough. He almost spilled the Canadian Club on the floor but managed to hand it back to Rudy before he bolted out the door in search of the water cooler. Rudy found Cooper sitting on the back porch, trying to smoke a cigarette. In a rare gesture of kindness, Rudy suggested, "Why don't you go up to your room and lie down for a while?"

The fourth load of towels was tumbling in the dryer, and the air in the room was hot. The laundry ladies had discarded their sweaters and taken off their sneakers and stockings, and they sat facing each with their toes wiggling to the rhythm of the washing machine. Even though they hadn't heard the faint wail of the noon whistle at the quarry across the lake, they had spread a napkin over the apple crate and were setting up for lunch.

Mercy opened a cigar box containing a tin of deviled ham, a pat of butter, two slices of whole wheat bread, a slice of dill pickle and two brownies. She buttered one slice of bread, opened the tin, and spread a thin layer of its contents on the second slice. Then with great ceremony, she joined the two pieces and cut the sandwich carefully into four equal segments. She arranged her creation on a small plate and placed the pickle delicately on the right side of the sandwich. Then she threw up her hands, smiled at her partner, and exclaimed, "There!"

Mercy simply went to her locker and came back with a child's small lunchbox covered with figures from *Snow White*. She removed a ham sandwich wrapped in wax paper, a small piece of white cheddar cheese, and a not-quite-ripe purple plum. She sat opposite Dorcas and said heartily, "There! Too!"

"Whose turn is it to say the blessing?" Dorcas asked.

"I believe it's yours," countered Mercy.

"All right, then," stated Dorcas, as her voice shifted to mellow, stained-glass tones. "Let's bow our heads and pray." She began by thanking the Almighty for a multitude of blessings—personal, local, national, and international. She informed her Creator of the weather, the local economy, and what seemed like the complete list of patients at the Middlebury Hospital. When she finally got to her "amen," Mercy said, "Well, that about covers it."

Each one took a bite or two before Mercy said, "Oh! I almost forgot the soda pop that Standish brought down from the kitchen—two bottles of orange tonic."

"Didn't he have any grape? He ought to know by now that grape is my favorite."

"Oh, Dorcas, Dorcas," said Mercy. "He's known that all summer and last summer, too. He came by when you were not available and wanted to tell you personally that they are out of the grape tonic, but they expect that the delivery man will be by this afternoon with a fresh supply."

"That was nice of him. That Standish is a nice boy." Dorcas took a sip of orange soda. She smacked her lips a time or two and then said, "Did he have anything else to say?"

"Oh, my, yes!" declared Mercy. "He just couldn't wait to tell me that our boy Cooper had too much to drink last night and that they had to stop the wagon so that Cooper could throw up on the side of the road. He said he was lucky that the young lad didn't 'puke' in the wagon."

"I don't like that word," said Dorcas. "It sounds so messy." She took a deep breath before saying, "Can we change the subject? I'd rather talk about something else while we're eating our lunch."

"Well, the reason I brought up the subject at all," Mercy explained, "was to say that I don't think Standish is particularly fond of young Cooper. I don't think he's said a kind word about him since he arrived."

"Noticed that, did you?" Dorcas snorted. She tilted her head and then asked, "You don't suppose he's a bit jealous, do you?"

"Why on earth would Standish be jealous of Cooper?" asked Mercy. "I mean, next year he'll be a junior at Harvard. He comes from an old Boston family and he has the top job here at the hotel. Why would he be jealous of a high school lad from Long Island?"

"Well, if you ask me, I don't his jealousy has anything to do with that. I think," Dorcas said sagely, "that it has to do with being the center of attention."

"Center of attention?"

"Yes, last summer everybody was talking about Standish. He was Mr. Bradford's fair-haired boy. All the waitresses and half of the widowed women were talking about him and flirting with him. They still do, but this year, the boy from Long Island is the one everybody wants to hear about."

※ ※ ※

It was three o'clock in the afternoon when Cooper re-entered the kitchen. No one was there except Benson, the dishwasher, who had just swept and mopped the floor. Cooper's nausea had passed and now his appetite was returning. He found a soup bowl and dished out some broth from the stockpot on the back of the stove. Then he located two bread rolls and sat down at the end of the staff table. Benson wrung out his mop on the back porch and joined Cooper at the table. He opened a large brown paper bag and asked, "Want some…want some chicken? Cooper?"

"Where'd you get the chicken?" asked Cooper.

"Oh…you know. It comes…back from the…dining…room. Nobody…has touched…it. I only…save…the pieces…that haven't been…touched. The other stuff…goes in… the bucket…I take …to feed the…pigs." Benson stuck his hand in the bag and retrieved a dark pink piece of meat. "Want some … ham…Cooper? The ham is…real good."

Benson's generosity set Cooper back about two hours. He did his best to look the other way and then excused himself, leaving behind a half-empty soup bowl and one bread roll. He was almost out the door when Benson called out, "Cooper! Cooper... I think you...got a letter."

❧ ❧ ❧

Cooper sat on the back porch and opened the package from his mother. It contained a sweatshirt with "Michigan" stenciled on front and back. He tried it on. It was about a size too large, but that was OK. He bloused it so that it fit like an Eisenhower jacket. He could see his reflection in one of the kitchen windows, and he liked what he saw. His shoulders were broad, and his waist and hips were slim. If he had dark hair instead of blond, he thought that he would look like Dana Andrews. He liked everything about Dana Andrews, except for the bad dreams he had in the movie. Too bad he hadn't had the shirt when he arrived at the Middlebury train station. His mother also sent a letter, which he put in his pocket. He would read it later, but first he wanted to see what the note from Guts had to say, but he didn't want to read it near the hotel kitchen, where Rudy could show up and put him back to work.

Cooper walked down the trail to the icehouse, where he had noticed a small path that continued along the edge of the lake. As he walked along the water's edge, it became obvious that the path wasn't a major walkway. There was at least a year's growth of pine and maple seedlings that were doing their best to take root in the hard soil. Wasn't there something in the Bible about seed falling on hard ground and being eaten by the birds or stepped on by travelers? About two hundred yards into this no-man's-land, he found an outcropping of granite rock and sat down to rest. This was as good a place as any to see what Guts had to say.

THE MORNING AFTER

Hey, Coop!

Wow! Did I just have the best Fourth of July ever. As you know, we had a long weekend, so I went out to the beach house as soon as school got out to help Pops get ready for the big day.

We dug over a bushel of clams in Mount Sinai Harbor for the chowder. The butcher in Port Jefferson had prepared twenty pounds of two-inch-thick steaks. We stopped at the vegetable stand on Old Country Road and practically bought them out of corn, potatoes, onions, and tomatoes. Pops got the tomatoes to go in the chowder. He says that's the only way to do it—not like they do it in New England with a lot of milk.

Speaking of "doing it," I finally hit a home run. You know this girl I was telling you about? The one I met at school? Her name is Bristol.

Well, back to the beach cottage. I got up early on the Fourth and took the clams down to the sound for their last drink of water. Then I helped Pops set up the picnic tables and start the fires in the grill.

As soon as just about everybody arrived, I told everyone hello and then got into my Humpmobile and took off. Just about everybody we know or are related to was there, except of course for your dad and Grandma Dawkins.

I took the Jericho Turnpike into Hicksville to pick up Bristol. She has light brown hair, almost blonde, and a gorgeous figure. We started eating lunch together at school, and then I started driving her home after school. We went to the drive-in movie a couple of times, but I wouldn't exactly say that we made out—nothing more than kissing and holding hands. I guess you could say that I got to first base.

Bristol's parents were having a picnic in the backyard with some of the neighbors. They insisted we stay and have some hot dogs and homemade ice cream. Bristol's father is in real estate and all he could talk about was Levittown and the building boom on Long Island.

He says that you and I better put our education into high gear or we may miss all the action.

He says that developers are buying up the potato fields all the way out to Riverhead.

Bristol and I headed for Jones Beach. The first three parking lots were full, but we finally found one with open space. It was still more than a half-mile walk to the beach. I guess it was the beach. We could hardly see the sand or find a place to put our blanket. It was really hot, and Bristol and I headed for the surf. We stayed in the water a long time and we really got close, if you know what I mean.

We watched the fireworks from our blanket and then we went back to the Humpmobile in the parking lot and had some real fireworks of our own. If we'd been playing baseball, you'd call it a home run! Wow! I hope you had a great

Fourth of July and enjoy your own ball game in the Green Mountains.
God bless America!
Your cousin and friend for life,
Guts!

P.S. Please destroy this letter when you have read it.

Cooper reread the letter twice and then exclaimed, "Lucky guy! Guts is a lucky guy." The sound of his voice startled two little red squirrels that had been observing him from a low branch of a maple tree. Cooper tore Guts' letter into tiny pieces and then walked to the edge of the lake and threw the pieces in the lake. Much to his surprise, there was a churning in the water as the remains of Guts' letter were attacked by a hungry school of lake trout. *That certainly takes care of Guts' request to destroy his letter*, Cooper thought.

He resumed his walk along the path, and as he walked, he relived the train ride with Ronnie from Grand Central all the way to Middlebury. He thought about the marine and that he had been outclassed until the beer party following the movie. Hadn't Ronnie turned her back on the marine and quite openly started flirting with him? Then he remembered puking at the side of the road and feeling that he had lost any chance he might have had with Ronnie. But then, what was she telling him that morning when she rubbed his neck and brought him the ginger ale? He shivered as he thought of her strong little hands on his body, and it awakened in him a whole new set of fantasies.

A branch brushed his face as he entered a small clearing and heard the sound of gurgling water. An old stone dam had been constructed to turn a meandering stream and assorted springs into the ten-mile lake system, which was named after the first Bradford settlers. There had been a lot of rain, and the water level was high, and so a silver sheet of water slid over the edge and pounded the rocks ten feet below. While the path had been virtually abandoned, there was evidence that boats had pulled up on the narrow sandy beach that separated the grass carpet from the lake.

Cooper stood at the water's edge and discovered his own image staring back at him. He liked what he saw—a tall young man wearing a Michigan sweatshirt and khaki trousers. He looked to the left and then to the right before posing with his hands on his hips. Yes. Yes! If the sweatshirt was an Ike jacket and his hair was darker, he would indeed look like Dana Andrews, except for the ugly pimple on his cheek. He took his handkerchief, covered the yellow dot on his face, and squeezed it with his thumb and forefinger. He kept on pressing until the yellow stain turned red. That was the advice that Guts had given him: "Get all the poison out until you start to bleed, or it will all come back again." Cooper could almost hear his cousin's voice.

Cooper looked back at his reflection in the lake and realized that the right side of his face was now quite red. He squatted at the water's edge and splashed his face. The swelling began to recede, and Cooper wondered how old he would have to be before the pimples would go away. They weren't as bad as they used to be. When they first started, they were all over his back, as well as his face. He felt like a walking pimple farm, and during that summer when they first appeared, he never took off his T-shirt in public, even when he went swimming. Pops said that they would stop when he had reached his full height. Guts' theory was that when you started having sex, the acne would go away. It was only a short step from that thought to Ronnie. *What a beautiful place to bring Ronnie*, he thought. Maybe they could get a bottle of wine and come out after dinner in the early evening. *After dinner!* "Oh, shit!" he yelled as he looked at his watch. It was time to report to Rudy for dinner. Cooper tried to run back to the hotel, but settled for a brisk walk.

Much to his surprise, the kitchen was empty except for Gretchen, who was working on the salads and desserts. "Cooper, you are feeling better, yah?"

"I'm doing much better. I think I'll make it. Thank you."

"When Rudy comes down, he has a big surprise for you. You will like what he is planning."

Cooper went over to the Coke machine, fished around in his pocket for a nickel, and pulled out a chair at the staff table. The Coke went down easily, but caused a large burp, which he deliberately refused to stifle. He picked up an old *Time* magazine and started to read the sports section. The National League was still up for grabs, but in the American, the Yankees had already taken a commanding lead for the pennant. Then he remembered the letter from his mother that he had put in his back pocket. He pulled it out, stared at it for a few seconds, and then grabbed a knife and sliced it open.

Dear Cooper,

We had our usual Fourth of July gathering at your grandfather's beach cottage. Everybody asked about you and wanted to be remembered to you.

We had a surprise visit from my cousin Matthew Goetz and his wife from Detroit, which is why I was able to send you the Michigan sweatshirt so quickly. I know you call him "Uncle Matthew," but in actuality he's your second cousin or your first cousin once removed. (I'm never sure just how that goes.)

Anyway, he and Aunt Lilly were on their way to France, where he is going to take a special summer course at the Sorbonne in Paris. They will be coming back through New York in time for the Labor Day weekend. As you know, he is the architect in Detroit who says that he will help you get into the University of Michigan.

Uncle Matthew hasn't seen you since before the war and he is eager to get to know you as an adult. I know that you are busy at the hotel and that you are having all kinds of wonderful new adventures this summer, but it is very important for your future that your Uncle Matthew gets to know you.

Do speak with that dear Dr. Martin and explain the situation, and I am sure that he will be glad to let you come home in time for the Labor Day weekend.

With much love,

Mother

How does she know that I'm working hard, Cooper thought, or that I'm "having all kinds of new adventures?" Does she know about the beer or the ginger ale or about Ronnie? It was a scary idea, but Cooper didn't have much time to follow that train of thought. Rudy entered the kitchen and said, "I see that our little party boy has re-entered the land of the living." This was about as close as Rudy got to humor and considering the time of day, to find him in a good mood was indeed something to be treasured. Cooper stood up and saluted. "Corporal Cooper returning from the infirmary and reporting for duty, sir!"

Gretchen interrupted, "Rudy, I told him that you had a surprise."

"Yah, but first we get ready for dinner and then we will have our big surprise."

The main item on the menu was a great loin of beef, served au jus with roasted potatoes, peas, string beans, and summer squash. Mercifully, someone already had shelled the peas and prepared the string beans and squash. "Go in the refrigerator and

THE MORNING AFTER

get the potatoes that you peeled yesterday that are soaking in the cold water. We will prepare them for baking," Rudy directed as he sharpened his long two-edged carving knife. "And then I will show you how to do the roast potatoes so that they are tender on the inside and crisp and brown on the outside."

Cooper realized that Rudy had described what he called "Sunday potatoes," the kind Gamma Dawkins used to fix for Sunday dinner to go along with the roast beef or leg of lamb. Gamma and his mother used to take turns on the Sunday dinner. Whoever was "on duty" would go to the early service at St. Phil's-on-the-Hill and then take over the kitchen when everybody else was leaving for church. Cooper never had seen his mother and grandmother in the kitchen at the same time. When the divorce started, he realized that the two most important women in his life did not get along all that well. They had been thrown together by the economic necessity of the Depression. Gamma, along with a number of unemployed relatives who were "between jobs," were in residence and always showed up for Sunday dinner at 1:00 p.m. Gamma received a small widow's pension and once a quarter, there was a dividend check from AT&T, or "Blessed Ma Bell," as she liked to call the phone company. All through the Depression the stock never missed a dividend. She contributed half of her dividends to the family till but insisted on controlling how the money was spent. Roast beef or leg of lamb, along with Sunday potatoes, were high on her priority list.

Rudy had trimmed some of the fat off of the roast and had rendered it in a cast-iron frying pan. "Make sure you grease the bottom of the baking pans," he instructed. "It is the fat that gives the potatoes their flavor. Don't ever use that cooking oil or Crisco. The potatoes will not taste right. Now we should put the peeled potatoes on the stove and bring their water to a boil for five minutes. Then we put the potatoes in the baking pans and sprinkle them with salt and pepper and a little bit of paprika. Don't throw out the potato water; put it in Gretchen's soup pot. Now put the potatoes in the oven and turn them over every ten minutes until they are brown and crisp on the outside."

Rudy was a master with the carving knife. The blade was eighteen inches long and was double-edged. He sharpened it constantly until it was like a razor, and in the wrong hands it could have been a lethal weapon. When he sliced the loin of beef, it was a precision cut. "Don't give them too much meat. It is the most expensive part of the meal. If they want more, we will give them a second helping. The slice should take up about 40 percent of the plate, and with the vegetables, it should look pretty. The presentation is very important. Don't ever throw the vegetables at the plate. A chef doesn't do that. That's what mess sergeants do to privates in basic training—they throw food at a metal tray and the poor soldier has to catch it. A good chef puts the potato next to the meat and then decorates with the green vegetables and parsley. You will like how it looks and if it looks good, it will taste better. Now, let me tell you a little secret about the meat." Rudy put his arm around Cooper's shoulder and pulled him closer, as if to whisper in his ear. "If the customer says the meat is too rare, put a little gravy on it and send it back to the dining room." He chuckled. "It works almost every time."

Cooper had mixed feelings about Rudy. He really didn't like him, but Rudy was his boss, and Cooper did everything to stay on his right side. Cooper listened to Rudy's cooking instructions but did his best to ignore Rudy's increasingly offensive remarks about Jews in general and Rosie in particular. And Rudy drank too much and could be mean and nasty to people who rubbed

THE MORNING AFTER

him the wrong way. On the other hand, Rudy had tried to help Cooper get over his hangover. And when it came to cooking, Rudy did seem to know what he was talking about.

Ronnie appeared at the serving counter, brushed her hair to one side, and smiled. "I see you're feeling a lot better, Cooper."

Cooper might have been a novice with the opposite sex, but he recognized an invitation when he saw one. "Well, I had a lot of expert help, especially when you rubbed the back of my neck."

"Any time, Cooper. Any time."

"How about after work?" Cooper asked, trying to judge her reaction. When he found no resistance, he ventured a bit further, "How about tonight?"

"OK."

"Where?"

"What about the dock?" she suggested.

"Don't keep the guests waiting!" Rudy boomed. "Take that food out to the dining room before it gets cold."

Cooper's mind went wild in anticipation of his rendezvous with Ronnie. In his fantasy he would run up to his room, take a shower, and put on fresh clothes. He'd make sure he had plenty of cigarettes and dry matches. He wouldn't go out through the kitchen but would exit through the front door, walk casually around the hotel, and head for the dock. He wouldn't want to appear too anxious. If Ronnie was already on the dock, he would begin the conversation with "Cigarette?" On the other hand, if he got there first, he would stand up when he heard her footsteps on the planks of the dock. Then he would offer her a cigarette and ask something like, "What do you hear from the folks back in New Jersey?" That would put them on common ground, commiserating on the burden of divorcing parents.

"If you don't stop daydreaming about that little blonde *Fräulein*, we'll never get to the surprise, much less finish serving dinner," Rudy scolded.

In plotting his encounter with Ronnie, Cooper had forgotten about his kitchen duties and the surprise Rudy had planned for after dinner. What did Rudy have in mind? How much time would it take? How long would Ronnie be willing to wait for him on the dock?

Rudy led Cooper into the cooler and pointed to two ten-gallon earthen crocks. Looking to Cooper for approval he declared, "This is where we begin the sauerbraten!" Cooper's mind was elsewhere, but he knew enough to respond with a smile and nod of approval. Rudy unwrapped large chunks of beef, which he placed on the bottom of the crocks. "Now we go outside, and you will help me make the juice." Rudy commandeered the largest pot in the kitchen and proceeded to pour in several gallons of red wine and red wine vinegar. He told Cooper to chop onions, carrots, celery, and several cloves of garlic. Then Rudy presented Cooper with a large tin of ginger snaps and ordered, "Get the rolling pin and crush these into a powder. Then put them in the pot with the wine and the vinegar, along with the vegetables." When that task was accomplished Rudy produced a gallon glass jar filled with grayish powder.

"What's that?" asked Cooper.

"That's the secret ingredient. Every chef has his secrets, and that's what makes him a chef. Otherwise anybody could get out a cookbook, and it would all come out the same. Now we mix this all up and then pour it over the meat in the crocks. It stays there in the refrigerator for five days, and every morning and every evening, you go in there and take a big fork and turn all the roasts over so they marinade good. Most cooks marinade the meat for only two or three days, but a real German chef lets them soak for at least five days."

It had been at least thirty minutes since Rudy started the sauerbraten preparation. Cooper followed instructions and did his best to look interested, but he wondered if Ronnie was still waiting for him on the dock.

Finally, Cooper faced Rudy and extended his hand to say good-bye and thank Rudy for the instruction, and Rudy placed a cold beer bottle in Cooper's hand. Even the sight of beer triggered a rumble in Cooper's stomach.

"This calls for a celebration. Ya?" said Rudy.

"I really have to go, Rudy. I really have to go."

"What's the hurry? You are meeting someone outside tonight? You have some plans? Maybe with that girl with the golden hair all over her face?"

Cooper blushed. "Well sort of…I…I…"

"Don't try to explain. I was a young man once myself. Go see your girlfriend. Go have a good time!"

Cooper abandoned his original plan for a change of clothes and a casual stroll across the hotel lawn. Instead, he dashed out the kitchen door and jumped off the loading dock, slowing his pace only as he walked on to the wooden pier. Each plank creaked with its own peculiar sound. The half moon was behind a cloud, so it was very dark. Only the scraping of cricket wings occasionally broke silence. A fish jumped near the stern of a secured rowboat as the moon came out of hiding…and revealed that the dock was empty.

CHAPTER TEN
TO STAY OR TO LEAVE?

"Cooper, there's a note for you on the bulletin board," Rosie said. She had slipped into the kitchen and was seated at the staff table, waiting for the coffee to brew. She was whistling the tune of "What a Difference a Day Makes."

How appropriate, thought Cooper. Yesterday my head was fuzzy and my body was hurting, but my heart was filled with all kinds of possibilities. Today, my head is as clear as the sky, but everything feels hopeless. He walked over to the bulletin board and detached the note, which read:

Cooper Dawkins
Call your mother collect at
Manhasset 3-1964

Cooper looked at his watch and put the note in his pocket. It was 6:50 a.m., and his mother would just be getting up and going through her morning routine before rushing to catch the

8:03 train for New York City. She would get off the train at Woodside, walk up the stairs, and board the IRT train for Times Square. It would be crowded, and she would have to stand, crushed up against a stranger, holding on to a strap and pretending to read the subway ads until the train stopped at Fifth Avenue. Then she would re-enter the world of fresh air and sunshine across from the New York Public Library and head south for B. Altman's. In the past she had strolled Fifth Avenue as a shopper. How many times had she reminded Cooper of the great change the separation from his father was making in her life? How many times, as she massaged her swollen feet, had she reminded him of their Christmas shopping trips to the city? Now, Fifth Avenue had become the last lap in a daily marathon as she rushed with all the other store clerks and office workers to get to her job and punch in before 9:30. All of this was very new for Victoria Goetz Dawkins, she had told her son. Nothing in her years at Smith College had prepared her for the daily commute or for standing behind a lingerie counter. Altman's strategy was to train her at the Manhattan store, and if she had any sales skills and could endure the pace, she would be transferred to the Manhasset store on the Miracle Mile. It was their plan that she could convert her social contacts into loyal customers. But as a divorcing woman, she would discover that her social life would be diminished, both by fatigue and by the protective instincts of her married friends, who seemed threatened by the presence of a soon-to-be-single woman in a social setting with their middle-aged husbands.

Cooper decided to wait until after supper to return the call. If it had been an emergency, she would have said so, or she would call again during her lunch break. He put the note in his pocket, drew a cup of coffee, and sat down at the table across from Rosie, who was reading the *New York Times*. "Will you look at this! Princess Elizabeth is engaged to be married to Lieutenant Mountbatten. He's a prince of Greece and Denmark in his own right and is now a British citizen and an officer in the British navy. It says here that the official announcement will be made on Sunday by King George VI. Will you look at that man! If he isn't a Prince Charming, I don't know who is." Cooper sipped his coffee and smoked a Camel as Rosie read all the royal details. "It says here," continued Rosie, "in Piccadilly Circus, after the announcement was published, there were scenes that have not been matched since Germany surrendered."

"Excuse me, Rosie," interrupted Cooper, "but I've got to get the bacon and oatmeal going, and I need to turn over the meat in the sauerbraten sauce."

Rosie looked up from her paper. "Cooper, things aren't always what they seem."

"What does that mean?"

"You'll find out soon enough, and I hope it isn't the hard way."

※ ※ ※

The chambermaids arrived early at the laundry with a day's load of soiled towels and sheets, along with a bundle of current gossip, all of which Dorcas began to sort out. When Mercy arrived, Dorcas opened with, "As you know, the waitresses and some of the maids often gather after hours in one of the larger bedrooms on the fourth floor to smoke, joke, and chatter about the events of the day. Seems they're all a twitter about Dr. Martin's student from Long Island—you know, that Cooper lad. Well, it seems that he's only sixteen, and they have decided that he's still a virgin, which is what he's supposed to be. In fact, that's what those college girls are supposed to be, too! Making love is for the marriage bed. Joseph and I were both virgins when we tied the knot. Neither one of us really knew what we were supposed to do when we got into our matrimonial bed, but pretty soon we figured it all out and, like I say, we haven't slept apart one night since we took our vows. That's the way it's supposed to be."

"What does your matrimonial bed have to do with Cooper and the waitresses?" queried Mercy.

"Be patient, Mercy. I'm getting to that."

"Well, don't dawdle so much, or it will be time to put the sheets in the tumbler."

"As I was saying, the ladies of the dining room see Cooper as something of a challenge. They say that he has one of those rubber things in his wallet and that he is keen to…what do they call it now? 'Go all the way'? That one who looks like the movie star with her blonde hair all over her face had something of a wager going with Sheila, and she started flirting with the boy up at the Middlebury Inn, and then last night she was supposed to meet him out on the dock after work, but she lost her nerve and didn't show up. It seems that instead of going to the dock, she went to the big rocks down by the cottages. She stayed there, smoking one cigarette after another, for almost two hours, and then tried to sneak into her bedroom without talking to the other girls. They caught her, and practically dragged her down the hall, and kept her there until she told them everything, which wasn't much. They say she said that she just couldn't do that with a high school virgin, even if he looked like a college student. She cried a lot and said that Cooper's a nice kid, and she sort of liked him in a sisterly way, if you receive my meaning. She told them that she thought that Cooper was a decent young man and that she didn't want to lead him on. The maids said she told them that she just didn't want to be a tease, but that's not the word she used. I'm sorry; I can't repeat it."

"Did it have anything to do with a respectable rooster?"

"That's close enough," said Dorcas. "The maids said she started to cry again and announced that all bets were off and that she was going to go to bed alone, and then she ran down the hall to her room and slammed the door."

"I have one more question," said Mercy.

"And what would that be?"

"Did you bring the tea?"

✤ ✤ ✤

Cooper managed to make it through breakfast and lunch without giving much thought to what was going on around him. There was the beef in the sauerbraten crocks to turn over, the coffee to brew, eggs to fry, pancake batter to dribble on the hot grill, hash browns to toss, the potatoes to peel, and the vegetables to prepare. Rudy was reasonably sober, and every once in a while he would smile at Cooper, chuckle, and say something like, "You have a good time last night? Yah?" Cooper would smile back but remain silent. He intentionally stayed away from the staff table, where the guys were talking baseball and the possibility of a subway series, and the girls were oohing and ahhing over the pictures of Princess Elizabeth and Prince Philip in the Sunday *Times* magazine section. Then all of a sudden, Cooper came out of the storeroom with a bushel of potatoes to be peeled and ran smack into Ronnie, who had a tray of dirty dishes.

"Oops! Oh, hi Cooper. I...I..."

"Hey, Ronnie. I missed you last night. I mean, I waited out on the dock after work for an hour. I mean, I thought you and I...were..."

"Oh, I'm sorry. I mean, I didn't think there was anything definite. I...I...was planning to wash my hair."

Cooper didn't know how to respond to her excuse, so he said, "OK. See ya around the lake."

"Yeah, OK. See ya," said Ronnie. She rushed her dishes over to Benson, who was scraping the plates into his pig pail and stacking the dishes in the washer.

"Hi, R-r-ronnie," stuttered Benson. "How ya...d-d-doing?"

"Fine, Benson, just fine," Ronnie said as she ran out the kitchen door and headed for her room on the fourth floor.

Benson called after her. "I'm sorry...Ronnie. I...didn't... mean to...hurt your feelings." He shrugged and turned to find Cooper for support, but Cooper had gone back to the storage room.

❦ ❦ ❦

Cooper gave the sauerbraten crocks one more poke and then took off his apron and went out the kitchen door. He walked down to the path to the icehouse and then headed along the abandoned path by the lake to the dam. He realized that after supper he would have to return his mother's phone call. He really didn't know how he felt about his mother. He was mad at both his mother and father for breaking up the family. Life had been so simple, and now it was so complicated. For one thing, he and Guts had been betting that a romance was developing between Grandpa Goetz and Grandma Dawkins. Both were widowed, they were always together at family gatherings, and Pops had invited her to a yacht club party or two. But now that was over and according to Guts, she wasn't even at the Fourth of July picnic.

Cooper really didn't know why his parents couldn't get along. All he knew was that with each promotion, from first lieutenant to colonel, his father had been home less and less, even though he was only stationed in Manhattan. Moving in with Grandpa Goetz was OK, and it did mean that he could still go to Manhasset High School and that he could still see his friends and he could sail his boat in Manhasset Bay. But things were different. His mother was different, and somehow she seemed to want Cooper to feel responsible for her feelings. She often said, "Now you've got to be the man in the house." When he had first heard that phrase, it was during the war, when his father first got a commission in the army, and Cooper was put in charge of shoveling coal into the furnace. "Isn't he wonderful?" his mother had said. "He's the little man of the house!" One good thing about moving into Pops' house—it had an oil burner.

Once, Cooper had a dream that he was the star end on the Michigan team, and both his parents had flown out to Detroit to see the Michigan–Ohio State game. They sat next to each other, and when he intercepted a forward pass on the twenty-yard line and ran it back for a touchdown, his mother and father jumped up and down and yelled and screamed. And the next thing he knew, they were hugging each other.

There were only two problems: one, it was a dream; and two, Cooper didn't play football. He played soccer.

The person he really wanted to talk to was Guts. Guts would help him sort things out; he always did. His parents said that he was smarter than Guts, which was why Guts was going to a trade school, while Cooper was heading for the University of

Michigan. Well, that's what his parents said, anyway. Maybe Guts' grades weren't that good and maybe he barely passed the New York State Board of Regents exams, but Guts knew a lot about people and how to get along. And judging from his last letter, Guts knew a lot more about girls than Cooper did. Maybe Guts could help him understand just what had happened with Ronnie. She had done nothing but flirt with him for two days— heck, she had done more than flirt! She had rubbed his neck, and put her hand on his knee, and even rubbed his lap when the beer had spilled on his trousers. She had done everything but send him an engraved invitation. What had gone wrong? When they had first met on the train, they had a lot to talk about, and they had a lot in common. He wanted to make out with her, but he also really liked her and thought she liked him. What had he done that had scared her away?

Cooper reached the grassy clearing by the old stone dam. Two blue jays fluttered to a higher perch and announced his arrival with cries of "Thief! Thief!" Cooper kicked a pinecone, which sent an inquisitive squirrel scampering. The lake was down a bit, and the waterfall had been reduced to a few trickles over the rocks. Cooper looked down below the dam and discovered a small pond that had been created by a family of beavers, who were busy reinforcing their bulkhead of timber and mud. Cooper watched the beaver family at work. It all looked so simple and so orderly. Each beaver had its role and place and function. There was no question who was in charge. They all worked in harmony, like the Rockettes at the Christmas show at the Radio City Music Hall. When Cooper was little, that's the way he thought his family worked—all together, all dancing to the same tune. But apparently that wasn't so. Were all families like that or just his?

Cooper sat down on the grass by the lake and listened to the breeze gently moving through the trees. It was almost as if the trees were singing or speaking to each other in a secret language all of their own. The spruces and the pines had a high-pitched purr, while the birches swayed in the breeze and sounded very gentle and motherly. Cooper remembered the year his father had purchased an eight-foot blue spruce for a Christmas tree, with the intention of planting it in the front yard on January sixth. The only problem was that there was a blizzard right after Christmas, and the ground was frozen solid. The spruce stayed in the living room and after enjoying another week of spring-like temperatures indoors, it began to sprout pale green "candles" at the end of all of its branches. It was Palm Sunday before the tree made it into the front yard and two years before it readjusted its rhythms to those of Mother Nature.

The sound of a gray squirrel scampering from branch to branch brought him back to the reality of the Vermont forest. Birch leaves played out their rhythms in lower octaves, and their rustlings sounded like the distant conversation that came out of a Boy Scout tent after lights out and taps had sounded. When Cooper had been a Boy Scout, he earned a merit badge by constructing a miniature Indian village, like the ones that had dotted the north shore of Long Island before the Dutch and English arrived. From the bark of the birch, he had fashioned a small fleet of canoes.

Now he turned to the old maple. It had a more demanding voice and stood taller than the other trees; it insisted on providing the harmony. Cooper noted that the old maple bore only the faint scars of the syrup trade. It was, in fact, the only maple on the lake's edge. Its siblings and cousins were clustered on higher ground on the sides of the hills. Then he looked across the lake at the distant range of the Green Mountains. He noted a sailboat way down the lake and realized that he had never been able to take Graham up on his offer to help out with sailing lessons. He stood up to see if there were any more sailboats, and once again looked at his image in the smooth surface of the lake.

For some reason, watching his own reflection reminded him of the year that he and Guts had signed up for the Charles Atlas body-building course. The course was advertised on the back cover of all of the comic books, and one of the games that Guts and Cooper would play when they were at Pops' beach cottage was the ninety-five-pound weakling getting sand kicked in his face on the beach. The two boys would take turns as victim and villain and would end up wrestling on the beach and then in the water. Guts saved up his allowance and subscribed to the body-building course, which came weekly in a plain envelope. After about three months, when Guts began feeling and seeing the results, he passed the lessons on to Cooper, who began following them religiously but secretly. He kept them hidden, along with his collection of *Esquire* magazines and their centerfolds of Vargas Girls. One thing Cooper didn't do, however, was take off all his clothes, even though Charles Atlas advised that his exercises should be conducted in the nude in front of a mirror. The best Cooper could muster was to strip to his Fruit of the Loom briefs. He did his best to keep up with the exercises at Lake Bradford, but the only mirror in his room was small, and he wasn't about to go down to the bathroom and exercise in front of the mirrors and all the other guys.

But there he was in his own private grove by the old dam, and the lake was smooth, so he stripped to his shorts, folded his khaki trousers and Michigan sweatshirt carefully, along with his socks and shoes, and waded into the lake. He pressed his right fist against the palm of his left hand and struck a pose that accentuated his developing chest muscles. He put his hands behind his head and turned to the left and then to the right. He noted that even though it was blond, he could see the hair in his armpits. His stomach muscles had yet to develop the washboard ripple effect that Guts had achieved, but his baby fat had all but disappeared. Cooper liked what he saw. He decided that he was pleased with the man that he was becoming.

Suddenly, his self-absorption was invaded by the sound of an outboard motor that was coming from somewhere behind the trees to the left. When the bow of the boat broke into view, he dove into the lake. When he surfaced, he saw Ronnie's golden hair at the bow and the familiar profile of the marine with his hand on the throttle of the Evinrude engine. When they spotted Cooper, the boat did a quick turnabout and sped off in another direction.

✤ ✤ ✤

Cooper entered the empty kitchen, put on his apron, and went into the refrigerator to turn over the chunks of meat marinating in the sauerbraten sauce. Then he walked over to the staff dining area to get a Coke and check his mailbox and the message board. A bottle clanked out of the machine just as a voice behind him called out, "Goy-boy! Do you have two nickels for a dime? Or if you only have one nickel, will you buy me a Coke?"

"Rosie! When did you come in? I thought I was all alone."

"You're a loner, that's for sure. But if you want privacy, you'd better go someplace else. I doubt if the management will let you have the exclusive use of their kitchen complex."

Cooper fished in his pocket and realized that he was still wearing his soggy underwear. "How about a nickel and five pennies? Or if you've got a quarter I can give you two dimes and a nickel. Or why don't I just break down and buy you a Coke?"

"You've got a deal!" said Rosie as she headed for the staff mailboxes. She brought back one letter for Cooper and one for herself. They both pulled up chairs at the old oak table that had been painted over with a coat of white enamel. Cooper immediately recognized Guts' bold handwriting.

> Dear Coop,
> This is gonna be a short one, but I had to tell someone, and you're the only one who I can trust to keep a secret. The big news—but you can't tell anybody—is that Bristol and I are in love. I don't mean that we love making love. That, too! But I'm in love with Bristol. I've never felt this way before. No wonder they write all those songs about falling in love. It's true, and everything that they say about being in love is wonderful. I love Bristol, and she loves me, and we're talking about getting married. You might say that we're almost engaged. But don't tell anybody, and burn this letter when you've read it.
> Your cousin and friend for life,
> Guts
>
> P.S. I can't wait for you to meet Bristol. You'll love her, too.

Cooper read the letter twice before he walked out onto the kitchen platform, struck a match, and lit the corner of the letter. He held it with his thumb and forefinger until it was almost consumed and then dropped it onto the driveway below. Noticing that the charred paper was still all of a piece, he jumped off the platform and stomped on the letter until it was nothing but black dust. He gave the ashes one more glance and exclaimed, "Wow!"

So intent was he on following Guts' directions that he hadn't noticed that Rosie had followed him and was standing on the edge of the platform with Coke in hand. Looking down at Cooper, she inquired, "What's with the burnt offering? Is that something you Christians do at the full of the moon or what?"

"It was a letter."

"So, was it good news or bad?" asked Rosie.

"Good news."

"So what's the good news?"

"I can't tell you."

"Why not?"

"The letter said to burn it when I'd read it."

"So you've already told me part of the letter," pushed Rosie.

"I've already told you too much."

"Who's it from?"

"My cousin Guts."

"Is that his real name?"

"No."

"So, what's his real name?"

"His real name is John C. Goetz, the third."

"So, who's the first?"

"My grandfather."

"And his name is?"

"John C. Goetz."

"Is that a German name?"

"I guess it is."

"Do you guess, or do you know?"

"Goetz has been an American name for over one hundred years. The Goetzes came to America during the Revolutionary War. They were mercenaries, hired by the English to put down the American rebellion. When the British left, the Goetzes stayed. Most of them settled in New York, but some of them went on to Cincinnati."

"I don't like Germans."

"Why not?"

"Guess!"

"Adolf Hitler?"

"Yah!"

"Well, all Germans aren't like Hitler. My grandfather is a patriotic American," Cooper said defensively. "When America entered World War I, he headed up the Liberty Bond Committee and stopped speaking German at home. He was ashamed of what happened in Germany, and when World War II broke out, he even tried to enlist in the army, except that he was well into his sixties."

"Take a look at this," said Rosie. She handed him a thick envelope containing all kinds of clippings from New York newspapers that listed agencies that would search for missing Jewish relatives in Europe. There was the JDC, the Joint Distribution Committee, known as "the Joint," and then there was HIAS, the Hebrew Immigrant Aid Society, offering to help locate missing relatives. The Yiddish and the German clippings also contained personals such as, "If anybody knows anything about Aaron and Sophie Schwartz, whose last known address was…"

TO STAY OR TO LEAVE?

The scraps of newsprint were accompanied by a letter from Sophie's father, who related the sad news that he had received a cablegram from the International Red Cross in Geneva saying that Rosie's grandmother, along with two great-uncles and one great-aunt had been shipped to the death camps and were presumed dead. One aunt, her father's youngest sister, had somehow survived and had been found alive in Auschwitz when the army of liberation broke through the gates of the concentration camp. Rosie's father was making arrangements to get the aunt a visa and bring her to the United States.

Cooper looked up from the letter. Rosie was puffing wildly at her cigarette and fighting back the tears. "Why do people hate us so? Why does everybody hate the Jews?"

Unable to answer, he put his hand gently on her shoulder. He really couldn't think of anything to say and was relieved when he heard his name shouted out from the other side of the kitchen. Rudy calling him to work, and his German accent sounded more pronounced than ever.

※ ※ ※

Cooper did his job, took care of his chores, and avoided eye contact with Ronnie throughout the evening meal. When he hung up his apron, he headed for the one phone booth in the hotel lobby. There were three guests in line ahead of him. The only other phones were in the office and in Mr. Bradford's cabin. The hotel had an intercom system of sorts, which had been installed around 1928 and connected the guestrooms with the front desk. It also had extensions in the dining room, kitchen, and laundry. A well-kept secret was that by flipping the right switch, the person at the desk could hear what was going on in the kitchen, dining room, laundry, or even the bedrooms. When it was Cooper's turn, he looked again at the note that instructed him to call his mother. which read, "Cooper call your mother collect at Manhasset-3-1964." He checked his pockets for a nickel. He had never placed a collect call from a pay phone, but he assumed that he would need a nickel to wake up the operator and that she would return it when he placed the call.

"Number, please." The voice sounded quite different from the nasal sound of New York operators. When Cooper was a little boy, he was allowed to call his grandmother on her birthday. He memorized the number in preparation for his first call and delivered it with as much maturity as a six-year-old could muster. But on Grandma's birthday, the phone didn't ring; it buzzed and the operator informed Cooper, "The lion is busy." This threw six-year-old Cooper off balance as he imagined a very nervous golden feline pacing up and down behind the operators at the phone company.

"Number, please" was followed by a friendly New England twang. "Operator. May I help you?"

"Yes...oh, yes," said Cooper. "I want to place a collect call to Manhasset 3-1964, please."

"Manhasset? Is Manhasset in Vermont?

"No, Manhasset is on Long Island. That's in New York."

"In York State? I'll have to put you through to Rutland. Hold on for a minute while I take care of this local call." The line went dead except for some intermittent static and the faint sound of voices in conversation. Then there was the ringing sound.

"Rutland operator. Rutland operator."

"Rutland, this is Middlebury."

"Middlebury! Haven't heard from Middlebury all day. How's the weather up there? We've had some fierce summer storms down here. Some maple trees are down, and some lights are out."

"It's clear as a bell up here in Middlebury. A little fog in the morning, but no rain at all. Rutland, I've got a young man here with a collect call to Manhasset 3-1964. That's Manhasset on Long Island in New York."

"I'll have to put you through to Albany. I don't have any open lines to New York City. Let me try Albany." There were several busy signals before there was an answer across the state border.

"Albany operator."

"Albany, this is Rutland. Rutland, Vermont. How's the weather over there?"

"Hot!"

"Any storms?"

"No, it's just hot and muggy. Been that way for days. No wind. No breeze. Not even a ripple on the river. Everything is still. The Roxy Theater is packed. It's the only air-conditioned building in the city. People are lining up for hours on the street just to stay cool for a short time inside."

"Albany, I've got a young fellow up here in Middlebury who wants to place a collect call to Manhasset, Long Island. Can you help us out?"

"I'll have to put you through to New York City." This declaration was followed by a series of rings.

A nasal, no-nonsense voice answered, "New York operator. New York operator."

"New York, this is Albany."

"Go ahead, dear."

"I have a young man who is placing a collect call to Manhasset 3-1964."

"What is the name of the party placing the call?"

Cooper jumped in. "Cooper Dawkins."

"And what is the name of the person to whom you wish to speak and reverse the charges?"

Cooper hesitated. What was his mother's name now that she was divorced? Was she Mrs. Frank Dawkins? No, that wouldn't be right. "I'm calling Mrs. Victoria Goetz Dawkins. She's my mother, and I'm calling collect."

"How do you spell that?"

"That's V-i-c-t-o—"

"No, I mean the last name, dear."

"That's Dawkins. D-a-w-k-i-n-s."

"And what is your name?"

"I'm Cooper Dawkins. I'm her son."

"One moment, please!" There was a series of busy signals followed by the announcement, "The lion is busy. Hold on! I'll try that again."

"Manhasset operator." The voice still had a New York sound, but it was a bit softer, gentler.

"Manhasset," said New York, "I have a collect call for Mrs. Victoria Dawkins at Manhasset 3-1964 from a Cooper Dawkins in Middlebury, Vermont."

"Would you give me that number again, please?"

"Manhasset 3-1964."

"Hello? Hello?" said Cooper's mother.

"Mrs. Dawkins?"

"Yes, this is she."

"Mrs. Dawkins, I have a collect call from Cooper Dawkins in Middlebury, Vermont. Will you accept the charges?"

"Oh, yes, yes. I'll accept the charges. Hello, Cooper."

"Just a minute, ma'am. I'll put your party through."

"Hello, Cooper."

"Hi, Mom."

"Oh, it's so good to hear your voice."

"Same here."

"Did you get my letter?'

"Which one?"

"The one about talking to Dr. Martin about coming home a little early for Labor Day so that you and Uncle Matt can talk about going to the University of Michigan to study architecture."

"I thought that was all set."

"Well, it is, sort of, but it's important that you get to know Uncle Matt. He's on the alumni board, and he has a large architectural firm in Detroit. He's a big man in the Midwest, and he has a lot of influence. Uncle Matt really isn't your uncle, actually my first cousin, but he's always been like a brother to me." Cooper's mother paused and then added, "Have you talked with Dr. Martin? I'm sure he'll understand." There were several seconds of silence before she asked, "Cooper, are you there? Can you hear me?"

"Yes, Mom, I'm here. I can hear you."

"Well, have you talked to Dr. Martin?"

"Not yet."

"Not yet?"

"You see, I've really been awfully busy. They've been working me really hard, and there's a lot going on. I don't see Dr. Martin that much, and Labor Day is still a month away."

"Oh, Cooper, please! This is very important. It's important to me, and it's very important for your future. Promise me you'll talk to Dr. Martin this week and then call me again. Promise?"

"OK."

"Promise!"

"OK, cross my heart and hope to die. Hope a cat spits in my eye."

"That's my boy!" she said. "This is a good time to call. It's practically seven o'clock when I get home, and by eight-thirty I'm soaking in a hot bathtub, or I'm in bed. Commuting to the city on the Long Island Railroad is a day's job in itself, especially in the summer heat, and standing all day behind a counter is making my feet and ankles swell."

Cooper felt sorry for his mother. The shift from Manhasset matron to commuting sales clerk was taking its toll, but Cooper wasn't sure just how to express his sympathy. The best he could do was to say, "Gee, Mom, it sounds rough down there. I sure hope you feel better. How's everybody else doing?"

"I hardly see anybody these days. I haven't been out to the beach cottage since the Fourth of July. Your grandfather calls every now and then to see how I'm doing. He says he hasn't seen much of your cousin, John III, the one you call Guts.

"OK, Mom. This call is costing you a lot of money. I'd better say good-bye."

"Good-bye, son. Now, don't forget to talk to Dr. Martin, and don't forget to call me collect."

"Good-bye, Mom."

"Good-bye, Cooper."

CHAPTER ELEVEN
SUNDAY

As the summer drew on, the days and nights at Lake Bradford took on a rhythm, and one week blurred into the next without much pause or punctuation. July was almost over when Cooper realized that he hadn't been to church since he'd left Long Island. There was a community service on Sunday morning at eleven in the hotel parlor, conducted by a retired Congregational minister from Boston. Dr. Lawrence had been doing the service since the end of World War I. He had a loyal but shrinking following a piano player who liked to begin the service with "We Gather Together," and a soloist from the First Unitarian Church of Lowell, Massachusetts, who had a fondness for the "Battle Hymn of the Republic." Cooper was not uncomfortable with the Congregational way of doing things. In fact, the nearest church to Pops' beach cottage was the white clapboard Congregational Church overlooking Mount Sinai Harbor. It was often more convenient to go there than into Port Jefferson or Setauket for an Episcopal service. But Sunday at the Lake Bradford Inn was a workday for Cooper like any other, except that the main meal was in the middle of the day, and Sunday night supper was a picnic down by the lake. This meant that Cooper had to report back to the kitchen by 11:15 a.m. in order to help Rudy with the big Sunday feast.

So he tried to find an earlier Episcopal service. At age thirteen, Cooper had been confirmed at Saint Philip's Episcopal Church. His parents had been married there. He had been baptized there. Pops had been on the vestry and had even been the senior warden of the parish. Grandpa Dawkins and Grandma Goetz were both buried in the churchyard there. After confirmation, Cooper had become an acolyte, and he'd learned to like serving at the 8:00 a.m. communion service in the summer before heading on his bicycle down to his sailboat in Manhasset Bay. During school months, the ladies of the church had volunteered to serve juice, hot chocolate, and scrambled eggs to the young people after the service. The charge was twenty-five cents, and the breakfast became quite popular, especially with the high school seniors who were known to party past midnight and then play bridge until daybreak, go to church, and head home for bed.

Cooper checked out the listing of local church services at the front desk in the lobby and in the local newspaper. Just like back home, the Episcopal Church in Middlebury had services at eight and eleven. The Catholics had masses every ninety minutes. The standard for all the other Protestant churches was 11:00 a.m. Cooper approached Dr. Martin, who advised, "Rudy always tries to do something special for Sunday dinner, so we really need you in the kitchen to help prepare for the big meal. We could probably cover for you at breakfast, if you could find a guest who was going into town for the early service." But Cooper discovered that the guests who got up early on Sunday morning either weren't Episcopalians or if they were, they were on vacation from church as well as business. Sheila mentioned that there was a group of guests and staff who made a run into town for the 9:30 mass and maybe they could squeeze him in if he wanted to come along.

Cooper had never been to mass in a Catholic Church. Once, during the Christmas season, his mother had taken him into St. Patrick's Cathedral on Fifth Avenue in New York City. He was only five or six at the time. He and his mother had been shopping, but it had started to snow and he had gotten restless, and his mother's feet were sore. So she slipped into the back of the cathedral and sat down in an empty pew. When his eyes grew accustomed to the dim light, his attention was drawn to the candles flickering in the little red jelly glasses. He discovered that behind the candles were statues on shelves, filling every cubby hole and corner along both walls of the massive stone structure. He watched as people with very serious expressions deposited coins, lighted candles, crossed their hearts, and appeared to be talking to the statues. Quietly, he climbed onto the pew, stood up to better observe what was going on, and then boldly declared to his mother and everyone else in the church, "Mother, look at all the people worshipping the idols!" He must have been at the dead acoustical center of the nave, because his announcement triggered not only disapproving glares but also a squad of priests and nuns who surrounded him. At first he thought that they were there to answer his questions, but his mother read their dour expressions differently. She smiled sheepishly, gathered her shopping bags with one hand and her loud-mouthed son with the other hand, directed by the holy escorts, headed out to Fifth Avenue and into the snowstorm.

Cooper wondered what his grandfather would have to say about his attending a Catholic church. Pops was a big man in the Masonic order and also the Shriners. Pops was proud of the fact that Christians and Jews belonged to his lodge but unhappy that Catholics weren't allowed to join. Pops thought that the Catholic Church and Tammany Hall were in cahoots. Cooper decided that it would be best to let his visit go unreported as far as the folks back home were concerned.

He'd decided to join the group heading to 9:30 Mass that Sunday, and now he followed his group into the church. They all dipped their fingers into a bowl of holy water near the door and crossed themselves when they entered the pew. The church was full, and the service had already begun. The priest, with his back to the congregation, recited the mass in an expressionless Latin. The people were kneeling, saying their prayers, and many were busying themselves with rosary beads. It struck Cooper that there were really two programs going on simultaneously: the priest and his servers were doing one thing at the altar, and the folks in the pews were busy with their own agendas. Now and then an altar boy would ring some bells, and the priest and congregation came together with a brief exchange of Latin phrases, which sounded like "Domino biscuits," followed by "Et gum spirits chewy." Cooper observed that everyone took what they were doing very seriously; he appeared to be the only one looking about. Whatever these Catholics were doing, they were very intent about it. As he made this observation, his eye caught the candles flickering at the side altars, and he recalled being escorted out of St. Patrick's some ten years before. The images of that experience were still playing in his mind when he became aware of Sheila's kneeling beside him. The exotic odor of incense competed with the gentle gardenia scent of her perfume. The left side of his leg, from his knee back to his hip, was growing warm. Sheila's thigh was pressing against him and stirring a most un-childlike response. He glanced at Sheila. She was looking intently at the priest in his robes at the altar. Cooper decided that they were packed into the pew like sardines and that Sheila wasn't even aware of the reaction she was igniting. He was ashamed of having such feelings during a church service, and even though it wasn't his own church and he didn't really understand what was going on, he hoped that the good Lord would forgive him for such thoughts. He adjusted his leg and tried to concentrate on saying his own prayers. All he seemed able to do was go down the family roster, beginning with his grandparents. The choir was singing something in Latin, and a few people in the front of the church were lining up to receive communion. Cooper wondered if he should go up for communion. The last time he received communion was back in June before he left for Vermont. Would it be a sin to take communion in a Catholic church? Who would know? Danny and Kevin and Sheila would know. Besides, they weren't going up to the altar. They had said something in the car about not being allowed to take communion if they hadn't been to confession the day before. Then Cooper felt the warmth of Sheila's leg again. *This is no accident*, he thought. She's doing this on purpose!

At 10:22 they were back in the station wagon and heading down Route 7 for the hotel. Cooper was in the backseat with Sheila and two other passengers. There was talk about Major League Baseball. It looked like a subway series was in the making. On Saturday, the Brooklyn Dodgers had taken a doubleheader from the Chicago Cubs. It was 7–2 and 6–3, giving them a solid three and a half game lead in the National League. Cooper had heard the news on WOR, which he picked up on his radio late at night.

To make space in the backseat, Cooper rested his weight on his left hip and had his back to the door. Sheila had her back to Cooper and was wedged in between him and another girl. As they turned the corner by the stately First Congregational Church, Sheila's backside pressed against Cooper. He was embarrassed by his automatic response but could do nothing to disengage. All he could do was relax and enjoy the ride, which was especially exciting when the car bumped across the covered bridge. When they pulled up to the kitchen door, Cooper took his time getting out of the car. He carefully slipped out of his jacket and draped it over his arm in front of his trousers. Sheila held the kitchen door open for him, smiled, and said, "I enjoyed the ride."

※ ※ ※

The noon meal on Sunday was the big one of the week and always included roast beef, along with leg of lamb or turkey. For the waitresses, it was also pay day. This was the day they got their tips. They received no salary, only room and board and tips from satisfied guests. If they were good at what they did, however, they could easily bring home five hundred dollars by the end of the summer. Each waitress could handle four or five tables, depending on the size of the family. There was nothing in writing, but the generally accepted standard tip was a dollar a day per adult and fifty cents per day per child over five years old.

The college men and the veterans were making twenty dollars a week at the hotel, but Benson received minimum wage of seventy-five cents an hour. Cooper had signed on at $12.50 a week, plus room and board, and a round trip ticket from Manhasset to

Middlebury. He could have made more money back home—if he could have gotten a job. But the veterans were given preferential treatment, so local jobs for high school juniors were not all that plentiful. And if he had gone to work at an office in the city, there would have been expenses—bus or train fare, lunches, dry cleaning—and he would have been back home, right in the middle of his parents' divorce.

The Broadsmiths had been in the dining room for four weeks. Jonathan Broadsmith had a law practice in Hartford and motored up to Vermont every weekend to join his family. Spending a month at Lake Bradford was his wife, Claire's, idea. Cooper learned she had come there with her parents as a child and also as a teenager and thought that it would be a nice place for a family vacation. But with three children, aged six, eleven, and thirteen, she more than had her hands full, and at mealtimes, her problem became Rosie's problem.

Stephanie Broadsmith was thirteen going on twenty-two. She wore a brassiere, although she really didn't need one. She had long blonde hair and affected a Veronica Lake hairstyle until she saw Ronnie, who so outclassed her in a blouse, sweater, or bathing suit that she switched to a ponytail in the daytime and a bun on more formal occasions. She was one of the young ladies who had offered to help Cooper with the hot dogs and hamburgers on Independence Day. Her idea of acting "grown up" was to be rude, picky, and critical. Rosie privately called her Goldilocks because the food was either too hot or too cold for Stephanie, but never just right. Jonathan Junior., the eleven-year-old, was a pleasant kid with the appetite of a college fullback. He cleaned his plate in record time and always asked for seconds, if not thirds. Douglas, age six, always spilled things. He spilled his milk, the gravy, the maple syrup, and the ice cream, not to mention dropping the silverware, the napkins, and lots of peas. Douglas also picked up new words from the older children at the hotel, which he tried out on Rosie at the dinner table, like, "Rosie, what's a penis?"

"Ask your mother."

"She doesn't have one."

"Then ask your father."

Rosie's only consolation was that the Broadsmiths gave her something to talk about or laugh about at the staff table. She was also looking forward to a big tip. She figured that $2.50 a day times twenty-eight days would amount to seventy dollars, plus Mr. Broadsmith's weekend visits would run the figure to over seventy-five dollars.

Jonathan Broadsmith, Sr. sat with his family at their final meal at the hotel. When it was over, they would return to their rooms, finish packing, change into their traveling clothes, and head down the road to Hartford. Everyone but little Douglas ordered the roast beef. Stephanie claimed that hers was too rare, so Rosie took it back to Rudy, who put some dark gravy on it, and there was no further complaint. Douglas's vocabulary was under control, but he did spill some milk into his mashed potatoes, which he then consumed with a spoon, making loud slurps, to the annoyance of his mother and the delight of his older siblings. Rosie served the apple pie à la mode and refilled Mr. Broadsmith's coffee cup. Then she asked, "Will there be anything else?"

"No," said Claire Broadsmith as she handed Rosie an envelope. "Thank you so much for your wonderful service. We all appreciate your hard work and putting up with our lively family." Douglas rolled his eyes and let out a loud burp, while his brother and sister giggled. "So," she continued, "we want you to have this as a token of our appreciation."

Rosie smiled, did a small curtsy, and replied, "It's been a pleasure knowing you and serving you."

Almost on cue, the other waitresses followed Rosie into the kitchen and surrounded her as she opened the envelope, which contained a flowery note card and five one-dollar bills. Rosie emitted a muffled scream, followed by, "That bitch! That damn bitch." The other waitresses chimed in with their disapproval.

"That's an insult," said Audrey.

"I'd give it back," added Ronnie. "Don't let her get away with it, or we'll all get short-changed and work all summer for nothing."

"That bitch! That damn bitch!" repeated Rosie. "I'm going back in the dining room, put the bills on the table, and tell her, 'Mrs. Broadsmith, I believe you need this more than I do!'"

Benson had stopped the dishwasher to listen to Rosie's complaint and yelled his approval. "G-g-go…go, Rosie! Go!"

The cheer was picked up by all the waitresses and the kitchen crew. "Go, Rosie, go! Go, Rosie, go!"

Rosie had turned and was headed for the dining room when Dr. Martin stepped into the kitchen. He had been at the front desk and just by chance had turned on the intercom connection with the kitchen. When he entered the room, the noise came to an abrupt halt. "What's going on?" he asked. There was a chorus of complaints, and Dr. Martin held up his hand. "One voice at a time. What's going on?" He looked at Cooper, so Cooper explained, "Rosie waited on the Broadsmiths for four weeks and all the thanks she got was five dollars."

Rosie interjected, "I'm going to give it back to her and tell her that she needs the money more than I do."

"No, Rosie," Dr. Martin said calmly. "Let me handle this. Rosie, you stay in the kitchen." Then, turning to the assembled waitresses, he said, "Now, you girls go back and wait on your tables. This isn't the end of the world. This problem can be solved, if we don't turn it into World War III."

Dr. Martin entered the dining room, followed by the dining room staff, each to her own table, with the exception of Rosie. She went to the staff table, bought herself a Coke, lit a cigarette, and proceeded to cry. Cooper started to cross the kitchen to see if he could comfort her when he heard Rudy's guttural voice. "Stay here, Cooper. We have much work to do. Let that Jew-girl cry her eyes out. All she cares about is money. That Jew-girl is nothing but trouble."

※ ※ ※

The Sunday evening picnic seemed like a simple thing to the guests, but for the staff, it was a lot of work. Not only were there tables and chairs to be set up on the lawn, but all the food had to be hauled out from the kitchen and then all the leftovers returned. For Benson, it was a gold mine of slops. He filled his buckets with the plate scrapings from the guests and the half-empty bowls of potato salad, coleslaw, baked beans, and bread, which would provide a special treat for the pigs he pampered.

By the time Rudy had finished carving the cold ham and roast beef, he was showing signs of having consumed the contents of the flask he carried at all times in his back pocket. Gretchen approached him rather coyly with the suggestion, "Why don't we go back to our room. We can let Cooper finish the cleaning up and putting away." She smiled at him and raised her eye-

SUNDAY

brows in a wifely way as she took him by the hand. "Come, we go back to the room."

Rudy held Gretchen's hand and toddled off like a little child. Cooper watched them leave and wondered if Rudy would be able to climb the stairs to his room, much less claim the prize that Gretchen seemed to be offering.

"Hi, Cooper," Sheila called to him from the end of the serving table. "I enjoyed riding back from church with you."

"Oh, h-h-h-hi Sh-ei-la," stuttered Cooper. "I enjoyed the r-r-r-ride, too."

Sheila was still wearing her white starched waitress uniform, covered in part by a red-and-white checkered apron, which matched the tablecloths on the picnic tables. Even so, she had a sensuous look about her. Unlike Ronnie, it wasn't her coiffure that was appealing. Sheila's hair was dark brown and short, parted in the middle, and barely covered her ears. Cooper suspected that it would have hung straight down if it weren't for a nightly application of curlers. It reminded him of his oldest sister, who spent half her life with her hair either in curlers or tied up in little knots with strips of white cloth. Sheila had something of a pug nose, and her lips were full and slightly turned up at the edges, giving her a permanent grin. She wore a thick coat of deep red lipstick, and when she turned her grin into a smile, she was careful not to part her lips and expose the space between her two front teeth. Sheila's eyes, however, were her major feature. They were large, round and blue–almost an ice-blue–that sparkled even in the dimmest light, coming alive whenever someone lighted a match or even took a deep drag on a cigarette. Cooper wondered if her long eyelashes were real or had just been touched up with one of those little brushes his sisters used. Sheila inhaled her cigarette, fluttered her eyelashes, and asked, "Is there anything I can do to help you clean up?"

"Not really," returned Cooper. "Everything is pretty much under control. All I have left to do is take this stuff back into the kitchen and put it away. Then, thank God, I'll be through for the evening."

"Why don't I keep you company while you sort things out. Then, maybe, I can help you carry some of these things into the kitchen."

Cooper nodded his assent and then silently proceeded to fill a bushel basket with condiments and utensils. He placed what was left of the ham and roast beef on a stack of platters. He kept looking at Sheila; Sheila smiled at him each time. He handed her a ketchup bottle, and she found room for it in the basket. He wasn't quite sure what he was supposed to say, but something deep within his body remembered the warmth of her body pressing against him in the car ride back from church.

Sheila took one last drag on her cigarette, and its glow reflected in her eyes. She smiled at Cooper, picked up the basket, looked over her shoulder, smiled, and said, "Let's go." Cooper dutifully followed her into the kitchen. They deposited the dirty plates and utensils by the silent dishwasher and then entered the walk-in cooler to store the meats and relish.

When Cooper had covered the unsliced meat with an old dented tureen cover, he turned to Sheila and declared, "That does it!"

In response, she faced Cooper, stood on tiptoe, reached behind his neck and untied his apron, which fell at their feet. Then she kissed him, first softly and then with a full, open mouth. Cooper pulled her close and began to return the favor, but Sheila pushed him gently and firmly away. "Let's get cleaned up and go someplace more private," she said.

"Who would ever want to look in the refrigerator at this time of the evening?" asked Cooper.

"You never know. Besides, you're all greasy, and I would feel more comfortable in something a bit more casual. Why don't we do a quick change and meet out on the dock in about twenty minutes."

The suggestion of a rendezvous on the dock sent a wave of panic through Cooper, as he remembered being stood up by Ronnie. "Can we meet somewhere else?" pleaded Cooper. "I mean, the dock is so public, and the planks squeak and make a lot of noise when you walk on them."

Almost by telepathy, Sheila picked up on the source of Cooper's anxiety and quickly suggested that they meet down by the laundry room door. She sent him off to his room with a deep kiss, after which he bounded up the stairs to his room, three steps at a time. When he reached his room he quickly stripped, leaving his greasy trousers, shorts, and work shirt in a heap on the floor by the side of his bed. Then he grabbed a towel and headed for the shower. One look in the mirror revealed a deep red smudge from his upper lip to his chin. He thought he looked like a circus clown. Thank God, no one was in bathroom, or they'd know what he was up to. He jumped in the shower, soaped up, quickly rinsed off and ran the towel over his body. A quick glance in the mirror indicated that he didn't need a shave, but just for good measure he splashed aftershave over his face and then went over his teeth with a toothbrush loaded with a thick helping of Pepsodent. In less than ten minutes he had on fresh skivvies, slacks, and his new Michigan sweatshirt. He decided against socks, just slipping his bare feet into his loafers. Then he checked his wallet for the Trojan he had placed there weeks before. Remembering Sheila's thick coat of lipstick, he grabbed a clean but impressed handkerchief from his dresser drawer. Cooper was about to leap down the stairs but thought that perhaps a bit of restraint was in order, so as not to give away his game plan. When he reached the first floor, he quietly opened the screen door that led to the loading platform, carefully navigated the stairs to the driveway, and headed for the entrance to the laundry. Sheila was already waiting for him and signaled her presence by drawing deeply on her cigarette so that its tip glowed a bright red.

"Is that you, Cooper?"

"It's me…I mean, it is I. Yeah, it's just me."

Sheila dropped her cigarette on the ground and twisted the sole of her shoe over it until its life was gone and it disappeared into the dirt. Then she took a tissue and wiped her lips. "I won't be needing any lipstick in the dark." She pressed against Cooper, kissed him deeply, and then took his hand and gently led him in the direction of the icehouse.

The hasp on the door was not secured. The door opened with little effort on Sheila's part, but the hinges still squeaked. Cooper remembered the day he had gone for the ice and discovered Harvard and Radcliff. He even remembered that he had planned to come back with a can of oil to get rid of that eerie *Inner Sanctum* wail. Too late now.

The interior of the icehouse was dark, and Cooper was literally in Sheila's hands as she led him across the thick bed of sawdust that insulated the remaining blocks of ice below. Suddenly, the grainy texture underfoot gave way to a softer, firmer footing. "Here," whispered Sheila, "let's sit down here."

Cooper realized that they were standing on a cotton blanket. He lowered himself to his knees and reached out to Sheila. She kissed him gently on the lips, and then he realized that she was fiddling with the waistband of his sweatshirt. "Here, let me help you out of that," she said. Cooper couldn't believe this was happening as she peeled his shirt over his shoulders and down his arms. After she had completed this task, she ran her fingers gently over his shoulders, arms, and chest. "Are you sure you haven't been lying about your age?"

Good grief, thought Cooper. Does she think I'm younger than sixteen-and-a-half?

But Sheila wasn't so much asking a question as paying him a compliment. "Your body isn't a kid's body. It's the body of a grown man." She kissed him gently on the neck and then said, "Now, it's your turn."

Cooper's eyes had adjusted to the darkness, which was penetrated by thin strands of moonlight through tiny cracks in the roof. He could actually see Sheila in front of him. He was in ecstasy as he fumbled with the buttons on her blouse and discovered, to his surprise and delight, that she wasn't wearing a bra. He found her lips and was pressing himself against her when he heard a sneeze. Startled, he pulled back from their embrace and called out, "What was that?"

Sheila did her best to rescue the situation by sniffling. "I guess I have a bit of hay fever from the sawdust or something."

"But Sheila," said Cooper, "you couldn't have been sneezing and kissing me at the same time."

Then there was another sneeze. Sheila did her best to cover it with a faint "Ah-choo."

"Someone's in here!" gasped Cooper.

With that, Kevin and Danny broke out in peals of laughter.

"Oh, shit!" Cooper cried out. Grabbing his shirt and groping through the sawdust, he fought off a wave of nausea as he lurched toward the icehouse door.

❧ ❧ ❧

Gasping for breath, Cooper stumbled out into the dark and instinctively made his way to his secret path along the edge of the lake. His head was spinning and his breathing shallow, but finally he heard the trickle of water over the edge of the dam. He leaned back against a birch tree and lowered himself to the ground. "That bitch! That goddamn bitch! And she thinks she's a good Catholic, too. That sleazy cock-teaser!" The sound of his voice awakened a nearby chipmunk, which scampered into the forest. Cooper couldn't believe that Sheila had intended to seduce him in front of an audience that was hiding behind a pile of sawdust in the icehouse. Maybe "seduce" was the wrong word. Cooper was a willing accomplice as far as the sex was concerned, but he couldn't believe that anyone, male or female, would want to do such a thing in front of an audience! Maybe Sheila didn't know she had an audience. It was still bad, but maybe not that bad. He decided that he would never know the answer to that one. He tapped out a Camel and torched it with his lighter, which was reflected in the eyes of a dozen creatures that had come back to observe the human invader from a safe distance. Cooper breathed a deep, despairing sigh, which caught a cloud of smoke and sent him into a coughing spasm. Damn it to hell! He couldn't even smoke like an adult. All the little critter eyes disappeared. He crushed his cigarette in the grass and stumbled over to the dam to wash his face and wash his mouth out with a handful of water. Then he made a small pile of pine needles into a pillow and stretched out on the grass. A slight breeze produced gentle rustling sounds in the trees, and now and then a lake trout splashed in the water.

Cooper looked up at the sky and realized the stars were brighter than he had ever seen them. There seemed to be were more of them than he had ever seen, except that time that Pops had taken him and Guts to the planetarium. He had asked Pops why the stars were so bright in the planetarium and so fuzzy over the sky in Manhasset. Pops had explained that the lights of New York City were so bright that they competed with the night lights that God had put in the sky.

The next time Cooper and Guts were at the beach cottage, they took a blanket down by the shore and stared up into the night sky. The new moon was just a sliver, so the stars were almost as bright as in the planetarium. They quickly found the Big Dipper and the North Star and the great blanket of light in the Milky Way. They looked for Mars but couldn't find it. Their favorite comic book character was Buck Rogers, and the two young boys chattered on about boarding a rocket ship, circling the moon, and then heading out for the Red Planet.

What fun it would be to explore the grand canals of Mars! Cooper looked again at the Vermont sky. If anything, it was brighter than the one he and his cousin had observed on Long Island. Some music started running through his head. What was it? He realized that he had heard it in church when the voices of St. Phil's choir triumphantly declared, "The heavens are telling." But what were the heavens saying? Were they telling God and the whole world what a big fool he was? Were the heavens telling the stars that Cooper Dawkins, at age sixteen, had tried to pass himself off as a college student and that he was spotted as a phony on his first day in Vermont? Were the heavens telling the planets that all Cooper could think about was getting laid and that as far as the other staff members were concerned, he was a big joke? But maybe the heavens were silent. Maybe nobody up there really cared what happened to Cooper Dawkins from Manhasset, Long Island.

Cooper had no idea how long he had been lying on the ground before he realized that it was getting cold and he was starting to shiver. He stood up, brushed the leaves and pine needles off his shirt and slacks, then headed back to the hotel. Just short of the icehouse, he stopped and listened. There was nothing but the sound of crickets, so he headed for the kitchen door and the staircase that led to the fourth floor.

Once in his room, he realized that between the sawdust from the icehouse and the pine needles down by the dam, he needed a shower. He wrapped a towel around his waist and went down the hall. None of the rooms had their own toilets and only a few had wash basins. Most were equipped with a washstand, a pitcher of water, and a ceramic basin with a drain that led to a galvanized bucket below. If you needed to do anything more serious than wash your face or brush your teeth, you headed down the hall to what became known as the "community privy." The room had three door-less stalls with overhead oak water tanks. Everything else was out in the open. An area opposite the wash basins had been tiled and contained three showerheads. To get to the toilets you practically had to take a shower. The college jocks and the guys who had been in the service didn't seem to mind the lack of privacy. Some even wallowed in it, walking into the bathroom with nothing more than a towel draped around their necks, showing off their physiques, and shaving in the nude. Cooper was never completely comfortable in this setting, and while he stopped wearing his bathrobe after the first week, he always covered up with a towel or wore his shorts in the community privy. Before entering the bathroom now, Cooper checked it out to see if it was empty. Relieved, he took a deep breath, draped his towel over a stall and adjusted the shower faucets for a quick rinse. He was washing the leaves and sawdust out of his hair when he heard the familiar refrain of the "Whiffenpoof Song" coming down the hall. *Oh, my God*, he thought. *It's Kevin and Danny. The little black sheep have gone astray and they're heading my way, and they sound like they're drunk.* Cooper turned off the shower, grabbed his towel, and slipped into a stall as the Seton Hall boys stumbled into the room, naked except for the towels around their necks.

After the final "baa" of the song, Kevin asked, "I still don't understand. How come Sheila slapped your face and told you to get lost?"

"All I did," said Danny, "was offer, in a very gentlemanly way, to help her with her problem."

"And what was that?'

"I just offered to take care of her need. You know, I offered to finish off what she tried to start with that kid."

"That was very gentlemanly of you."

"I thought so," said Danny, "but she didn't just say get lost. She said, 'Fuck off, you Irish bastard!'"

"That's no way for a nice Catholic girl to talk, now is it?"

"She may be Catholic, but I wouldn't call her any kind of a nice girl. I mean, you might get a nice Catholic girl to do it, to go all the way. I mean, if you told her that you loved her and pretended that you wanted to marry her as soon as you got out of college and that you wouldn't tell your friends or your parish priest. That would be a nice Catholic girl. But Jesus, Mary, and

Joseph! To do it with a high school kid in front of your friends! I wouldn't call her a nice Catholic girl."

They started soaping each other's backs and tried another chorus: "From the tables down at Mory's."

When Cooper heard them stumbling over the "baas," he thought he had a chance to make a quick dash for the door. Then Kevin saw him out of the corner of his eye and almost slipped to the floor as he grabbed Cooper by the arm. At the same time, Danny grabbed at Cooper's waist and was left with a blue towel in his hand. "Fe-fi-fo-fum, I see the butt of an Englishman," chanted Kevin.

They pulled Cooper into the shower area and held him under the faucet. "Well, look who's here! It's the little high school kid. It's Cooper. Coop, Coop, chicken Coop, the red-hot lover from Long Island," Kevin taunted.

"Did you like what Sheila showed you when you took off her blouse? She's got a nice pair of jugs. Did she let you touch them?" Danny sneered. "I'll bet she got you real hot. You know what you need? You need to cool off."

Danny reached for the faucet to turn up the cold water as he and Kevin tried to center Cooper under the near-freezing stream of mountain water. Somehow, Cooper wrenched himself loose and scrambled down the hall, stark naked. He slammed and bolted his door and then headed for the wash basin. If Danny and Kevin had tried to open his door, he wouldn't have heard them over the sound of his retching. When the spasms in his stomach finally subsided, the heavens took over, and thunder claps bounced back and forth from mountain to mountain. His mind went back to his earlier thought: *the heavens are telling*. They were trying to tell him something, but what? Then he remembered the fury of the thunderstorms at the summer cottage. One night, when the lightning struck a nearby telephone pole, he ran trembling into his parents' bedroom and crawled under the covers next to his mother. She tried to comfort him by reciting the Twenty-third Psalm. Now, as the storm rumbled through the Green Mountains, he tried to remember the psalm. But all he could remember were the first five words, "The Lord is my Shepherd." It was first light before Cooper finally fell asleep.

CHAPTER TWELVE

THE NIGHT OF THE SAUERBRATEN

"What happened to you?" asked Dorcas as Mercy entered the laundry room with a red face and breathing deeply. "Here it is, twenty past the hour, and you're just arriving. I was getting a bit worried. I thought maybe you'd been in an accident."

"Nothing so dramatic," stated Mercy. "I just ran out of gas. Simple as that. I should have filled up the tank last night on my way home. It seemed like just yesterday that I put a dollar's worth of gas in the tank. But there I was, halfway down Route 7, and next thing you know the old jalopy was coughing and wheezing like a three-year-old with the croup. And then she just stopped! Right in the middle of the road. A truck barreled down the hill and almost hit me in the rear. Then two veterans on their way to Rutland pulled over. They didn't have any gas, and they were in a big hurry, something about an appointment for a job interview. So they couldn't help me get the gas, but they did push me off onto the grass on the side of the road. Then, who should come along but Dr. Martin. He'd been in to Middlebury on hotel business. He's a nice man, that Dr. Martin. I remember when he was a college student, before the war, working at the hotel. He was a real gay bachelor, he was. All the young ladies were crazy about him, including that Broadsmith woman from Hartford, before she had those three awful kids."

"Ever wonder what life would have been like for Dr. Martin if Libby hadn't charmed him away from Mrs. Broadsmith?" questioned Dorcas.

"Well, for one thing he'd have had some children, but I doubt if he'd have wanted the litter that woman would have given him."

"It was too bad about Libby and all those miscarriages and the one little boy that she did birth, only to lose him to the measles when he was three. I remember that summer before he died. When was it, 1933 or '34? They had him up here, and he was so cute. He'd be sixteen or seventeen, by now, if he had lived."

"Well mannered, too! Not like the Broadsmith children," said Mercy. "When the dining room laundry comes down, you can always tell which one was on the Broadsmiths' table. It's always covered with ketchup and mustard, gravy, milk, maple syrup, ice cream, what have you. Take one look at the tablecloth, and I could tell right away what Rudy was serving for dinner."

"Get to the point, Mercy, or we'll be here all day getting your car off the road."

"Well, that nice Dr. Martin drove me back to the Esso station outside of Middlebury. They lent him a five-gallon gas can, and he had them fill it up. Remind me to pay him for the gas. I owe him seventy-five cents." She paused, searched her sweater pockets for her coin purse, opened it, and fingered the coins until she has assured herself that she did indeed have the necessary money to repay Dr. Martin. Then she continued, "Anyway, while we were driving back to the car, I told him that I had heard that the Broadsmith woman had given that Jewish girl a five-dollar tip for a month of serving food to those difficult children of hers. Dr. Martin allowed that she didn't get away with it. After he stopped Rosie from giving Mrs. Broadsmith back the five dollars. Within an hour, everybody in the hotel knew what had happened, and everybody was rooting for Rosie. Dr. Martin said that when Mr. Broadsmith was settling his account at the front desk, Dr. Martin took him into the office and explained the situation to him. The poor man was embarrassed as all get out and gave Dr. Martin one hundred dollars for the waitress and fifty for the maid who'd cleaned their rooms and made the beds every day. Dr. Martin said that he was going to surprise the two girls with the money right after breakfast."

❖ ❖ ❖

Breakfast was not finished yet but Cooper already felt like a zombie. He went about his morning chores as if he was setting pins in a bowling alley, with his mind on another planet. He kept his distance from everybody but Benson, assuming that everyone else had been in the icehouse or, by now, had heard about him and Sheila. He was drinking coffee at the staff table when Kevin and Danny came in and poured themselves some orange juice. The memory of their encounter in the shower the night before sent a shockwave through his body, and Cooper left his coffee cup on the table and returned to the stove to check on the bacon in the oven. He was developing a plan. He would tell

Dr. Martin that the whole summer idea was a mistake and that he wasn't ready to compete in a world of college students and returning vets. He would thank Dr. Martin, but tell him that he wanted to go home. Actually, he really didn't want to go home. He really didn't know where home was anymore. Was it at his father's house overlooking the bay, or was it with his mother in her childhood home on Plandome Road? Neither of these places was really home. The closest thing to home was Pops' place at the beach. That was it. When he got to New York, he'd catch the Long Island Railroad to Port Jefferson rather than Manhasset. He'd hitchhike out Old Country Road to Pops's place. Pops would take him in. Even if Pops had a lot of company, Cooper could sleep on a couch on the porch or down in the cellar. He'd stay out of everybody's way and use the old outhouse rather than the inside toilet. That was it! He would go to Pops' place, and then when he rode his bicycle to pick up the mail at the Mt. Sinai Post Office, he might follow one of the monks down to the monastery. He could become a monk, and then he wouldn't have to worry about competing with the veterans for the girls or getting laid or any of that stuff. That was what he would do—he'd become an Episcopal monk!

"Hey! Cooper! Wake up!" Rosie snapped at him. "I've got a breakfast order here: two Vermont special flapjacks with sausage, one scrambled with bacon, and one kippered herring." Cooper was certain that she knew what had happened to him in the icehouse. The sooner he got away from everybody the better. "Cooper! Are you listening? I need two cakes with sausage, one scrambled with bacon, and a kippered herring," Rosie repeated.

"OK, OK," returned Cooper, "I've got it. Go get the maple syrup and come back in five minutes, and it will all be ready." He poured the pancake batter in small puddles on the griddle.

THE NIGHT OF THE SAUERBRATEN

The scrambled eggs, sausage, and bacon were all done and waiting in the warmer. Opening the tin of kippered herring was the part he didn't like. Rudy said that you needed three hands to open the herring: two to open the can and one to hold your nose. Nonetheless, in five minutes all was ready and waiting for Rosie when she returned.

"What happened to you?" asked Rosie. "You look like yesterday's pancakes."

"I didn't get much sleep," Cooper muttered.

"I didn't get much sleep, either," said Rosie. "I stayed awake most of the night. I guess you heard what happened.'

Happened? What didn't happen and who didn't know?

"You know," said Rosie. "How that Mrs. Broadsmith from Hartford gave me only five bucks for a whole month of serving her and her bratty kids."

"Oh, that!"

"I guess you heard what I wanted to tell her to do with her five dollars."

"Yeah, I heard."

"But if the truth be known," stated Rosie "I do need the money. I need every penny of it for books and tuition this fall, or I won't be able to go back to Columbia. My abba told me to watch out for the gentiles. He said that they're not very good tippers, especially when the hotel is on the American plan, and that I probably wouldn't make as much money this summer as I thought. He wanted me to apply for a job in the Catskills, where the tips are better, the food is kosher, and I might meet a nice Jewish boy who was going to be a doctor or a lawyer."

"*Why are you still standing* when there is work to do?" bellowed Rudy, and everyone in the kitchen started looking busy. Rosie picked up her tray and headed into the dining room. Rudy lowered his voice and spoke directly to Cooper. "Why are you wasting time talking to that Jew-girl. She is nothing but trouble. What she wanted to do yesterday was very bad. The tip she got was just what she deserved." Then suddenly Rudy straightened his back and stuck out his stomach. His countenance changed from grim to joyful as he proudly announced, "Today is the day we cook the sauerbraten."

❖ ❖ ❖

There was a commotion at the staff table as Cooper entered the kitchen to report for luncheon duty. It centered around Rosie, who was waving five twenty-dollar bills over her head and shouting, "I won. I won!"

Stan, who was making one of his rare appearances at the staff table, observed, "You know, Rosie, when I saw you heading into the dining room to return the five dollars to Mrs. Broadsmith, I thought you'd be going back to the Bronx on the next southbound train. But the other guests were delighted with the outcome. I think they'd had it with those bratty kids. Not only that, but you did everybody a favor. We'll all get better tips because you stood up to that woman and her cheap ways."

"I don't...get...any tips," Benson commented. He'd come over from his dishwasher to see what all the excitement was all about.

"That's right," said Stan, "you get an hourly wage."

"And all you can eat," offered Ronnie.

"And all your pigs can eat, too," added the marine.

"Are...you...making f-f-fun of me?"

"No, no, Benson," said Stan. "We're just pointing out that the hotel pays you one way, and it pays the waitresses another.

THE NIGHT OF THE SAUERBRATEN

The waitresses don't get paid anything by the hotel. They get three meals a day and a place to sleep. The only money they get is from their tips, and they don't get to feed the pigs."

"Oh, I don't know about that," said Rosie. "Did you ever watch those Broadsmith kids mess up a table?"

"Hey, where's Sheila?" asked Stan. "Two of her big tables are checking out at the end of the week. She's bound to benefit from Rosie's successful protest."

"She's in her room. She doesn't feel well," said Rosie.

"We've all agreed to take care of her tables for the noon meal," added Ronnie.

"What's the matter with her?" queried Kevin. "She having her monthly visitor?"

"What'd she do, fall off the roof?" chimed in Danny.

"At least we know she didn't get knocked up in the icehouse," offered Kevin. He looked around the table expecting approving laughter but received none.

"Oh, shut up," retorted Rosie. "You need to send your brains down to Dorcas and Mercy for a good cleanup job."

The conversation came to an abrupt halt when Rudy bellowed Cooper's name from across the kitchen.

The staff table broke into laughter again as someone quipped *"Achtung!"* followed by a barely audible *"Heil, Hitler."* Cooper did a quick about-face and joined Rudy at his station in front of the stoves.

"What were they all laughing about?" Rudy wanted to know. "What was so funny? Do they think that reporting for work is a big joke?"

"Oh, that bunch of jerks—they're just telling college jokes," Cooper improvised. "You know, they're always telling stupid stories."

"That's stupid! I told you that you were wasting your time and would only get in trouble around that Jew-girl. Now, you are here, and we have work to do. We serve the lunch, and we get ready the sauerbraten."

When lunch was over Rudy and Cooper went into the refrigerator and removed the large chunks of beef from the pungent marinade where they had been soaking for the past six days. First, Rudy dried off the meat and dusted it with flour, salt, and pepper. Then he had Cooper heat up two of the largest cast-iron skillets in the kitchen. He rendered some fat in each frying pan and then carefully seared the large pieces of beef. "We sear the beef so that the juices stay in. Otherwise you end up with slices of rubber." Rudy carefully turned each piece of meat until the outside was a golden brown. The meat was then placed in large cast iron pots, washed with the marinade, and set over a low flame to simmer for the afternoon. "Cook it slowly, and it will be tender," advised Rudy. "Now there are two more important steps in preparing a perfect sauerbraten meal. One is the gravy, which I will fix just before we serve the dinner, and the other is the potato dumplings, which I will show you how to fix. That will be your duty tonight, while I am carving the meat you will be making the dumplings. Did you peel the potatoes like I told you?"

Rudy instructed Cooper to boil the potatoes until they were very soft and then to drain the water off and mash them. Unfortunately the mashing was a manual operation, as the old mixer had broken down and had yet to be repaired. The masher resembled a small garden rake, but Cooper mastered the art of pulverizing the potatoes after Rudy pointed out that by adding a saucepan of hot milk, the job would be a lot easier and the potatoes a lot smoother. As he mashed the potatoes, Cooper noticed that

Rudy was making frequent trips into the cooler, but he never brought anything back. Cooper assumed that Rudy was visiting his secret stash of whiskey.

"Now I will show you how to make the potato dumplings, or what your grandmother's cousin called *kartoffelklosse*. First we want to experiment a bit so we don't ruin the whole pot of mashed potatoes. We cut up an onion into little tiny pieces and cook it in a frying pan until it is transparent. Then, put four cups of the mashed potatoes in a bowl. Add the onions, a tablespoon of butter, one egg, and a half-cup of flour, and mix it with some salt and pepper and just a pinch of nutmeg. Now, we need a gallon saucepan. Fill it with three quarts of water and add a cup of the marinade, to give it some flavor. Put it on the stove and while you are waiting for it to boil, take the potatoes and shape them into little golf balls."

When the saucepan came to a boil, Rudy dropped the first potato golf ball into the water. It bobbed up and down two or three times and then fell apart. "That is not good," instructed Rudy. "That means that we need a little more flour." So Cooper put the lumps of potatoes back into the mixing bowl, added about a third of a cup of flour, and reformed the balls. This time when they were lowered into the water, they remained intact. It was almost ten minutes later when Rudy announced that the dumplings were ready. He fished them out with a slotted spoon and lined them up on a plate. "Now, we taste and see," stated Rudy as he plunged his fork into one of the puffy white clusters and opened wide. After smacking his lips several times, he smiled and handed a sample to Cooper. "Yah, *das ist gut!* Try it. Maybe it needs a little more salt, but it is good! Very good!"

Cooper was then dismissed but instructed to be back in the kitchen by five o'clock to and start the *kartoffelklosse.*

A SUMMER REMEMBERED

❖ ❖ ❖

Before reporting for the evening meal, or what Cooper was beginning to think of as the sauerbraten extravaganza, he sat down on the kitchen porch for one last cigarette. He barely remembered returning to his room after lunch and falling into bed, but he had slept for a good three solid hours before he was awakened by a full bladder and the need to trot down the hall. He was still half asleep when he took a deep drag on his Camel and looked up to see Sheila standing in the cloud of his smoke. Her hair was uncombed and matted and her eyes were puffy and red.

"C-cooper," she stammered, "I've got to talk to you."

He looked up in amzement. Sheila was the last person in the world he wanted to see. In fact, he never wanted to see her again. If he could take a sponge and wipe the blackboard of all the ugly episodes in his life, last night with Sheila in the icehouse would be the first to go.

"Cooper, I've got to tell you something," she insisted. She took a deep breath. "I am…I am so sorry for what I did last night. I am such a slut…and I started the whole thing in church…during mass." Then she broke down and started to cry.

Part of Cooper wanted to reach out to Sheila, but the other part yelled an emphatic *No! Don't go near that girl. Don't touch her ever again!* One thing was for sure: Cooper was now wide awake.

"I am so sorry," Sheila said again. "I was a real bitch. I couldn't sleep all night after what I did to you and in front of all those people. Honestly, I didn't know they would be there. They all thought it was a joke, but it was a sin. A real sin. A mortal sin. Nothing as simple as eating meat on Friday or missing mass. That was a 'Go to hell; go straight to hell. Don't pass go and don't collect two hundred dollars'—*that* kind of sin. I've got to go to confession, or I'll go to hell. Pray that I'm not struck by lightning or hit by a truck before I go to confession. I tried to get a ride into town to see the priest, but no one was going, and I couldn't tell anybody why I needed to go. So I went to the reverend from Boston. He was very nice. He didn't call me any names or anything. He did sigh and say 'Oh, dear, oh, dear.' He said that he thought going to the priest for confession was a good idea, but he also said that I needed to tell you that I'm sorry and ask you to forgive me. And then he said that I shouldn't be too surprised if you didn't—not at first, anyway."

Sheila took out a handkerchief, blew her nose, and started to sob. Cooper was immobilized. He had no idea what he was supposed to do or what he wanted to do. No one had ever apologized to him like this. On the other hand, no female had ever tried to undress him in front of an audience. Then again, he recalled that he had started out as a willing partner. He hadn't exactly gone into the icehouse to play patty cake. Cooper was about to reach out to Sheila when he heard Rudy's all-too-familiar bellow. This late in the afternoon, the jolliness was gone and meanness was charging in. "Cooper! Cooper! Don't be still standing! It is time we make the sauerbraten." For once, Cooper was relieved to hear Rudy's call to duty. He shrugged his shoulders, crushed his cigarette in the ash tray, turned his back on Sheila, and headed for the serving counter.

A bit on the confused side, with his mind torn between what he had just heard from Sheila and the summons from his harsh taskmaster, Cooper donned his apron. He set a large pot of water on the stove to boil, added a few cups of marinade, and then started to mix a bowl of mashed potatoes, onions, butter, eggs, and flour before creating those little golf balls of batter. The marine wandered through the kitchen and stopped to observe Cooper. "What are you trying to do now, Cooper? Lay some eggs?" he quipped.

Somehow Cooper managed to keep his cool and without looking up, he retorted, "No. I'm making golf balls!"

"Well, that proves what I've always contended—you do have balls, even if they're only made out of potatoes."

Even Cooper thought that was rather funny, but he wasn't about to give the marine the satisfaction of laughing at his joke. So he bit his lip and reminded himself that in the morning, he was going to tell Dr. Martin that he was going to go home, wherever that was, or maybe he would just get off the train and hitchhike to the monastery.

Rudy, in the meantime, had made another trip to the refrigerator and was now checking his chunks of beef for tenderness. He nibbled on a small slice, broke into a smile, and offered Cooper a sample. "Taste this and see if it doesn't bring back memories of happy times with your grandparents and your German relatives." Cooper savored the pungent odor, chewed, swallowed, and nodded his approval.

About that time, Rosie came bouncing up to the serving counter, sniffed the air, and then took a deep breath. She made a funny face and exclaimed to all, "What's that funny smell? Something smells sour." Rudy barked back, "It's supposed to smell sour. That's why they call it sauerbraten." And Rosie had the good sense to do a quiet about-face and join the other waitresses at the staff table at the other end of the kitchen. Rudy's face was almost purple when he turned to Cooper and announced that it was now time to prepare the gravy, and then he muttered, "That stupid Hebrew bitch."

THE NIGHT OF THE SAUERBRATEN

Cooper cringed at Rudy's offensive statement. He said nothing but instinctively turned his head and busied himself with forming golf-ball-sized clumps of potato batter until Rudy's face returned to its normal bright red color.

"Now I will show you the secret ingredient in the gravy," Rudy announced. "Go into the storeroom and get those big boxes of ginger snaps and bring them here." Cooper did as directed and then watched intently as Rudy took a rolling pin and pulverized the ginger snaps into a fine powder. This he mixed in with flour and proceeded to make a thick gravy with the meat juices. After dipping a spoon into the golden-brown liquid, he offered it to Cooper. "Now taste this and see. As I told you, the difference between a chef and a cook is in the sauces. It is the sauces that make the meal. You can take a piece of cardboard and make it taste good with the right sauce." Cooper tasted the gravy, touched his tongue to his lips, and again nodded his approval.

It was the custom at the Lake Bradford Hotel to offer one main dish at the evening meal, which was often served family-style. This usually satisfied nine out of ten of the guests. Individuals with special dietary needs or finicky eating habits could always make a selection from the short-order menu. There was always the choice of pork or lamb chops, cold meats, or Salisbury steak. The most popular item among the children was hot dogs. Even when the main course was something exotic, like Maine lobster, most of the youngsters still ordered hot dogs.

When the dining room opened, Rudy put on a fresh apron and a crisp chef's cap. The sharp aroma of the sauerbraten permeated the kitchen and crept into the dining room. Rudy sharpened his long, double-edged carving knife to razor-sharp perfection and proceeded to fill the serving platters with slices of his German specialty. After a couple of false starts, Cooper had managed to stock the warming oven with a large supply of perfectly formed potato dumplings, which accompanied the sauerbraten on the serving platters.

But within ten minutes, Rudy's countenance had changed from regal triumph to hang-dog despair. Waitresses were returning half-filled platters of meat and placing orders for chops and hot dogs—anything but the sauerbraten. "What's going on here?" shouted Rudy. "What is happening? Don't they know what a special treat we are serving?"

"They say they've never heard of sauerbraten," offered Audrey. "They don't know what it is."

Rudy barked back, "They don't know good food when it's served to them on a platter."

Rosie was next in line and added, "They don't like the smell. They say it smells rotten. They don't want to eat it."

With that, Rudy turned purple. He started swearing at Rosie in German, and even Cooper could pick up that every third word was *Juden*. Rudy had his carving knife in his hand and tapped the blade on the counter in rhythm to his litany of contempt. Rosie put her platter down on the counter and placed her hands on her hips. She said nothing but stared defiantly back at Rudy.

Rudy leaned forward and pressed his large German belly against the edge of the serving counter as his rage increased. His foul breath was only inches from Rosie's face as he spewed insults. She winced but refused to cower and run. Cooper's understanding of German wasn't the best, but he thought Rudy said something to the effect that Hitler was right about the Jews.

Then, without warning, Rudy whipped the flat surface of his knife under her chin and pressed her head back. From where Cooper was standing—behind Rudy and slightly to his right—he found himself looking up Rosie's flared nostrils. Her eyes were bulging, dilated, and moist. Her lips were quivering. Rudy shouted in English, "I don't need any advice from a fat Jew-girl."

Cooper watched in horror as Rudy held his razor-sharp carving knife at Rosie's throat. Perspiration had broken out on Rudy's neck, and the back of his shirt was soaking wet. The rancid odor of Rudy's sweat and the pungent aroma of the sauerbraten was joined by a third odor—Rudy had passed some gas. The mixture was nauseating; Cooper thought he might throw up. *If hatred and evil had a smell*, thought Cooper, *this is it*.

The room was suddenly silent. Benson turned off the dishwasher. Chatter at the staff table ceased. Ronnie, just returning from the dining room with a tray of dirty dishes, stood trembling as the soiled crockery rattled. Audrey was frozen in place next to Benson. The guests in the dining room, sensing that something was amiss, ceased their conversations. The faint hiss of steam from the boiler in the laundry room and the crackle of hot grease in a frying pan could be heard. The hum of the kitchen's exhaust fan and the rhythm of heavy breathing became the dominant sounds. Somewhere in the hotel a radio or phonograph was playing "String of Pearls," but there was no tapping of feet.

Cooper knew he had to do something, but what? Rudy had the knife under Rosie's chin. He considered lunging at Rudy but realized that Rosie's throat would probably be sliced open in the process.

"All you Jew girls are interested in is the money," Rudy snarled. "You want the big tip. That's all you care about."

Then, three things happen almost simultaneously.

Rosie's face suddenly turned from an angry bright red to a fearful gray-green. She looked like she was about to faint, and her body swayed slightly.

Dr. Martin, who had heard Rudy's tirade on the intercom at the front desk, entered the kitchen.

And Cooper realized that he could reach the frying pan without Rudy's seeing him do so.

"*Ruhe! Und nicht bewegen!*" barked Dr. Martin, ordering Rudy to freeze. The command resonated off the high ceiling of the kitchen complex. Rudy was startled by the voice and looked around to determine its point of origin.

"Drop that knife, Rudy!"

Rudy pulled the knife back from Rosie's chin, at which point Rosie's eyes rolled back, and she fell, bumping her head on the kitchen floor. Then Rudy turned toward Dr. Martin, raising his knife as if he was ready to kill.

Cooper had no immediate memory of what happened next, but there were a dozen eye witnesses who later were more than happy to fill him in on the details. They all agreed that when Rudy raised the carving knife, Cooper swung the iron skillet and whacked Rudy on the side of his head. Rudy hit the floor— and Cooper fainted. Dr. Martin rushed in and planted his foot on Rudy's wrist. Danny, Kevin, and the marine, who had been smoking and drinking coffee at the staff table, charged over when Rudy hit the floor. The marine sat on Rudy's chest. Kevin and Danny each took a leg, while Dr. Martin pried the knife out of Rudy's clenched fist. Stan was directed to call the sheriff's office, and Dr. Schuller came in from the dining room to check Rudy's body for vital signs. Then he moved his attention to Rosie, who came to with the help of some ice water over her head. Audrey and Ronnie were at her side, holding her hands and assuring her that it was all over and that Rudy couldn't hurt her any more.

Gretchen charged across the kitchen floor, screaming, "You killed my Rudy! You killed my Rudy!" But she was assured that he would soon be awake, although with a bump and a burn on his forehead and one big hangover. Gretchen fetched some ice, cradled Rudy's head in her lap, and rubbed the top of his head with ice as she sang a German lullaby.

Cooper was the last one to come to. With Ronnie and Audrey attending Rosie, Sheila made a move in Cooper's direction but then thought the better of it and stepped back. By this time Libby Martin had joined the scene with a bucket of ice, water, and a towel. She knelt at Cooper's side, dipped the towel in the cool water, and used it to caress his face—first his forehead, then his eyelids, his cheeks, and his neck, as she cooed, "You poor baby. You poor baby. You were such a brave little man."

By the second round of Libby's ministrations, Cooper opened his eyes. Many of the guests from the dining room also had entered the kitchen and were clustered above him. "What happened?" one asked. "Is he hurt?" asked another. "What did he do?"

CHAPTER THIRTEEN
AFTER RUDY

Except for the bump on the back of his head, Cooper felt fine the next morning and, almost by rote, made it down the stairs to begin the breakfast routine. When he arrived in the kitchen, he found Dr. Martin, who had already started the coffee and was boiling water for the oatmeal.

"Good morning, Cooper," said Dr. Martin as he handed him a cup of coffee. "That was quite a night we all had. How are you feeling?"

"Oh, I guess I'll be all right," answered Cooper. "The back of my head's a bit sore, but I'll make it all right. What are you doing down in the kitchen so early in the morning?"

"I wasn't sure what shape you'd be in, so I came down to fix the breakfast, but if you feel that you're up to it, I'll go back to the front desk. Are you sure you can handle things?"

"I'll be OK."

Dr. Martin nodded and patted Cooper's shoulder. "Call me if you need any help."

"Yes, sir," said Cooper. "I'll do that." He put some cream and sugar in his coffee and took up his post in front of the stoves, powdering the bacon with flour before putting it in the oven to bake and then cutting up a batch of potatoes for the hash browns. He had the breakfast routine down pat. He had, after all, been doing most of the breakfast by himself for the past couple of weeks, as Rudy made his grand entrance later and later each morning.

A short time later, Dr. Martin stuck his head back in the kitchen. "Everything under control, Cooper?"

"Yes, sir."

"Sure you're feeling OK?"

"Yes, sir. I think I'll make it through breakfast just fine." Cooper almost added that after breakfast he would like to talk to Dr. Martin about the big mistake he'd made in coming to the hotel and that it would be better if he just packed up and returned to Long Island. But Dr. Martin was heading back to the dining room. After breakfast, Cooper decided, he would clean up the kitchen and then go see Dr. Martin in his office.

Dr. Martin paused a moment and turned to Cooper. "You were really quite the hero last night. No telling what Rudy would have done if you hadn't hit him with the frying pan."

Cooper's strongest memory of the evening was the horror of Rudy holding the knife up to Rosie's throat and yelling at her in German. He had no idea what the foreign words meant, but the sound was pure hate, and the look on Rosie's face was undiluted fear. He only had a vague recollection of swinging the frying pan. Then there was Mrs. Martin, stroking his face, and all the guests staring at him from what seemed like a hundred feet above him. After that, there was Dr. Schuller bending over him, checking his pulse, and telling Stan and the marine to take him up to his room, give him two aspirin, and put him to bed.

※ ※ ※

"Well, he's gone," said Mercy. "The sheriff came by, and put the handcuffs on him, and took him off to Middlebury, and locked him up in the Addison County Jail. Good riddance, I say. Good riddance!"

"Did they throw away the key?" asked Dorcas.

"Wish they had. Sheriff asked Dr. Martin and Mr. Bradford if they wanted to press charges. Standish brought me the whole story just before you got here this morning. He said that Dr. Martin and Mr. Bradford went off into the office for ten minutes to confer in private. Standish said that he could hear them through the door, talking about what to do, and when they came out of the office they allowed that a trial would bring a lot of bad publicity to the hotel. And it probably wouldn't happen until after Labor Day when the judge gets back from Cape Cod, so they would have to bring all the witnesses back up here from school. They asked the sheriff if there was some way to get him out of town and make sure he never came back to Addison County. If the sheriff could do that, it would be just fine with them."

"So what did they decide?"

"Well," continued Dorcas, "sometime this afternoon, after they fingerprint them and take their pictures, they're going to escort them over to York State and let them know that if they ever come back to Vermont, that they will end up in jail."

"I feel sorry for Gretchen," said Mercy.

"I don't. When they put the handcuffs on Rudy, she started yelling and hitting the officer, so they put cuffs on her, too, and took her off to jail with Rudy. Besides, a woman shouldn't have to put up with a man like that. He is a monster. He had no business coming to work here at Lake Bradford. He should've gone to work in one of those German-American hotels over in the Adirondacks in York State where they like to eat that sour... sour...what did he call that pot roast that nobody liked?"

"Sour-bracket?"

"Something like that."

"Do you think he would have gotten along any better over there? I mean, with his drinking and all?" asked Mercy.

"Probably not," agreed Dorcas, "and I don't think he would have treated Gretchen any better. If I were a wagering woman, I'd bet you he roughs her up a lot. How many times have you seen her in the morning with really puffy eyes, like she'd spent most of the night crying?"

"What's a woman to do? She promised for better or for worse."

"I don't believe in divorce, you understand. But there are limits to what a woman should have to put up with. The Bible may say that wives are to obey their husbands, but the husbands are supposed to love their wives. If Rudy had loved her, he wouldn't have treated her the way he did. It says so right in the Bible. My mother made me memorize that before Joseph and I got married, and we haven't slept apart in forty-six years."

"What happened to the Jewish girl?" asked Mercy. "How's she doing?"

"Doc Schuller said that she would be OK," answered Dorcas. "She got a lump on the back of her head when she fainted. He also said that there was a tiny cut under her chin. Shows you how close that animal came to cutting her throat. When she woke up, she started to cry. All the girls held her and hugged her and told her not to be afraid. Doc went back to his cottage and brought her one of those fein-o-bar-bee-tall pills to calm her down. Mrs. Martin took her up to her room and told her not to worry about her tables and to stay in bed in the morning."

"When all that was settled last night," continued Dorcas. "Dr. Martin went into the dining room and announced, 'As you all know by now, we've had some trouble in the kitchen. Everything is under control. Mr. Hoffman, our former chef '—and he emphasized *former*—'has been taken to the Addison County Jail. His employment has been terminated. He will never come back to the Lake Bradford Inn, Middlebury, or the state of Vermont.' The guests gasped, Standish said, and some politely applauded. Then he continued. 'Miriam Morris, our fine waitress, and Cooper Dawkins, our kitchen assistant, are both a bit shaken by the experience, but with a good night's sleep, Dr. Schuller says they will be just fine.' There was another round of hand claps. 'Now, I imagine you're wondering about your dinner. Personally, I'm very fond of sauerbraten. It's a very spicy Teutonic way of making pot roast. However, there is plenty of good sirloin steak, lamb chops, and pork chops in the cooler for any guest who would like to switch from the pot roast to the grill.' There was more applause and then he concluded with, 'And, oh yes, we'll be uncorking the champagne for the adults and doubling the ice cream for the children.' Someone called out 'Here, here!' and Libby Martin came in and started pouring the champagne."

"That Dr. Martin is something special," said Mercy.

"Always has been," added Dorcas, "Ever since he first came up here as a college student."

Stan was at the front desk when Cooper came by at midmorning, looking for Dr. Martin. "I'm afraid he isn't here," said Stan officiously. "He's gone into town on business, part of which is stopping by the sheriff's office to sign some papers. He said to tell you that he wouldn't be able to help with the lunch. Mr. Bradford is going to take charge of that, and Mrs. Martin is going to take over Gretchen's post and fix the dessert and salads."

"What am I supposed to do?" asked Cooper.

"Whatever Rudy had you do between breakfast and lunch. I don't know. Go do something. Look busy. The kitchen isn't my department."

Cooper was taken aback by Stan's demeanor. He always projected something of Cambridge superiority, but this was different from the guy who had welcomed him to the hotel almost two months ago. Cooper shook his head and had started back to the kitchen when he heard Mr. Bradford call out, "Cooper Dawkins! I've been meaning to come back to the kitchen all morning to commend you for your very manly and responsible actions in the kitchen last night. You were splendid, just splendid!"

Cooper grinned, and his face turned a darker shade of pink. He wondered if he should tell Mr. Bradford rather than Dr. Martin that he was going to leave the hotel and go home.

Mr. Bradford made the decision for him by announcing, "Now, Dr. Martin and I want to talk with you this afternoon when he comes back, but in the meantime, I'm going to depend on you to help me with the lunch. Let's go back in the kitchen and see what we can put together."

It was a warm day, so they decided on a cold lunch. Libby Martin was busy dishing out the fruit cup. There was a large cauldron of boiled potatoes in the walk-in refrigerator that were quickly turned into potato salad. The store room had an unlimited supply of baked beans and enough potato chips to feed an army. The meat locker had a half dozen picnic hams, which filled out the menu. For the little kids who didn't like ham or ham sandwiches, there were always the hot dogs. Mr. Bradford allowed that before he had gone to Yale, "back when the first Roosevelt was president, I used to help out in the kitchen. I peeled the potatoes, shelled the peas, and even made the ice cream with ice from the icehouse, salt from the cellar, cream from the dairy, and one of those hand-crank churns they don't have in the stores anymore."

※ ※ ※

Cooper rehearsed his speech six or seven times before he headed for the front office to see Dr. Martin and Mr. Bradford. He planned to say right off, "I'm here to submit my resignation, effective immediately." He thought that would be better than bluntly saying, "I quit." He realized that he would have to be polite; after all, he would have to face Dr. Martin back at Manhasset High in the fall. Then he would direct his remarks to Dr. Martin and say, "You were very kind to invite me up here for the summer. I really appreciate it, but it really hasn't worked. I got off on the wrong foot by trying to pass myself off as a college student, and I became something of a joke." Did Dr. Martin know about what happened in the icehouse with Sheila? He had probably heard about it from Stan. How would he tell Dr. Martin what a fool he had been, how willingly he had walked into that trap, and how Danny and Kevin, especially, had given him a hard time ever since? Cooper decided to skip that part and just politely submit his resignation and go back to his room and start packing. He looked at his watch. It was 2:25. He had five more minutes, so he decided to have one more cigarette before walking up the front steps to the lobby. As he took drag after drag in rapid succession, pacing back and forth in the driveway, he didn't realize was Dr. Martin and Mr. Bradford were watching him from their office window.

"The kid looks nervous," said Mr. Bradford.

"Well, look at all he's been through in the past twenty-four hours. Let's meet him as he comes in the front door and get right down to business," said Dr. Martin. The two men went into the lobby to greet the Cooper as if he were a swell from New York City or a politician from Boston.

They both smiled as they extended their hands and almost in unison said, "Good to see you, Cooper. Please come into the office. Take a seat. Would you care for a cigarette?"

Stan busied himself at the front desk and pretended not to notice the royal greeting extended to Dr. Martin's Long Island legacy.

Cooper politely turned down his teacher's offer of a Lucky Strike and took out his own pack of Camels. He inhaled deeply, with the intent that the first exhale of smoke would introduce his resignation speech, but before the first stream of smoke came out of his mouth, Dr. Martin began. "We were very impressed with your brave action last night. You are to be commended for saving Rosie's life, and we want you to know how much everybody here admires you."

"You were splendid, just splendid," added Mr. Bradford.

"But that's not the only reason we've asked you to meet with us this afternoon. We have also been impressed with how quickly you have caught on to the whole kitchen operation. We know that Rudy wasn't an easy man to work with. Quite frankly, I wouldn't have blamed you if you had just packed your bags and gone home." Cooper shifted uncomfortably in his seat. "We were seriously thinking of letting Rudy go early. Then the decision was made for us last night. But in spite of Rudy's many faults, he knew his business, and you managed to learn a lot from him. What I'm getting to is that we want to increase your responsibilities and also increase your salary. Mr. Bradford and I will be responsible for the meats at dinner. The rest will be yours. We're going to promote you to assistant chef. My wife will take over Gretchen's duties, and if you like, we'll get Benson to come over and help you peel the potatoes and prepare the vegetables. You think you can work with Benson?"

Cooper almost choked on his cigarette, which the two men took as an affirmative answer.

"Splendid!" said Mr. Bradford.

"Now," continued Dr. Martin, "how much are we paying you?"

"It's twelve-fifty a week."

"Well, we'll double that and make it retroactive to the first of July. How's that sound to you?"

Cooper's head was swimming as he tried to calculate what twenty-five dollars would mean. Could he take home enough to make a down payment on one of those Model A Fords on the used car lot on Northern Boulevard? "I'm...I'm not...not sure," he stammered.

"Not sure of what?" countered Dr. Martin. "Not sure that you can do the job? Not sure you're up to the responsibility?"

"Well, sir...well, sir...I mean..."

"Cooper, if you could put up with all the garbage you were getting from Rudy and at the same time learn his trade, you can do just about anything. I was proud of your actions last night, but I've also been proud of the way you have handled your job in the kitchen."

"Well, I—"

"Cooper, we need you. I don't think we can finish the season without you."

Cooper stared back in amazement. "Can I think it over?"

"Of course you can. You need to take some time off this afternoon. Mr. Bradford and I are going to fix roast beef for dinner, along with baked potatoes and some garden vegetables. Take some time off this afternoon—go for a swim, or take out one of the sailboats. Think it over, and don't worry about preparing anything for the dinner. You can come in around six and help us serve, if you like."

The two men stood up and extended their hands to Cooper. He stared at them in amazement and silently shook each of their hands. He left the room and walked by Stan at the front desk. Stan pretended not to see him as he turned to put some mail in the guests' boxes.

I'll bet Stan knows, Cooper thought, and I'll bet he's really pissed.

※ ※ ※

"To leave or not to leave," mumbled Cooper as he walked across the empty dining room and through the swinging doors into the kitchen. Twenty-four hours ago he'd felt like the bastard child at a family reunion and now, all of a sudden, he was the guest of honor. To stay or to leave—what should he do? He didn't think of himself as a hero. He had just done what he had to do—he hit Rudy when he had the chance. But being offered a promotion was another thing. The only person who had ever said he needed him was Pops, when he asked Cooper and Guts to help him make an appraisal by holding the other end of the measuring tape. But Dr. Martin and Mr. Bradford had not only complimented him on his work in the kitchen, they had said that they needed him. They *needed* him.

Cooper didn't see Rosie, who was sitting at the staff table, when he put the nickel in the Coke machine and pulled the crank. She had a cup of black coffee in one hand and a cigarette in the other.

"What time is it?" she asked. Her voice was groggy and one octave lower than usual.

Cooper jumped at the sound of her voice, and then turned to her and answered, "It's almost a quarter to three. You look like you've been out drinking all night."

"I wish I had. I don't know what was in that pill Doc gave me last night, but it's powerful stuff. I vaguely remember getting up to tinkle around daybreak, but that's all I remember until about half an hour ago. I must have slept for eighteen hours."

"Do you remember anything about last night in the kitchen?"

"Oh, God, do I ever! That bastard was ready to cut my throat, and he would have if Dr. Martin hadn't yelled at him, and you hadn't hit him with the frying pan."

"And if you hadn't fainted backwards. I hate to think of what would have happened if you had gone down face first," said Cooper.

"Oh, God," replied Rosie as she crushed the stub of her cigarette in the cereal bowl that was subbing as an ashtray, "I don't even want to think about it. Do you realize how close he came to cutting my throat? Look at this," said Rosie as she lifted her head and ran her finger across the scratch under her chin. "That's how close the Nazi bastard came."

Cooper put his index finger under Rosie's chin and lifted it so that he could get a better look. When he took his finger away, their faces remained only inches apart. Something was happening, but neither Cooper nor Rosie was able to say what it was. Finally, after what seemed like minutes of looking into each other's eyes, Rosie said, "Did you bring any cigarettes with you?"

Cooper placed two cigarettes in his mouth, lit both of them, and put one between Rosie's lips. He had never done this before, but he remembered seeing Humphrey Bogart do it in *Casablanca*. Rosie leaned back, inhaled deeply, puckered up her lips, and then formed three perfect smoke rings. Cooper attempted to spear one of the rings with a long, slow, blue stream of smoke, but his trajectory was slightly off course. The circle and the arrow formed a puffy little cloud. They stared at each other before they both made noises halfway between a guffaw and a giggle.

Cooper crushed out his cigarette and announced, "Dr. Martin gave you the day off, right?" Rosie nodded. "Well, he and Mr. Bradford told me to take the afternoon off and not to come in until around six. So I have a whole three hours off." He grinned at her again. "Rosie, have you ever been sailing?"

"Never!"

"Never been on a boat?"

"That's not what you asked. Didn't I tell you that when I was little, I liked to ride ferry boats. I've been on the Staten Island ferry. And my abba took me on the College Point ferry, just before they closed it down when they finished the Whitestone Bridge. You asked me if I had ever been sailing, not if I had ever been on a boat."

"OK, would you like to go for a sail on the lake?"

"I'm not a very good swimmer."

"That's no problem," Cooper said confidently. "I won't be dumping you in the water. And besides, we're supposed to wear life jackets anyway. Let's go down to the dock and ask Graham if we can take one of the boats out for a sail. I'll be the captain, and you can be my first mate."

"I'm not sure I would know what to do," Rosie protested.

"Don't worry about it. There's a first time for everything."

※ ※ ※

"You're in luck," said Graham. "Doc Schuller's children just brought this one back about ten minutes ago."

"Rosie's never been in a sailboat before," announced Cooper, "so this is going to be the short course in Sailing 101."

"The first thing you've got to do," said Graham, "is take off those shoes."

Rosie looked down at her penny loafers. "What's wrong with my shoes?"

"Nothing's wrong with them, except the leather soles will slip and slide as well as mark up the deck. You're either going to have to put on sneakers or go barefoot."

"Let's take off our shoes," said Cooper, even though sneakers had been part of his daily kitchen garb ever since he had slipped when he was mopping the floor that first week on the job.

"The next thing is to put on your life jackets," directed Graham.

"Rosie needs one, but I'm a good swimmer," countered Cooper. "I'll just keep a cushion handy by the tiller."

"No way!" Graham declared in his most official naval reserve officer's voice. "Everybody wears a life jacket when they're out in one of the hotel's boats. It's a good safety rule, and besides, the insurance company insists on it."

Cooper reluctantly donned his jacket and helped Rosie into hers.

"If this is Rosie's first time out," Graham said, "you'll need to explain to her about the boom."

"What's a boom?" inquired Rosie.

"It's that big pole that sticks out from the mast when you get underway and raise the mainsail," Graham explained. "When the boat comes about—I mean, when it changes course…when it turns around—the sail and the boom will swing from one side of the boat to the other. It's really simple. When Cooper yells 'coming about,' you need to duck. Keep your head down and your bottom down, and be prepared to move to the other side of the boat."

"That's all I need," Rosie groused, "is another bump on my head or a splinter in my tush."

Then Graham advised, "Cooper, there's almost no wind here at the dock, and only a gentle breeze out farther on the lake. The boat's already rigged, so what I would advise you to do is paddle out about a hundred yards and then raise the sail. Otherwise, you will be becalmed ten feet from the dock. There's a paddle under the deck, and I'll get you another one for Rosie."

Cooper untangled the bow and stern lines from the galvanized cleats on the dock. Graham gave Rosie her paddle and then took an oar and pushed the two of them off into the lake. Rosie not only was a beginner when it came to sailing; she was also a beginner at paddling. Finally, Cooper rolled up his trousers, positioned himself with a paddle at the bow, and had Rosie sit at the stern and steer the boat. It took a while, but eventually she got the knack of it. "I've got to remember, she said, "if I want to go to the right, I push this stick—er, the tiller—to the left. Right?"

"Right! Er, I mean, left. I mean, correct," said Cooper. "Now the next lesson is that on a boat, starboard is right and port is left." Cooper was enjoying his new role as the teacher for a change. "Remember that, because there will be a test."

"What happens if I flunk the test?"

"We'll have to do it all over again. Now, the next lesson is that the front of the boat is called the bow and the rear is called the stern."

"Is that the same as tush in Yiddish?" Rosie teased.

The banter continued until they felt a gentle breeze bouncing off the nearby hills. Cooper returned to the cockpit, hoisted the jib and mainsail, handed the jib line to Rosie, and settled down with the tiller in one hand and the main sheet in the other. There was just enough of a breeze to move the boat gently across the shining surface of the water. When they got to the middle of the lake, Cooper warned Rosie that they were about to come about and to keep her head down. The new tack took them directly to Cooper's special place by the dam. He explained that they were about to run the boat up on the beach and showed her how to pull up the centerboard when he gave the signal. Once ashore, he lowered the sails and ran a line from the bow of the boat to a nearby birch tree and then helped Rosie on to the sandy beach. He showed her the old man-made dam that had created the lake system many years before and then pointed to the beaver's housing project some twenty feet below. They sat cross-legged on the grass, and Cooper offered Rosie a cigarette.

"This is a beautiful place," she said as she exhaled her first puff of smoke. "How did you find it?"

"I wandered out here one afternoon, and then I came back here a couple of nights ago."

"Was that after you met Sheila in the icehouse?"

"You know about the icehouse?"

"Everybody knows about the icehouse."

"Everybody?"

"That's right. Everybody."

"That was the most horrible experience of my life. If I had had a rope, I would have hanged myself. If I'd been on a bridge, I would have jumped off. When I heard Kevin and Danny laugh, I ran out the icehouse door and into the woods. If I could have kept running, I would have high-tailed it right back to Long Island so that I would never, ever have to face anybody in Vermont again. Once I got into the woods, I found the remnants of an old trail that followed the shoreline and finally brought me to this clearing. This is my private place. I come here to be alone and to think."

"You know, Sheila is very sorry about what happened in the icehouse."

"Yeah, I know. She told me so yesterday."

"She wants you to forgive her."

"I know; she said that, too."

"Well?"

"Well, what?"

"Well, why don't you forgive her?"

Cooper thought for a moment. "I'm not sure I know how to do that. I mean, what am I supposed to say? 'Don't worry about it. Sheila; it really didn't matter. Who cares if you took off your blouse and started to unzip my trousers in front of an audience. It was really just one big laugh, and the Seton Hall boys got a big kick out of it. Ha. Ha. Ha.' Am I supposed to say it didn't matter and it didn't hurt?"

"If it didn't matter and it didn't hurt, what's to forgive?" Rosie was silent for a moment and then added, "Sheila's hurting really bad right now."

"Serves her right."

"And you're still hurting."

"Maybe it serves me right, too, for being such a damn fool."

"Maybe if you could find a way to forgive Sheila, you could forgive yourself. Then maybe you wouldn't hurt so much."

"I hurt so bad," declared Cooper, "that last night I was going to go to Dr. Martin and tell him that I was quitting, that coming here was a big mistake, and that I was going to go home."

"I thought you didn't want to go home," said Rosie. "I thought the reason you wanted to come here in the first place was to get away from your parents and their nasty divorce."

"If I went back to Long Island, I wouldn't go home to Manhasset. I'd go out to Pops's beach cottage and stay away from my mother and father. Or maybe I'd go to the monastery and become a monk."

"Do you have any idea of why they got a divorce?"

"I really don't know, and I really don't care," said Cooper. "I just want to get on with my life. When Mother told my sisters and me that we would be moving over to Pops' place in Manhasset, she wanted to explain why this was happening, but I left the house and went out for a long walk."

"Didn't you want to hear what your mom had to say?" asked Rosie.

"I guess I didn't know how to listen. All I could think of was that the family I knew and counted on was coming apart. I wanted to cry, but I didn't know how to do that either. When I heard that Grandmother Dawkins, my father's mother, Gamma, was coming back from California, I couldn't wait to tell her how much I was hurting, but…"

"But what?"

"But she wasn't the same."

"What do you mean?"

"Well, when I was a little kid," continued Cooper, "Gamma was the one I would run to when I fell off my bike or skinned my knee. She'd pick me up, sit me on her lap, put her arms around me, and rock me back and forth until I stopped crying. Then she would give me an extra big hug, kiss me, and tell me to be her brave little man."

"Is that what you expected?" Asked Rosie."

"I don't know what I expected. Instead of a big hug, she took off her glove, extended her hand, and greeted me with a frosty, 'Hello, Cooper.' I tried to hug and kiss her, but all I was allowed was a peck on the cheek. And then she said, 'My, how you've grown. You're as tall as your father. You're a young man now.' Then my mother entered the room and very formally put out her hand and announced that she had just put the kettle on and that tea would be ready in just a few minutes."

"Then what happened?"

"Well, Gamma went into the back parlor and sat down in one of the big wingback chairs by the fireplace. Mother wheeled in the tea cart and sat opposite Gamma. They took a long time pouring the tea, deciding how many lumps of sugar they would use, and whether they wanted lemon or cream. You know, all that stuff women do over a cup of tea."

"Where were you when all of this was going on?"

"I was hiding in the front parlor, behind the sliding doors."

"What did they talk about?"

"Gamma did most of the talking. She told Mother that she was making a terrible mistake, which most marriages go through a crisis, especially when the children are almost grown and are ready to go off on their own. She said something about having an 'empty nest.'"

"Are you the only child?"

"No, I have two older sisters. They're both off in college"

"So, it's just you and your mother at home?"

"Well, home is at Grandfather Goetz's, but he's not there too much. He's either down in Florida in the winter or out at the beach cottage in the summer."

"So, what did your mother say to your grandmother?"

"Grandmother Dawkins wasn't finished. It sounded more like a lecture than a conversation. I remember she told Mother that she wasn't getting any younger and that—and I remember the exact words—'when a woman is going through the change is no time to be making decisions.'"

"Your mother is into menopause?"

"What's that?"

"Change of life. When a woman stops having her period and can't have any more babies. Some women have a really hard time with their menopause. They get very emotional. For no good reason they'll break out in a sweat. If the truth be told, it's not an easy time for anybody."

Cooper's mind started to match this information with his mother's behavior. "Oh. Oh, yeah. Poor Mom. Poor everybody."

"So, how did your mother take your grandmother's lecture?"

"She didn't say a word. I couldn't see her face. All I could hear was the sound of her spoon clinking around and round in the tea cup."

"Was that it?"

"Oh, no! Gamma told Mother that this was 'no time for hurt feelings' but the time to be practical."

"What did she mean by that?"

"She said men begin to realize that they are getting older and that they tend to wander a bit. She said that my dad was still a good-looking man and didn't look anywhere near his forty-six years. Being an officer during the war had a lot of glamour attached to it. And then she said, 'It's in your best interest to look the other way.' She said that's what she and most of the women she knew had to do. And she told my mother, 'Leave them alone, and they'll come home, wagging their tails behind them.'"

"How'd your mother take that?"

"She sniffled a bit, blew her nose, and asked Gamma if she'd like more tea."

"Was that the end of the tea party?"

"Oh, no," said Cooper. "She told Mother that it was time to think of her children and their inheritance. She pointed out that if she had divorced my grandfather when he wandered off, there would not have been any money to help my father start his business and that my mother wouldn't be enjoying the luxury of living in a big house in Manhasset."

"Then what happened?"

"The tea party was over. Mother began to cry. Gamma called a taxi, put on her gloves, and walked out the door. She didn't even say good-bye."

"What did you do?"

"I wanted to cry. I thought Gamma would at least give me a hug like she used to do when I was a little guy. My head was swimming, so I went for a long walk."

Rosie could see that Cooper's eyes were moist. She ran her hand through his hair, saying, "You know, I think the Irish have the best system."

"How's that?"

"My mother says that the men don't get married until they're close to forty, and they marry a girl who's still in her teens. So, by the time she's had ten kids, like a good Catholic girl should, she's ready to give it a rest, and he's so old that he'd just as soon go down to the pub, have a pint or two, shoot some darts, and smoke his pipe."

Cooper nodded, more to acknowledge that he'd heard Rosie than to agree with her. "Anyway, if I quit here, I wasn't going home to my mother or my father. I just wanted to get out of here. I was going to quit last night, but then there was that mess with Rudy."

"Mess is the understatement of the year," Rosie said.

"Yeah, I guess so. Anyway, I went in to see Dr. Martin and Mr. Bradford, but before I could hand in my resignation, they said they were going to promote me to assistant chef and double my salary. They said that I had learned a lot in a short time and that they really needed me."

"Wow! They really said that?"

"That was about it, except Mr. Bradford used the word 'splendid' a lot, and they also praised me for hitting Rudy with the frying pan."

"You saved my life," said Rosie. "He'd have cut my throat. It was a mistake for me to come here. I should have gotten a job in the Catskills. As nice as Mr. Bradford is, he probably didn't realize that I was Jewish. I was ready to pack my bags, too. I'd had it with Rudy's nasty jibes about Jews and the hateful way he'd look at me. And I'm sure last night he thought he'd be doing the world a favor by getting rid of one more Jew." Rosie choked up and started to cry. Cooper reached out to comfort her and held her tightly against his body as her crying turned to gasping sobs. "Why do they hate us so? Why do they hate us so?"

Cooper rocked her in his arms as he stroked her hair and patted her on the head. He wanted desperately to take away her pain and to protect her from all of the wicked Rudys of the world. To his pats and strokes, he added a gentle kiss on her forehead and then started crooning, "You poor baby!" Little by little Rosie's sobs subsided, and she snuggled securely into his embrace. Responding to his gentle kisses on her forehead, she stroked the back of his neck and kissed him on the neck and then quickly on the lips. Cooper felt himself being transferred into another world, and he pressed himself against the softness of her body and kissed back with great eagerness. How long they held on to each other was difficult to tell. They had lost all sense of time until the faint sound of the dinner bell drifted across the lake and entered their consciousness.

"We'd better head on back to the hotel," said Rosie as she stood up and brushed the pine needles off her shirt.

"Do we have to?" asked Cooper as he stumbled to his feet.

"We have to," said Rosie. "Now turn around while I brush the grass and leaves off your tush."

Cooper did the same for Rosie and then turned her around for one final kiss.

"We have to go," Rosie whispered, "but that doesn't mean we can't come back."

❖ ❖ ❖

Cooper and Rosie split when they got to the kitchen porch. She had decided to put on her uniform and wait on her regular tables. Cooper rolled down his trousers and entered the kitchen to find both Mr. Bradford and Dr. Martin decked out in white aprons standing behind the serving counter in front of the stove. "I know we said that you didn't have to worry about dinner tonight, but we sure could use some help back here," stated Dr. Martin.

"Whatever I can do," said Cooper as he took his apron from its appointed hook.

When Rosie appeared in her fresh waitress outfit, there was a spontaneous roar from the kitchen crew. Ever the performer, she raised her arms in ballerina style over her head, did a double twirl, and took a bow. Then Mr. Bradford moved from behind the serving counter to the center of the kitchen floor. He raised his hand for silence and announced, "I want to thank all of you for your splendid behavior and perseverance under very trying circumstances. You'll be happy to know that we won't be seeing the likes of Rudolph Hoffman anymore." His speech was interrupted by shouts and the sound of clapping hands. "Mr. and Mrs. Hoffman were escorted to the New York State line, never to return." There was more applause. "Now I want to apologize to Miss Morris for the totally unacceptable behavior of our former chef and commend her for her courage under the most adverse circumstances." The crew applauded loudly, and there were shouts of, "Yeah, Rosie!" Mr. Bradford held up his hand again. "I'm not finished yet. I want to commend both Dr. Martin and Cooper Dawkins for their timely action in thwarting Mr. Hoffman's murderous actions last night." He paused and the two men took a bow. "I'm also happy to announce that Mr. Dawkins has been promoted to assistant chef and is therefore entitled to wear this chef's cap while on duty in the kitchen." The kitchen crew and many of the hotel guests who had slipped in from the dining room expressed their approval as the puffy white cap was placed like a monarch's crown on Cooper's head. "Splendid," declared Mr. Bradford, "Simply splendid!"

※ ※ ※

Working with Dr. Martin and Mr. Bradford was quite a change from working with Rudy. For one thing, they were both sober, and Cooper realized that he wasn't walking around on egg shells, trying not to upset his boss. Somehow, he had felt that it was his fault when Rudy got out of control. Even on that last night with the sauerbraten, he wondered if the German pot roast would have tasted better if he had done something different. Would the guests have praised Rudy rather than sending their food back to the kitchen?

With Mr. Bradford and Dr. Martin, it didn't feel that way. It felt more like Bradford, Martin, and Dawkins, Inc. The owner and the manager treated Cooper like a junior partner, not a serf or even an apprentice. The roast beef and baked potatoes were a big hit—no complaints and lots of requests for second helpings. As soon as the initial rush was over they started planning the menus for the rest of the week. They were just hanging up their aprons when Ronnie informed Cooper that there was a person-to-person long-distance phone call waiting for him in the office.

Stan was at the desk when he arrived and stated tersely, "The call is waiting on the office phone. I think it's your mother."

Cooper picked up the phone. "Hello, Mom."

It wasn't his mother but the operator at the Manhasset exchange. "I have a person-to-person call for a Mr. Cooper Dawkins. Are you Mr. Dawkins?"

"Yes, I am."

"Just a minute, and I'll connect you with the party placing the call."

Finally, he heard his mother's voice. "Hello, Cooper."

"Hi, Mom, what's up?"

There was a slight annoyance in her voice. "I haven't heard from you."

"Gee, Mom, it's really been busy up here. A lot of things have been happening, a lot of strange things."

"Did you speak to Dr. Martin?"

"About?"

"About coming home for the Labor Day weekend, of course! So that you can meet with Uncle Matthew from Detroit. Of course, he's really not your uncle. He's my first cousin—"

Cooper interrupted, "Yeah, Mother, I know that." He didn't like the way the conversation was going and while he was trying to think of what to say next, he noticed that Rosie was standing outside the office door. She smiled and waved to him and he waved back.

"Cooper? Are you still there?"

"Yes, Mom, I'm here."

"Well, have you spoken with Dr. Martin?" she asked.

"No, Mom, I haven't."

"Well, when are you going to speak to him?"

"About coming home early? For Labor Day?"

"Yes, that's very important."

Cooper looked again at Rosie standing at the door. They exchanged smiles. Cooper took a deep breath. He didn't want to hurt his mother, but he had made his decision. "Mother, a lot of things have been happening up here. They had to fire the chef and I've been promoted, and I've been given a raise."

His mother's voice quavered. "Cooper...Cooper, please! This is very important. It's important for your future." She hesitated, and it sounded like she was softly crying. "It's important to me. Please, Cooper, for my sake, please come home for Labor Day."

"Mother, I don't want to disappoint you, but I can't come home for Labor Day." There was no response, only gentle sobs. "Mother? Mother, I can't come home. I'm needed here. Maybe I could take some of the extra money I'm making this summer and fly out to Detroit to see Uncle Matthew for Columbus Day or Thanksgiving or something like that."

All Cooper heard was the soft sound of his mother's tears and then a discouraged, "OK." He heard a couple of sniffles and then his mother added. "I'll talk to you later."

"Bye, Mom. I love you."

There were more sobs, followed by a weak, "Bye, Cooper."

CHAPTER FOURTEEN
FUGITIVE FROM JUSTICE

Cooper wasn't sure what woke him up. Was it the cold gray light that invaded his sleep? Was it the scampering of squirrels on the roof above him that invaded his warm dream of frolicking in the water with Rosie? Was it the distant sound of Reverend Lawrence's fishing boat beginning its early morning search-and-capture mission at the far end of the lake? All Cooper knew was that it was very chilly, and it was time to get up. Responsibility for breakfast was all his now. If too many guests appeared in the dining room at one time, Dr. Martin helped with the fried eggs or the omelets, but he was only there to "help out." He wasn't there to give orders or to tell Cooper to hurry up. Sometimes Mr. Bradford would drop by to say good morning and then walk off chanting, "Splendid, splendid." There was a new climate in the kitchen, and Cooper liked it that way.

His morning went smoothly; there were no complaints from the guests, and the waitresses glided in and out of the dining room as if choreographed for a scene from a Broadway musical. For some reason, Dr. Martin and Mr. Bradford didn't come by. Cooper took this as a compliment. It never occurred to him that his bosses were tied up in the office with long-distance telephone calls and a visit from the sheriff.

Just before noon, the kitchen and dining room staff, with the exception of Cooper, gathered at the staff table, drinking Cokes, ice tea, and coffee and having a final cigarette before taking up their luncheon chores. Stan approached with a bundle of newspapers in his hand and announced, "This is interesting; this is really exciting. The news just came in this morning, and Dr. Martin said that I could share it with the staff. I don't think anyone will be particularly surprised, especially Rosie and Cooper." Stan looked around the table, taking silent attendance. Rosie blushed and studied her coffee cup. "Hey, Cooper," Stan shouted across the kitchen. "I don't care what you're doing. Come over here. I want you to hear this."

Cooper removed his chef's cap and moved slowly toward the staff gathering. He quietly relished his new status as *the* assistant chef. And he was now the highest paid staff member of the summer. He could look the veterans and college types in the eye, and they didn't give him a condescending "who-let-you-in?" smirk. He looked across the table and smiled at Rosie. She smiled back and gestured to an empty chair beside her. He acknowledged her gesture with a flushed complexion and a nod but remained standing at the other end of the table, opposite Stan.

"This will really interest all of us," Stan said again, "especially Cooper and Rosie." Cooper's face turned a deeper shade of pink as the coupling of his name with Rosie's not only brought back warm memories but a near panic attack when he thought that there might have been witnesses hiding behind the birch trees on the other side of the dam.

"Get...on...with it!" Benson called, which was echoed by a chorus of the entire staff.

"Yeah," yelled Kevin. "Tell us what Cooper and Rosie are up to."

"I didn't say it was *about* Rosie and Cooper," said Stan. "I said that it would be of especial interest to them. It's about Rudy."

"Rudy? I thought we got rid of that son of a bitch!" declared the marine. "Boy, was he ever a Nazi!"

"As a matter of fact, he was a Nazi. It seems that when Rudy was fired, Dr. Martin wrote a letter to the hotel manager in Palm Beach to let him know about Rudy's behavior up here, just in case Rudy showed up in Palm Beach this fall and wanted his old job back. Dr. Martin said that he did it as a professional courtesy. Anyway, last night the sheriff came by asking questions about Rudy and Gretchen, and then this morning Mr. Bradford got a long-distance phone call from the FBI."

"FBI!"

"Hold on," said Stan. "No sooner had Mr. Bradford put down the phone than it rang again, and this time it was the long-distance operator from Palm Beach, Florida."

"Long distance! All the way from Palm Beach, Florida!" said one of the staff.

"It was the manager of the Beachwater Club where Rudy said he had been the chef. He apologized for giving us misleading information. It seems that Rudy had worked there last winter, but he never was the executive chef. He started out as a kitchen helper, kind of like Cooper here, and then sort of worked his way up to assistant." Stan looked across the table at Cooper, who started to blush.

"That's it? So, what's the big deal?" said Rosie. "The FBI has nothing better to do than check the credentials of hamburger flippers? Is that a federal offense? That doesn't make the old drunk a Nazi, does it?"

"Be patient," said Stan. "I'll get to that in a minute."

"How about thirty seconds?" quipped Rosie.

"OK! OK! The fact of the matter is that Rudy really was a Nazi, or at least he was a sergeant in the German army and ended up as a prisoner of war. He was shipped to the Unites States and locked up in Camp Blanding."

"Where the hell is Camp Blanding? I've never heard of it," declared the marine.

"Camp Blanding is in Florida, out in the piney woods somewhere between Jacksonville and Gainesville. At first, it was sort of a makeshift army basic training center, but by the end of World War II, they had converted it into a prisoner of war camp and had some five thousand German POWS in tents behind barbed wire."

"So, what did Rudy do? Walk out the gate and catch a bus to Palm Beach?" questioned Kevin.

"It wasn't quite that simple," continued Stan. "Rudy escaped."

"Escaped!"

"That's right; he escaped in a delivery truck and, among other things, he is wanted for the murder of the truck driver."

"Murder!"

"The story is that Rudy was a mess sergeant in the German army. What he was before that, nobody seems to know."

The term "mess sergeant" triggered Cooper's memory of the Saturday during the war when his father had taken him to the military police headquarters at Pier 90 on the Hudson River. At noon they went into the mess hall, where the enlisted men were being served. The old Cunard Line terminal had not been equipped with cooking facilities, so they were getting by with a portable field kitchen. Under the circumstances, Colonel Dawkins said they were doing a pretty good job. The mess sergeant insisted that Colonel Dawkins, his commanding officer, and Cooper be served at one of the tables. Cooper had wished that he could have gone through the line with the troops. He watched with fascination as the men picked up metal trays and went through the line, as the servers, often with cigarettes dangling from their mouths, took delight in "throwing the mashed potatoes at the trays," just as Rudy had said. So Rudy had been a mess sergeant and a short-order cook and not a chef after all. Cooper's face broke into something between a grin and a smirk.

Stan sensed that Cooper was drifting off, so he asked, "Cooper, are you following me? We don't have much time before lunch, and we all have a lot of work to do, so please pay attention."

An unidentified voice from the other end of the table muttered, "Get rid of one Nazi and what do you know—we've got his replacement."

Stan was taken aback by the harshness of the statement. He went to the Coke machine, deposited a nickel, and, having regained his composure, returned to the table. "Now, back to Rudy."

"Oh, joy," said Rosie. "Do get back to our number one Nazi."

"When Rudy got to Camp Blanding in Florida, it wasn't long before they discovered his cooking talents and put him to work in the prison mess hall."

"I'll bet he served sauerbraten every other day," interjected the marine.

"I hope they liked it better at Camp Blanding than we did at Lake Bradford," offered Ronnie.

Stan glared in her direction. "We're never going to get through this before lunch unless you guys settle down,"

"I'm afraid we're going to have to continue this briefing later," said Dr. Martin, who had slipped in behind Cooper. It's time to serve lunch; the dining room is already filling up."

Cooper walked back to his post in front of the stove and put on his new cap. So Rudy was a real Nazi. He didn't just think like one; he really was one. Somehow, Cooper was relieved. Even though Pops was the greatest man he had ever known and the Goetz family had been American since the early 1800s, Cooper had never been comfortable talking about his German background with Rudy. Even great-grandmother Goetz, "*Grossmudder*," who had lived into her nineties, had many tales to tell from American, not German, history. She delighted the family by relating how, as a little girl, she had stood on the Manhattan Island sidewalk as President Lincoln's funeral carriage was drawn through town on its long journey back to Illinois. Cooper preferred the stories of the Dawkins family, who landed in Maine in the mid-1600s. Cooper was relieved that Rudy was gone and was sorry he had revealed his German ancestry to Rudy. Once Rudy knew of that, he'd tried to make a little Nazi out of Cooper, he realized. He breathed a sigh of relief as he realized that being German didn't automatically mean you thought Hitler was right or that you instinctively hated Jews. Cooper drew a deep breath, whistled, and started to carve the cold ham, which, along with hot dogs, potato salad, coleslaw, and baked beans, would be the main course for his summer lunch.

❖ ❖ ❖

At mid-morning Dorcas and Mercy were still wearing their sweaters. "When the squirrels start scampering on the rooftops, it's a sure sign that summer's almost over and autumn's on the way," stated Mercy matter-of-factly.

"Judging from this morning's weather, I'd say that autumn's already here," added Dorcas. "Before you know it, Labor Day will be here, the students will be going back to school, the leaves will turn, and we'll be closing down the old place one more time."

"Dr. Martin's told those two basketball players from that Catholic School in New Jersey that no matter what they'd been up to the night before, they were to get their bee-hinds out of bed and have fires going in the dining room and the main parlor before the guests came down for breakfast. I hear tell they didn't much like the idea, but this morning when I arrived, I could see smoke coming out of the chimneys. So I guess they took the orders whether they liked it or not."

"Well, that's not all that's going on up there. Priscilla Handford, whose cousin Bert works at the sheriff's office, said that they'd had a visit from somebody at the state attorney's office, asking about Rudy and Gretchen. They think Rudy was an escaped prisoner of war who's wanted for murder down in Florida."

"I thought he was a chef at a big resort hotel in Palm Beach."

"That's what he wanted us to think."

"What about Gretchen? Where did she come from? Was she a prisoner of war, too?"

"No, Priscilla said that her cousin Bert said that she grew up in a little village on the Saint John's River in Florida called New Saxony. It sounds kind of English, but it was settled by a group from the Saxony part of Germany. The first families came to Florida from Germany before the Civil War. They had a plantation with slaves and all that and farmed the land and fished the river. When the South surrendered, the slaves were freed and most of the colored workers left. They turned the plantation house into a hotel. Back then, the railroad only went as far as Jacksonville and when folks went down there from New York and Philadelphia and Boston, there were paddlewheel boats that took them up the river to all these old homes that had been turned into hotels. Actually, they were more like boarding houses, but they called them hotels and inns. Gretchen belonged to the family that owned the hotel. They spoke German to the children and English to the guests. When Rudy escaped from the prison camp, somehow he found his way to New Saxony, and Gretchen's family took him in. Gretchen was already in her thirties, without any local prospects of a husband. Well, one thing led to another and, as they say, nature took its course—and not a good one, if you receive my meaning."

※ ※ ※

The word had circulated that Dr. Martin wanted to meet with the staff at 5:00 p.m. promptly on the hour he entered the kitchen, accompanied by Mr. Bradford, Stan, and the county sheriff. Instinctively, the marine stood up in the presence of his commanding officer, and the rest of the staff followed. "Please keep your seats," declared Mr. Bradford. "You have all been through a great deal, and I personally want to apologize to all of you, and especially to Miss Morris, for bringing such a destructive person into the peace, quiet, and freedom-loving spirit of the Green Mountains. You've all handled this splendidly, especially you, Miss Morris, and our new assistant chef, Mr. Dawkins." The group applauded, and Cooper and Rosie blushed.

Mr. Bradford bowed in Rosie's direction, stepped back, and took a seat at the edge of the gathering. Dr. Martin came forward. "I know that Stan briefed you this morning on the fact that Mr. Hoffman was actually an escaped prisoner of war. In fact, he was a mess sergeant in the German army. He served under General Rommel and was captured fairly early in the war in the African campaign outside of Cairo. As Stan told you, he ended up in Florida and when they discovered he could cook, they put him to work in the kitchen. After only a month in the mess hall, he made friends with the driver of a delivery truck that brought fresh bread to the camp. As they say on those late night radio mysteries, this is where 'the plot thickens.' I'll turn it over to Sheriff Putney, who has all of the details from the FBI."

After exchanging greetings, the sheriff began. "Well, the interesting thing was that the truck driver's name was Rudolph Hoffman. He was about Rudy's age and size, and he spoke German."

The marine raised his hand. "You mean Rudy stole the guy's name, as well as his delivery truck?"

"More than that," replied the sheriff. "He took the guy's life. Rudy's real name was Carl Schumacher. As far as we can piece the story together, Rudy was last seen joking with the driver and walking him out to his truck. Three days later they found the abandoned vehicle out in the woods near Starke, Florida, on US Route 301, which they tell me is one of the main north/south highways into the state. The driver's decomposing naked body was found in the rear of the truck. His throat had been cut. The assumption was that Rudy had pocketed the poor guy's driver's license, draft card, and whatever money he had, and put on his clothes and headed either north or south on 301."

"Wow!" was the collective response.

Dr. Martin handed the sheriff a glass of water. He took a gulp and continued. "Actually, Rudy found his way to New Saxony on the Saint John's River. He was taken in by a German innkeeper, and when he married the innkeeper's daughter, the marriage license read Rudolph Hoffman and Gretchen Lowenstein. After the war was over, he renewed his driver's license, got a Social Security number, and burned his draft card. According to Social Security, he and Gretchen worked their way down Florida's east coast until they ended up at the Breakwater in Palm Beach last winter."

"Where's our old Nazi now?" Rosie asked the sheriff.

"We don't know, but we have an idea that he's heading back to Florida."

"Why, after all these years, is the FBI just now hot on his trail?"

"That's a good question," replied the sheriff. "It seems that after his escape, the FBI and the Florida State Patrol sent out bulletins looking for Carl Schumacher, but a picture they put on the post office wall wasn't all that good. It was taken right after Rudy's unit had surrendered to the Allies. He was a lot thinner then; it looks sort of like a passport photograph. You know, it was a bit fuzzy. He must've looked like a thousand German-Americans from Milwaukee or Cincinnati." The sheriff looked over at Cooper, who did his best to avoid eye contact. Cooper feared that with his blond hair, he might be singled out as a typical German-American look-alike.

"At any rate," the sheriff continued, "someone in Washington was reviewing the file and realized that Rudy had probably taken on his victim's identity and was going under the name of Hoffman. He put together a new wanted flyer and sent it out about two weeks ago. Then, four days ago, after we released Rudy and told him to get out of Vermont and never come back, Rudy stopped at a roadhouse outside of Albany, had a few too many beers, and got into a brawl with a bunch of local veterans. When the New York State Patrol was called in to break up the fight, they booked him, fingerprinted him, took his picture, and were about to put him in jail."

"Why didn't they lock him up?" asked the marine.

"They should have done that," the sheriff agreed, "except that Gretchen cried and pleaded with them. She said that her husband had just lost his job at a hotel over at Lake George and to please let him go, because he was trying to get to Atlantic City where he had heard there was work to be had. The day after Rudy and Gretchen took off, the officer just happened to come across the new bulletin and recognized the name Hoffman. I wish we had booked Rudy on attempted murder when he threatened Miss Morris with the carving knife. In fact, the FBI wants us to press that charge, so that they will have a case against him even if they can't prove that he was a German POW."

CHAPTER FIFTEEN
COOPER AND ROSIE

"Go light on lunch," Rosie whispered to Cooper at the staff table. "I've packed a little picnic to take down to your special place by the dam, what my mother would call 'a little nosh in case you should get hungry before dinner.'"

When lunch had been served, they slipped away from the kitchen and found the old path behind the icehouse. They followed it along the shoreline, speculating about Rudy's capture and arrest. "Do you think they'll find him?" queried Cooper.

"No question about it," replied Rosie. "Now that they know they're looking for Rudolph Hoffman instead of…what was his name in the German army?"

"Carl Schumacher, I think," Cooper said. "That was his name. Carl Schumacher was the prisoner of war, and Rudolph Hoffman was the name of the man he murdered."

"OK," continued Rosie, "now that they know who they're looking for, I'll bet that his picture is in every post office in the country."

"But I'll bet that their old Packard with the Florida license plates is what will give him away," speculated Cooper. "If I were Rudy, I think I'd ditch that car and get another."

"How could he do that? He doesn't have any money."

"Doesn't he have the money he and Gretchen earned this summer? I think he told me that they were paying him several thousand dollars for the summer. That would be more than enough to buy a new car."

"Providing he hadn't spent it all on beer and whiskey," countered Rosie.

"Well, how about this," Cooper suggested. "He finds a used car lot and parks the Packard way in the back and takes off the Florida plates. Then he finds one of the newer models up at the front of the lot—say, a Ford. He takes the license plates off of that car, but he doesn't replace them with his Florida plates. Instead, he switches the plates with another Ford on the front lot."

"You've got me confused," said Rosie.

"That's the whole point," returned Cooper. "The idea is to confuse everybody. When they discover the Packard with its plates missing, they'll be looking for the Florida plates, except Rudy will have thrown them in a trash bin someplace. Then when they drive off with the stolen Ford, it won't have its own plates. The police will be looking for another Ford with different plates."

"I'm still confused," Rosie admitted, "but it's fascinating to see your criminal mind at work. What other schemes have you been working on?"

Cooper blushed but didn't answer Rosie's question. They had reached the grassy clearing by the sandy beach so he simply stated, "We're here."

Rosie glanced around at her surroundings. Her ponytail swished back and forth while she looked for just the right place to set up the picnic. Then she faced Cooper. "There's only one problem with your story."

"What's that?"

"Rudy doesn't know that the FBI is looking for him and that they know he's a fugitive from justice. When the troopers escorted him to the state line, he thought he was a free man. My bet is that it's just a matter of time before someone spots that old Packard heading south or parked behind some tourist cabins along the way to Florida."

"Let's just forget about Rudy," said Cooper. "We've got better things to do." Then, like a proprietor, he surveyed his personal domain for signs of intruders. His private glen was especially warm for an August afternoon. The grass was soft and dry. The wind was still. No song came from the sheltering trees. Only the gentle trickle of water slipping over the dam broke the absolute silence of the place. Cooper took off his shoes and waded out knee-deep into the smooth water. Satisfied that there were no sailboats, canoes, or fishermen lurking off the beach to invade their privacy, he returned to the grove.

Rosie had taken off her loafers and socks and was unloading the contents of the big brown bag she had been carrying. First, she took a large white linen table cloth—borrowed from the closet in the pantry—and spread it over the grass. It struck Cooper that the contrast between the whiteness of the linen cloth and the dark green of the lawn was dramatic. Gently but deliberately she emptied the brown bag of its contents: a bottle of red wine, two glasses, Vermont cheddar cheese, crackers, bananas, oranges, and purple grapes, along with plates, a corkscrew, a knife, and a loaf of freshly baked dark bread. Then she untied the ribbon that secured her ponytail. Her auburn hair fell from its perch on the back of her head to frame her round face and cover her shoulders. Cooper had never seen her with her hair down. He was used to her ponytail and, on occasion, the more formal bun. Her dark tresses had just the hint of curl to make her look like one of the portraits he had seen when his class visited the Metropolitan Museum of Art. While Cooper stared at the sensual figure before him, Rosie reached into her picnic basket and withdrew a small hairbrush. With her eyes fixed on Cooper she smiled and stroked her locks until they were smooth and reflected the sunlight that was filtering through the arbor of branches overhead.

Cooper leaned over and kissed Rosie. "You think of everything."

"Everything?"

"Well, almost everything," he said as put his hand at the back of her head and tried for a deeper kiss.

"Not so fast, goy-boy. First, why don't you try to get the cork out of this bottle?" She handed him a corkscrew, and he grunted and groaned until the cork exited the bottle with a loud pop.

"There," said Cooper.

"A New York waiter couldn't have done it better!" observed Rosie. "Though he might have done it with a little less noise!"

As he poured the wine into the two glasses, Rosie handed him a Ritz cracker with a generous slice of cheese. "Here, try this homemade Addison County white Vermont cheddar, straight from Bradford Farms."

"Why don't you peel me a grape," requested Cooper as he settled down on the tablecloth. He had heard the line in a movie somewhere. Was it Charles Lawton playing Henry VIII?

Rosie laughed and complied. "Cooper, I know you've been wearing that Michigan sweater all summer, and I know that's where you want to go to college. How come you want to be an architect? Is that what you really want to be?"

"Oh, yes, I guess that's been my dream now since I was twelve. You know, my grandfather, Pops, is a builder—at least, before the Depression he was a builder. He put up some pretty big buildings in New York City and has built some libraries, schools, and a Masonic lodge on Long Island. Then after the Depression set in and during the war, there wasn't much new construction going on. Pops managed to make a living doing fire appraisals and sometimes getting the contract to reconstruct a damaged building. When my cousin Guts and I would sleep over at Pops' place, he would show us his scrapbooks filled with pictures of the buildings he had constructed. That was really neat."

"Well, why don't you just become a contractor?"

"I want to design the buildings. Guts is going to build them. That's the big family plan."

"What about your cousin's father? Where does he fit in? Isn't Guts planning to take over his father's business."

"Uncle Jack and Pops don't really work that well together. My mother said that Pops tried to break him into the business, but it didn't work out very well. Uncle Jack doesn't like his father telling him what to do."

"Who does?"

Cooper thought for a moment. Maybe that's what was going on between him and his dad. "Anyway, Uncle Jack went into real estate. He says that if we build it, he'll sell it."

"Sounds like you've got a deal. So you're going to go off to Ann Arbor to study architecture, not just build buildings, and you decided this about five years ago?"

Cooper nodded. "Two of my good friends at Manhasset High have fathers who are architects. They let me look at their professional magazines and their books. Have you ever read *The Fountainhead*?"

"By Ayn Rand? My educational philosophy professor at Columbia says that book is about what's wrong with America. Too much me, me, me, and not enough of us, us, us or what's good for the community."

"I don't understand," Cooper said.

"You will some day. But tell me, did you read the whole 694 pages?"

"Three times."

"Three times?" questioned Rosie as she ran her fingers through his hair.

"Actually, I have a copy of it up in my room here, and I've started into it for the fourth time. I've even memorized parts of it. The first chapter begins, 'Howard Roark laughed. He stood naked at the edge of the cliff.'" Cooper leaned over and kissed Rosie on the neck and whispered the time, "'The lake lay far below him.'"

"Stop that!"

"Why?"

"Because you haven't asked me what I want to be when I grow up."

Cooper pulled back from Rosie's body, placed his left elbow on the tablecloth, and propped up his head with his hand. "OK, but first let me finish and then you can tell me what you want to be when you grow up."

Rosie feigned a slight pout, which Cooper erased with a gentle kiss before he continued. "Have you ever seen pictures of the buildings that Frank Lloyd Wright designed?"

"I've heard the name. What did he do?"

"What did he do? What did he do? He's world famous! He's designed some of the most beautiful modern buildings in this century. Down in Pennsylvania, there's a fantastic house that's built right over a waterfall."

"Does it leak?"

"No, and it's beautiful," said Cooper as he leaned over to kiss Rosie again. "And you're beautiful, too."

Rosie put her hand up to stop his advancing lips. "Not so fast, goy-boy. You still haven't asked me—"

"Oh," he said as he took her hand and kissed her fingers. "OK, what do you want to do when you grow up? You're at Columbia, right? And then when you graduate from Columbia, you're going to...what are you going to do?"

"I'm going to work on my master's degree and maybe even my doctorate in education. I'll stay right at Columbia. It has the most progressive education program in the country."

"Progressive education?

"Have you ever heard of it?"

"Heard of it? The Muncey Park School, where I was a student, was the first grammar school in Manhasset to try it."

"How did you like it?"

"My parents were horrified," stated Cooper with a big grin on his face. "But we all liked it. We got to do just about anything we wanted."

"Well," replied Rosie, a bit on the defensive, "There's more to it than that. It follows the philosophy of John Dewey."

"I thought he was running for president?'

"No, that's Tom Dewey; he's governor of New York. He ran for president against Roosevelt in '44, and now they say he's going to try again."

"Is Governor Dewey the little guy with the mustache?"

"That's him. Everybody says that he looks like the groom on top of the wedding cake."

"But that's not your Dewey?"

"Definitely not! When the world has forgotten about Governor Dewey, or even—God forbid—President Dewey, Dr. John Dewey will be honored in every schoolhouse in the country."

"So, you're going to learn how to be a teacher?"

"More than that. I'm going to get my Ph.D."

"Wow! Dr. Morris, I presume."

"You can presume anything you want, but that's not what I really want to do. Every Jewish girl in the country wants to be a teacher or a school principal. If I make it through Columbia graduate school, that's what I'll be, but that's not what I really want to do."

"What's that?"

"Guess," said Rosie.

"Something to do with music?"

"How did you ever figure that out? Ever since I was a little girl, I've wanted to be a song and dance girl on the stage."

"You mean like the Rockettes at the Radio City Music Hall?"

"No! Like Ethel Merman in *Annie Get Your Gun*. When I was six years old my abba gave me a record of Ethel Merman singing 'I've Got Rhythm.' I played it on the Victrola until I almost wore it out. I learned to tap dance, and when all the relatives would come by for a visit, Abba would sit down at the piano, and I would dance and sing, and they would applaud. Once when a Shirley Temple movie was playing down on the Grand

Concourse, they made the mistake of taking me to see it. They thought that Shirley would inspire me. Boy, were they wrong! I hated her. The first time I saw her, I knew that I could do it better than she could. Even now, whenever I hear 'On the Good Ship Lollipop,' it makes me sick, and whenever I sing 'Anything you can do, I can do better,' I think of how I felt about Shirley Temple."

"I kinda liked Shirley Temple," ventured Cooper, but the minute he said it, he realized that he had said the wrong thing.

"That's because you never saw me do 'I've Got Rhythm.' When *Annie Get Your Gun* opened on Broadway, Abba's second cousin got me a job as an usher for the Saturday matinee. I have seen it more than forty times. I know every line, every tune. If Ethel should drop dead in midsentence, God forbid, I could beat the understudy to the stage, pick up her cowboy hat, and not miss a note. I've even picked out a stage name. I can't be Rosalyn Morris. That wouldn't look good on the marquee. Ethel Merman's real name was Ethel Zimmerman. Instead of Rosie Morris, I'll be known as Rosie Mirror, a reflection of beauty no matter how you look at it. You'll see my name on Broadway."

"I want a front-row seat."

Rosie pushed their plates and glasses to the edge of the tablecloth, snuggled up to Cooper, and said, "You've got one now."

They embraced with increasing intensity, with clothing being discarded in all directions. Their words gave way to sighs and purrs. With his right arm, Cooper tried to reach the pocket of his trousers without interrupting their kiss.

"What on earth are you doing?" asked Rosie somewhat breathlessly.

"I'm...I'm looking for one of those...you know, one of those things."

"You mean a rubber?"

"Yeah, so that I won't get you...er...pregnant."

"Don't worry about it. I'm not going to let you get me pregnant."

Cooper propped himself back on his elbow, moaned, and stared at Rosie. A thousand confused and mixed thoughts raced through his head. First it was Ronnie, then Sheila, and now Rosie. Rosie was his friend. How could she play with him like this?

Rosie reached out with her hand to touch the wounded look on his face. "Oh, Cooper. Dear goy-boy. I didn't come out here to tease you or to hurt you. That would be as bad, if not worse, than Sheila. But I promised my abba that I wouldn't let a man into my body until my wedding night. He didn't want me to have any unwanted babies, and he didn't want me to catch any horrible disease."

"That's why I brought those things along," Cooper said, still feeling awkward with calling them by name. "I brought them so that I wouldn't get you pregnant. And I've never been inside a woman. I don't have any disease."

"I know that," said Rosie, as she stroked his hair. "But there's more to it than that. Abba says that the Torah and the Talmud teach that what we call 'going all the way' is a beautiful thing and is for the bedroom of a married couple." She looked into his eyes for a second and then added, "I believe you'll find that in the New Testament as well as the Old." Then she pulled him toward her. "Don't look so sad. Maybe we can't go all the way together, but that doesn't mean that we can't be together. Here, give me your hand."

They kissed and touched and clung to each other until their moans gave way to sighs.

Cooper looked at Rosie. He was having feelings that he had never had before in his life. Was this what being in love was all about? They lay silently on their backs until Rosie asked, "Did you bring any cigarettes?" Cooper put two in his mouth, lighted them, and gave one to Rosie, who then puffed out three perfect smoke rings. Cooper exhaled a thin blue stream of smoke and this time managed to spear one right in the center. They laughed, and then Rosie suggested, "Let's go for a swim."

Cooper responded, "But I haven't got a—" and then stopped short of saying, "bathing suit" when he realized how ridiculous his objection would sound. He jumped to his feet and dashed onto the beach and into the water, with Rosie in full pursuit. Had they been wading, they would have stopped when the chilly water hit their knees, but their momentum carried them into the lake and under the surface. Their heads bobbed up barely a yard from each other. They were both gasping for breath and laughing at the same time. They reached out to each other and let their slick bodies touch.

After they had kissed, Rosie said, "I believe that's the coldest kiss I've ever received, unless you count the good-night peck on the cheek I got in a snowstorm when I was thirteen."

As their internal thermostats began to send warm blood to the surface of their bodies to compensate for the chilly lake water, their flesh turned a light maroon, and they felt a gentle warmth surge through them. They laughed and they romped. They splashed and they played. Cooper had never seen a naked woman before and his eyes followed Rosie as she skipped and danced in the shallow water. He had seen pictures of naked women, starting with the bare-breasted natives in the *National Geographic*. He had also seen the nude statues and paintings on exhibit in the Metropolitan Museum of Art, and one time he and his buddies had sneaked off to the burlesque theater across the Hudson River in Union City, New Jersey, to watch the strippers, but they never took everything off, no matter how loud the crowd yelled. But there was Rosie, without one thread of clothing. She wasn't thin, but she wasn't fat. She was round. She had lots of curves. There wasn't a straight line in her body. Maybe "chubby" and "bouncy" were the best words to describe her, along with "beautiful" and "appealing." Almost as if the scene had been choreographed, the two came back together, embraced, and returned to the linen picnic cloth.

They slept in each other's arms until they heard the crashing sound of branches breaking and boughs being pushed aside. "Good God, what was that?" said Cooper, jolted out of his slumber. He quickly grabbed his shirt and covered his lap. Rosie reached for the edge of the linen cloth and pulled it up to her chin. Their eyes darted about, expecting to find the Seton Hall boys out on a scouting mission.

"Over there," whispered Rosie, pointing to the other side of the dam, where a family of deer were now drinking from the lake. The buck, the doe, and the yearling all looked over at Cooper and Rosie.

"I think they've spotted us," said Cooper.

"I wonder what they're thinking."

"Did you ever read *Bambi*—the book about the little deer?"

"Of course I did," said Rosie. "Read the book, saw the movie. Doesn't everybody over eight know the story of Bambi?"

"Remember the alarm that went out across the forest?"

"What was that?"

"Man has entered the forest," stated Cooper.

"Is that like, 'There goes the neighborhood'?"

CHAPTER SIXTEEN
TALENT NIGHT AT THE HOTEL

Stan had called a staff meeting for 9:00 a.m., right after the breakfast tables had been cleared. Just about everybody except Cooper had gathered around the staff table, but no one was paying any attention to Stan. Spread out on the table was the sports sections of the *Times* and the *Boston Globe*.

"There's absolutely no way that either one of your teams can catch up," the marine announced to the table in general and to Graham and Stan in particular. "Look here, the Red Sox are twelve and half games behind the Yankees. There just aren't enough games left in the season. And over in the National League, Brooklyn beat Pittsburgh yesterday, 11–10. That puts them six full games ahead of St. Louis."

"Oh, boy!" chimed in Rosie. "That cinches it for a subway series. Yankee Stadium and Ebbets Field. Uncle Morris has a friend who can get me some tickets."

"So who are you rooting for?" asked Graham.

"I'm from the Bronx. Yankee Stadium is in the Bronx. Is the Pope a Catholic? No one in the Bronx would dare root for the Dodgers. Now, Cooper over there at the stove, he's for Brooklyn."

"How do you know so much about Cooper?" purred Ronnie.

"None of your business, dearie."

Stan thumped his empty coffee mug on the table. "OK, OK, let's have some order here!"

"Achtung!"

"OK, Kevin," demanded Stan, "Settle down. We have work to do. The talent show is only two days away, and Mr. Bradford thinks it would be 'splendid' to have the staff participate."

There were a few moans, and Kevin, in one last stab at being the class clown, added, "Do we have to?"

"You can go to your room and pout, if you like," suggested Rosie. Kevin made an attempt to stand up, but gave it up when he felt the restraining hand of the marine on his shoulder.

Stan rapped his coffee cup one more time on the table. "Now that I have your full attention," he declared with just a hint of sarcasm in his voice, "let's get down to work. First of all, Mr. Bradford thinks it would be splendid if Rosie would accompany the acts on the piano. Rosie, can we count on you for that?"

Rosie nodded her agreement, and the staff concurred with shouts of, "Go, Rosie, go!"

"Guests have been signing up for special numbers," continued Stan. "The Newhouse kid wants to do his magic act. The Stanley twins—you know, the two little six-year-olds—have been working on a number. Mrs. Danvers wants to sing 'The Battle Hymn of the Republic.'"

"But she does that every Sunday," objected Graham.

"I know," said Stan. "She says that not everybody comes to the Sunday service in the parlor and that maybe this will encourage more people to attend."

"Fat chance of that," quipped Ronnie.

"Well, anyway, her family has been coming here for two generations, if you understand what I mean," continued Stan, "and just to let you know that this is a family show, her granddaughter Melissa is going to do a Shirley Temple number."

Rosie moaned and looked up at Cooper, who had just joined the group. Cooper rolled his eyes and shrugged his shoulders as if to say, "That's show business."

"Moving right along," said Stan, "by popular request Mr. Bradford will do his Rudy Vallee routine, and Dr. and Mrs. Martin say they want to do a number, but won't tell me what it is. Now, there has to be some talent in this group. What does the staff want to do?"

Everyone looked at Rosie.

"Don't look at me. I'm already playing the piano," said Rosie.

Silence settled on the staff table as everyone suddenly developed interest in their fingernails. "From the looks of things," quipped Stan, "this could be the annual meeting of the Addison County Palm Reading Society."

Finally, the silence was broken when the marine raised his hand. "How about an Abbot and Costello 'Who's on First' routine? That would fit in with the World Series that's coming up."

"Do you know the routine?" asked Stan.

"No, but maybe somebody here does." A quick scan of the shaking heads gave him his answer. He shrugged his shoulders and said, "Well, it was just a thought."

More silence until Graham spoke up. "All of us vets could sing our service songs. You know, 'Anchors Away' and all that stuff." He looked at the marine, who nodded his approval.

Kevin chimed in, "Ronnie and I could do the Alan Ladd/Veronica Lake love scene from *The Blue Dahlia*."

"Cut it out," retorted Ronnie.

"I just thought I'd suggest it. It wouldn't take a lot of practice."

Ronnie blushed as she swept her hair back so that she could stare at Kevin with both eyes. Then she offered, "I have a better idea. Rosie, why don't you do one of your Ethel Merman routines?"

"Well, I'm already playing the piano for Shirley Temple," she said with a note of martyrdom.

"So what! There's no reason you can't do more than one thing," said Stan. "You're the closest thing we have to a professional entertainer." His remarks were met with applause and more shouts of "Go, Rosie. Go, Rosie, go, go, go."

Rosie raised her hands. "All right already, but on one condition. I just thought of something we can do for a grand finale. Do you remember the Hitler spoof song we used to sing during the war? You know the one that goes, 'When the Fuhrer says we is the master race, we go Heil pffdd, Heil pffdd, right in the Fuhrer's face'?" They all nodded their recognition. "Well, let's see if we can substitute Rudy for the Fuhrer."

Stan interrupted. "I'm afraid I'll have to clear that one with the front office."

"Clear it. Schmear it. You do that, Stan. In the meantime, we'll work on the lyrics."

❖ ❖ ❖

"Cooper, can we talk to you for a minute?" asked Danny. He was standing at the edge of the staff table with Kevin and Sheila.

There was a very cautious tone in Cooper's voice when he said, "What about?"

"It's something personal," said Kevin. "Could we go outside on the kitchen porch?"

Cooper stepped back a foot. He had no idea what they were all about. At school, an invitation to step outside was a challenge to put up your fists and fight it out. Cooper was in no mood for a fight and besides, each one of the Seton Hall basketball players outweighed him by thirty or forty pounds. What would they do? Take turns punching him out while Sheila stood on the sidelines and cheered? He looked over at Sheila, who stood behind the two men and never made eye contact. Finally, she looked up at Cooper and said, "We haven't come to argue or fight; we've come to apologize."

Sheila's eyes were moist as she looked up at Cooper. He in turn stared at her. *What is she up to now?* he wondered.

"Yeah," said Danny, "we've come to say we're sorry."

"We all just went to confession at Saint Mary's in Middlebury," added Kevin.

Cooper looked confused. "What does that have to do with me?"

Sheila stepped forward. "It was my idea at first. I asked Danny and Kevin if I could borrow the hotel truck to run a couple of errands in Middlebury. They said that they couldn't lend me the truck but would be happy to run me into town. Then I had to explain that I wanted to go to confession at St. Mary's. Well, one thing led to another." She took out her handkerchief and blew her nose. "They knew I was going to...relieve you of your virginity." She blew her nose again and started to cry. Kevin put his hand on her shoulder, but she pushed it away. Sheila took a deep breath and continued. "But when I led you into the icehouse, I didn't know that these two jerks would be there. Honest, I wouldn't have done it to you, not in front of an audience."

Sheila started to cry again. Kevin put his hand on her shoulder and this time she let it be as Danny declared, "That was our idea. It didn't take too much smarts to figure out what was going on. I mean, we saw you and Sheila go into the cooler and come out with lipstick all over your face. Then you ran up the stairs to change clothes and then, while you and Sheila were meeting down by the laundry room, we knew what you were up to and where you would probably go to do it. So we slipped into the icehouse and waited."

Cooper was speechless. He didn't know what to think, so he took out his Camels and tapped one cigarette out of the pack. He extended his arm in their direction, offering them a cigarette.

"Why don't we take these out on the porch and light up where the air is cooler," Kevin suggested.

They all moved out on the porch, and Cooper fumbled in his pocket for a match. Danny beat him to it with his lighter, but the breeze coming off the lake blew it out. Finally, Kevin stepped back into the kitchen, lighted his Camel, and then passed it around. The four of them formed a circle and finished their cigarettes. Sheila regained control and continued her story. "On the way into town, I told them that I felt like such a whore and told them to drive slowly so they wouldn't wreck the truck, because if we all got killed before we got to confession, we would all go straight to hell."

"Yeah, that really got to me," said Kevin. "I guess that old nun who liked to whack me with the ruler at St. Joseph's put the fear of God into me. We slowed the truck down to thirty miles an hour and prayed that we would find a priest to hear our confessions when we got to the church."

Cooper still wasn't sure what was going on or what they were asking him to do. His cigarette was practically burning his fingers, so he tapped out another Camel and lighted it from the glowing butt. As he stood in a tight circle with the other three, he finally realized that they were no longer his adversaries. Who and what they were remained to be seen, but they were no longer his enemies. The silence was broken when Sheila crushed her cigarette on the porch floor with the toe of her shoe and the three guys followed suit. "Cooper," she said, "I don't know if you remember my coming to you after I had talked with the old reverend from Lowell, Massachusetts."

Cooper nodded his head. Yes, he remembered. Sheila said she wanted him to forgive her, and Cooper hadn't known how he was supposed to do that. He remembered feeling like such a fool that he'd wanted to go home.

Danny said, "After Sheila tried to talk to you, she found Kevin and me and told us what had happened. Then, we told her about how we had harassed and made fun of you that night in the shower."

"Yeah," said Kevin. "After you ran out of the icehouse, we broke into the cooler and liberated a case of Rudy's beer. We were really out of it when we went into the shower and found you hiding back in one of the commodes."

"The three of us realized that we had really done a number on you," Danny said. "We wouldn't blame you if you hated us for the rest of your life. Sheila demanded that all three of us go to confession like the reverend suggested. We had to get a special appointment in the middle of the afternoon, when we could get away between lunch and dinner."

"Father O'Brien listened to each one of us in the little box," said Kevin. "He gave us absolution and then assigned us each a penance. I had to do a dozen laps around the rosary before he would let me leave the church. He must have thought it was real serious because the most I have ever had to do down in New Jersey was half of that."

Now it was Sheila's turn. "Before I left the confessional booth, he said a couple of things that involve you, Cooper." She moved a half-step closer to him. "He said that before I asked you to forgive me that I ought to apologize first. I needed to say that I'm sorry. He said that if I ask you to forgive me, it's like I'm asking you to give me something, which you may not want to do because I've already taken something from you. But if I apologize, then I'm giving you a gift, and then it's up to you whether or not you want to take it."

She looked pleadingly at Cooper, who tried to avoid eye contact. "Then, Father O'Brien made another point," said Sheila. "He told me that I had been forgiven, that I had received absolution from God and the church, which I was to 'go and sin no more,' but that I was to make one more attempt to apologize to you and then ask for your forgiveness. He said I should tell you that as long as you held back, that the hurt and humiliation of the icehouse and the shower room would continue for you."

Cooper looked at Sheila, Kevin, and Danny. "I'm not sure I know how to do that."

The four of them stood in awkward silence, until Danny offered, "Why don't we begin by shaking hands."

This was not an easy thing for Cooper to do. If he could have grabbed on to a rope ladder from a hot air balloon, he would have done so, but there was no easy escape. Finally, slowly, painfully, he forced his right hand out of his pocket. Danny grabbed it, then Kevin, and then Sheila. They smiled and looked at each other. Sheila gently gave him a hug. Danny slapped Cooper on the back, said "Take it easy, pal," and then walked away.

Alone on the loading platform, Cooper listened to the murmur of the wind sifting through the evergreens. He looked over at the icehouse and at the path along the lakeshore, which led to his special place. Then he headed for the stairs up to his room.

※ ※ ※

Rosie at the piano was in her element. The great entrance hall, which ran from the front door to the grand porch overlooking the lake, had been turned into the stage, with the sliding oak doors between the hall and the dining room serving as the curtain. The tables had been moved into the kitchen, and the chairs were arranged in a semicircle, facing the hall, with the grand piano in the dining room just left of the sliding doors.

Rosie pounded out all the Ethel Merman tunes she had ever learned, to the delight of the assembled audience who were occupying every seat. The little children sat on a carpet up front, and at least a dozen guests stood at the back. Rosie really wanted to sing as well as play, but that would come later. Two of the teenage guests served as usherettes and made sure that everyone had a mimeographed program. Propped up on the edge of the piano was a small mirror that allowed Rosie to get signals from backstage. When Stan gave her the go-ahead sign, she resolved her chords and then gave a bold fanfare on the keyboard, which was the cue for the usherettes to come forward and open the rolling doors.

Stan stood at center stage, wearing his preppy uniform along with a straw hat. "Welcome to the fortieth ever-popular Lake

Bradford talent night, first established at the dawn of the twentieth century and performed annually since 1901, with the exception of the two world wars." There was another fanfare on the piano. "And now, brought to you at great expense, we have the high honor of welcoming Mr. Rudy Vallee, of stage, screen, and radio."

There was another flourish on the keyboard, as the usherettes closed the doors and then reopened them to reveal Mr. Bradford with his hair parted in the middle, wearing a cheerleader's large-knit sweater highlighted with a gigantic "Y" for Yale, and holding a megaphone. For openers, he sang "Boola, Boola" to the squeals of the more mature ladies, who still preferred Rudy Vallee to Bing Crosby or that skinny Italian upstart, Frank Sinatra. Next, he took a bow and added his welcome to Stan's, concluding with, "And now, in the name of Mr. Vallee and all the guests at the Lake Bradford Hotel, we wish you to have a splendid time tonight." This was Rosie's cue to play the first few bars to introduce Rudy Vallee's theme song, "My Time Is Your Time."

The evening was off to a great start. The Stanley twins, with an assist from their grandmother, sang "I'm a little teapot, short and stout. Here's my handle, and here's my spout," and as predicted, they tipped over to the delight of the audience.

Gregory Simpson Clarke III, wearing a black silk hat, ran way over his allotted time and had to be escorted off the stage, but not before the rabbit he pulled out of the hat had freed his ears from Greg's grasp, hopped onto center stage, pooped on the floor, and then bounced out the door.

Libby Martin and Dr. Martin, who wore the uniform of a Canadian Mounted Policeman, almost stopped the show when they came on stage as Jeanette MacDonald and Nelson Eddy, giving their rendition of the "Indian Love Call," singing, "When

I'm calling you-ou-ou-ou-ou-ou. You will answer too-oo-oo-oo-oo-oo." Libby wore long false eyelashes and a wig of curly red hair that sat loosely on her head. As she sang, it started to shift to the side, giving her a cockeyed look, which amused her audience. Cooper, who was watching from backstage, seemed to be the only one to realize that Mrs. Martin had been into the champagne again and would have fallen on the floor if she hadn't been held up by her husband. Before the summer began, Cooper had known Dr. Martin only as a most interesting and entertaining history teacher. Now, he was seeing another side of the man, in part a manager to be admired but also a rather tragic figure who was doing his best to cover the weaknesses of an unstable wife.

The veterans marched in singing "Let's Remember Pearl Harbor" and then sang the songs of the army, navy, marines, and army air corp. No one could remember the Coast Guard Song, so they ended with "Eternal Father Strong to Save," which Stan declared covered "everything that floats and flies."

In the grand finale, Cooper appeared with a pillow stuffed in his shirt, wearing his chef's hat, and sporting a black mustache. The entire staff goose-stepped across the stage, giving the Nazi salute and singing:

> When old Rudy says ve is der master race,
> Ve go heil pffdd, heil pffdd right in old Rudy's face.
> Ven old Rudy says ve make kartoffelklosse,
> Ve go heil pffdd, heil pffdd right in old Rudy's face.
> Not to love old Rudy is a great disgrace,
> So, ve heil pffdd, heil pffdd right in old Rudy's face.

The song went on and on to the delight of the guests and staff. The fact that some of the verses didn't rhyme or make much sense didn't seem to bother anybody. When they finally marched off stage to loud shouts of "Encore! Encore!" Cooper and Rosie were prepared to do a quick change and return with the scene from *Annie Get Your Gun*, from which Rosie planned to sing, "You Can't Get a Man with a Gun."

But Mr. Bradford caught Cooper as he ran off stage. "Cooper, there's a long-distance phone call for you in the office."

Thinking it was his mother calling again about coming home for the Labor Day weekend, he said, "Tell her I'll call back later."

Mr. Bradford returned to the phone in his office and then dutifully returned to Cooper in the hall. "The operator says it's an emergency."

It occurred to Cooper as he picked up the phone that everything was becoming an emergency with his mother.

"I have a person-to-person call to Mr. Cooper Dawkins," announced the New York operator. "Is this Mr. Dawkins?"

Cooper could barely hear the operator. Evidently, Mr. Bradford had told Rosie to go on with the show, and she was belting out, "You can't get a man with a gun."

"Just a minute, operator, I can barely hear you. There's a party going on in the hotel. Let me shut the door." He quickly gave the door a shove with his foot and then said, "OK, operator, please say that again."

She repeated her standard declaration and asked again, "Is this Mr. Dawkins?"

"Yes, it is," Cooper answered.

"I will connect you with the party in Manhasset."

"Cooper?" It was, as he'd expected, his mother, but her voice was weak and wavering. Did they have a bad connection, he wondered, or had she been crying?

"Mother?"

There was a long pause. It sounded as though she was gasping for breath. Finally, she said, "Something terrible has happened."

"Is it Pops?"

"No, it isn't your grandfather. It's your cousin."

"Guts?"

"Yes, your Uncle Jack's son."

"What's happened?"

"He was in an accident."

"Is he going to be OK?" Even as Cooper asked, he realized it must be bad news. It sounded like his mother was blowing her nose. Then she gasped for breath and whimpered, "No, he isn't all right. He died in the Port Jefferson Hospital just a little while ago."

"Mother! Mother! Mother!" Cooper repeated over and over, but all he could hear was his mother's sobs.

She finally managed to say, "I just can't talk now. I'll talk to you later. I love you. Good-bye, son."

Cooper was stunned. He sat down in the chair by Mr. Bradford's desk. Outside the door he could hear the applause and shouts of "More! More!" His mind went from blank to the news that Guts was dead and then back to blank. How long he sat there, he had no idea. Finally, Mr. Bradford opened the office door with a polite but tentative inquiry. "Is everything all right?"

Cooper only stared straight ahead. Dr. Martin entered the room, followed by Rosie. All three looked at Cooper, but all he could do was stare back. Finally, Rosie went over to him and ran her fingers through his hair. "Cooper, is something wrong? Bad news?"

He looked up at Rosie and opened and closed his mouth, but no words came out. Finally, he said, "Guts is dead. My cousin Guts is dead. I've got to go home. I've got to go home now."

"We'll get you out of here tonight," said Dr. Martin as he took charge. "We don't have time to get you on the train out of

Middlebury or Rutland, but there's a through-train from Montreal to New York that follows the New York State border and will get you into Grand Central in the morning around eight o'clock. Just take one suitcase, and we'll pack the rest of your stuff in your trunk, and if you don't get back, we'll ship it down to you."

"I'm going with you," declared Rosie.

CHAPTER SEVENTEEN
ON THE NIGHT TRAIN

Later that night, the Lake Bradford wagon rolled into the parking lot at the Ticonderoga Station. The station was deserted, with the exception of one taxi cab and a 1940 DeSoto. There was a chill in the air, and a light fog had rolled in from the nearby lakes. Each platform light was wrapped in a white gauze of fog, giving the whole setting the eerie look of a second-rate black-and-white movie set in London. A redcap shuffled out of the station house to offer his services, but Stan waved him off. "Thank you, I think we can handle it."

"Jeeze, it's cold," whistled Sheila as she and the others piled out of the vehicle.

"Hey, you guys," Stan called to them, "help me get these suitcases off the roof."

Audrey was the last one to leave the wagon and she stood in the parking lot, looking at the Victorian-era train station.

"Ticonderoga? Didn't something important happen here? I mean, weren't we supposed to remember that name for a history quiz?"

"There was a fort here," announced Stan, "and two battles were fought here: one in the French and Indian War and one in the American Revolution."

"So who was Ticonderoga?" queried the Marine. "Some kind of Indian chief or what?"

Stan shifted into his tour guide voice. "Actually, Ticonderoga comes from an Iroquois word that means 'where the waters meet,' referring to the La Chute River, which joins Lake George and Lake Champlain. This is also the site of America's oldest operating ferry. It's been here since 1755. Unfortunately, it doesn't run after 8:00 p.m. Otherwise, we would have gotten here about twenty minutes earlier."

"Speaking of old ferries," quipped Kevin.

"Oh, shut up," countered Rosie.

"Who cares?" declared Sheila. "Let's go inside the station before we freeze to death." Everyone went inside except for Cooper and Rosie, who wore raincoats over their college sweatshirts. They stood on the platform, facing north, holding hands and looking down the track for signs of their train. *Stop, look, and listen, Gamma Dawkins used to say*, Cooper laughed to himself. Rosie was looking, and he was listening for the crackling sound in the track that carried the first sign of the approaching train.

"Rosie," he whispered as he squeezed her hand, "I think she's coming. Can you hear that sound?"

Rosie leaned back and started to hum the tune to "Sentimental Journey."

First the train's headlight and then its whistle broke the dark silence of the night. The hotel gang moved out the station door and surrounded Cooper and Rosie with hugs and good wishes.

Sheila came up to Cooper, hesitated, and then put her arms around his shoulders and whispered something in his ear. Rosie instinctively tightened her grip on him.

"Let me put these bags on the train for you," Stan offered. There was a blast on the whistle as the conductor announced the train's departure. Rosie and Cooper climbed aboard as their colleagues broke into song.

Good night, sweethearts;
Till we meet tomorrow.
Good night, sweethearts;
Parting is such sweet sorrow.

They looked out the window and waved good-bye to everyone from the Lake Bradford Hotel. Cooper and Rosie found their seats and put their two suitcases in the overhead rack.

"I'm glad our seats are on the right side of the coach," stated Cooper.

"Why's that?"

"So we can see the river when morning comes."

"It's already morning," countered Rosie.

Cooper smiled and kissed Rosie on the forehead. "Oh, you know what I mean." He then excused himself, saying that he needed to talk to the conductor. Cooper handed the conductor his tickets and asked, "Would it be possible to get a bunk or a roomette in one of the Pullman cars? If I paid the extra fares?"

"Well, first of all you'd have to have a first-class ticket," stated the conductor. "Second, we'd have to have an empty berth or room available, and finally, you and the missus would have to have some kind of identification. You know, something like two drivers' licenses with the same address and the same last name."

He smiled. "If you know what I mean. But there's no need get out your wallet because the train is full. Every bed is taken in the Pullman cars and practically all the seats in coach. You know, with the big holiday weekend coming up, you and your...wife were lucky to get two seats together."

The big weekend! Oh, my God, thought Cooper. It's the Labor Day weekend coming up. Mother gets her way after all. I am going to be home for Labor Day, home for Guts' funeral. He started to choke up so he stood in the aisle taking deep breaths before returning to Rosie.

"What was all that about?" she asked when Cooper slid into the seat beside her.

"Oh, nothing. Just checking the time of arrival in New York and where we'll be when the sun comes up."

"I'll bet you were trying to get the conductor to let you have a bed in the sleeping car."

Cooper blushed. Rosie had read his mind, just like his mother. Could all women do that? "Just doing what comes naturally," he told her.

She handed him a pillow. "What's natural at two in the morning is to sleep. Here, put your head on this and snuggle up, and let's get some sleep."

"I'm not sleepy."

"What are you thinking about?"

"Next weekend is Labor Day weekend. All summer long my mother has been writing me and phoning me long distance, urging me to quit my job early and come home for the big family gathering."

"So?"

"Well, it's all so strange. I mean, here I am on my way home, and Labor Day is coming up, but it's not the way anybody would have imagined it. I mean, I'm going home for...for..." He couldn't say his cousin's name.

Rosie patted his hand understandingly. "You guys were really close, weren't you?"

Cooper nodded.

"Come here, goy-boy," soothed Rosie as she wrapped her arms around Cooper. "Put your head here, and just let me hold you."

❖ ❖ ❖

Cooper and Rosie were still asleep, curled up under their blanket, when the conductor walked down the aisle announcing, "First call for breakfast. The dining car will open in five minutes." Cooper opened one eye and looked over Rosie's shoulder at the golden glow of the sunrise highlighting the hills and villages on the western banks of the Hudson River. Rosie was still asleep as he cuddled closer, moved his left hand a bit higher, kissed her neck, and whispered, "Rosie, I love you." She mumbled something and pushed his hand back down to her waist.

Cooper had no idea where they were. He had a faint recollection of the conductor announcing, "Albany...Albany. Change here for northbound trains to Vermont and western trains for Buffalo, Chicago, and points in between." That meant that they still had at least two and a half hours to go. Cooper laughed to himself at the thought that this was the first time he had actually slept with a woman, although the possibilities of that phrase were not exhausted by the cramped conditions of two reclining coach seats with two small pillows and only a thin blanket to shield them from the chill and an incessant parade of passengers. Nonetheless, there was something warm and secure about being pressed up against her soft body, feeling the beat of her heart, and falling asleep to the rhythm of her breathing. Somewhere in his half-asleep, misty mind, he started composing a letter to Guts, to tell him about falling in love with Rosie. Then, the half-awake side of his brain brought him back to reality. He was sorry that he had never written Guts about Rosie. His sorrow was intense, but somehow, being close to Rosie made it just a little more bearable.

The conductor announced, "Harmon... Harmon, New York. We will stop in Harmon for fifteen minutes while we change to the electric engine, which will take us into Grand Central Station."

Rosie stirred and turned to Cooper. She kissed him on the cheek. He tried to kiss her on the lips, but she put her hand over his mouth, "Not now, goy-boy. If the truth be told, one whiff of my breath, and the conductor would be carrying you off the train on a stretcher. As a matter of fact, your mouth isn't exactly the perfume counter at Bloomingdale's." Cooper pretended to pout, and Rosie responded, "Don't look so sad, goy-boy. I need to brush my teeth, comb my hair, and take care of a few other things. Do you want to go first or shall I?"

"I don't think either of us can use the bathroom until the train leaves the station. The conductor just locked the door."

"I'm not sure I can wait fifteen minutes." Rosie began whistling a bouncy tune until Cooper asked her what all that was about. "Didn't you learn that song in the Boy Scouts or summer camp after they turned the lights out? I'll sing a bit, and I'll bet you'll remember: Prostitutes and shady ladies please refrain from having babies while the train is at the railroad stop."

"That's it? I mean, isn't there a second verse?"

"Oh, yes."

"Well, sing it."

"I can't remember it, but it has something to do with flushing the crapper and splatting all over people standing on the platform waving good-bye to their relatives. I understand that the New York Central got a lot of complaints about that."

"They probably filed the letters under, 'Don't give me that shit.'"

They laughed and hugged as their train started to glide out of station.

When they both had brushed their teeth, they threw themselves into each other's arms, only to be interrupted when they overheard the conversation between two fellow passengers.

"Will you look at those two go at it? You'd think they could wait until they got home."

"Maybe someone ought to throw a pail of cold water at them."

Cooper and Rosie pulled back. "Are you ready for breakfast?" asked Cooper.

"I'm not sure I'm hungry. I don't think I could eat a whole breakfast. Besides, do we have time?"

"How about the club car? I'll bet we could get some coffee and a doughnut."

"What about a bagel?"

"Let's go find out."

They purchased their coffee at the bar, where there was a selection of packaged chocolate and plain doughnuts, cupcakes, and something that called itself an apple pie, but no bagels. "I'll settle for a plain donut," said Rosie, so Cooper picked up two and headed for a couch in front of a little round cocktail table.

They sat sipping their coffee, munching on their doughnuts, and watching the river go by.

"I know there was a Last Supper," Rosie said, "but is there anything called a Last Breakfast?"

"I don't think so. I've never heard of one," said Cooper.

"Well, I guess that's what we're having."

"What do you mean? I thought when you said, 'I'm going with you,' that you meant you were going to go home with me all the way to Manhasset."

Rosie put her hand on Cooper's shoulder. "Oh, Cooper, I am sorry. I didn't mean that. I meant that I didn't want you to get on the night train all by yourself and ride down to New York alone, thinking about your cousin and all. When you get to Long Island you're going to be OK. You're going to be surrounded by family. They'll take care of you."

"But Rosie, I want you to meet my family, and I want to take care of you. I want us to take care of each other the way we did at Lake Bradford. Rosie, I want us to be together for the rest of our lives. Rosie…Rosie, I want…I want to marry you."

"We can't get married."

"Why not? I love you, and you said that you love me. Why can't we get married?"

"I do love you, but it just wouldn't work. For one thing, you're sixteen—"

"I'll be seventeen in November," he interrupted.

"And I'm twenty-one, and I'll be twenty-two in March."

"That's only five years," pleaded Cooper.

"Right now five years doesn't seem like such a big difference, but it is. You're in high school, and I'm in college. There's a big difference between Columbia and Manhasset High School. And then, if the truth be told, when I'm forty-six and having hot flashes, you'll be forty-one and having the hots for some cute blonde in your office."

"Rosie, I love you. You're talking about something that may never happen twenty-five years from now. I want to marry you.

I want you to go home with me now. I want you to meet my family."

"Look, goy-boy. You're the cutest, nicest guy I've ever met. I'll never forget you. You saved my life, and you've been a very special friend, and I love you, but our families would never mix. Mine are Jewish—very observant Jewish, very observant Bronx Jewish. My grandfather was very unhappy with my working at a hotel that didn't keep kosher. Your family is Christian, and not just *Christian* but Episcopalian Christians; North Shore Long Island Episcopal Gentile Christians. Maybe they don't teach their children to call Jews 'Christ killers,' but no matter how much you argue that they're not anti-Semitic, the North Shore is littered with yacht clubs and golf courses that screen their membership applications to keep out Jews. The deeds to their houses say that they can't sell to Jews or Negroes."

"I didn't know that. Are you sure about that?"

"Trust me. That's the way it is."

"Maybe that will change," argued Cooper.

"I certainly hope so, but change takes time. We can't live in the future. We've got to live in the here and now. You live on the North Shore; I live in the Bronx."

"When we get married, I'll move to the Bronx. We'll live in the Bronx."

"You wouldn't like it, and I don't think they would like you. I mean, you're sweet and smart, and you're handsome, and you're going to be an architect and all that, but if the truth be told, they wouldn't like you. I can hear my grandfather right now saying, 'What's wrong with Rosalyn? All that time at Columbia, and she couldn't find a nice Jewish boy? All she could come up with was a goy from Manhasset?' All the trouble doesn't rest on your side of the Whitestone Bridge. Do you know what the

Orthodox do when someone converts to Christianity or even if they marry outside the faith? They hold a funeral, as if that person has died—dead, gone forever—and they never mention his or her name again. It's called 'shanda.' Now, if the truth be told, my abba is Reform, but his abba, the cantor, follows the old traditions. They say Kaddish and everything."

"What's Kaddish?"

"Kaddish is the Jewish prayer for the dead."

"Oh."

Cooper had considered the fact that a Jewish bride in the Dawkins and Goetz family would pose some problems, but it had never occurred to him that the Morris family might object to their daughter marrying a gentile. The conversation definitely wasn't going his way. He sighed. "We're sort of like Romeo and Juliet."

Rosie, without a blink, countered, "And look where they ended up! Dead in the family tomb."

The conductor announced the train's imminent arrival at 125th Street.

Rosie jumped out of her chair and started to weave her way through the passengers in two coach cars. Cooper tried to follow, yelling, "What's wrong, Rosie? What's wrong?"

She answered over her shoulder, "I've got to get back to my seat. I've got to get my luggage. This is where I get off."

"Get off? I thought you were going to go with me to New York!"

"This is New York. This is where I got on the train to Vermont, and this is where I get off."

By now the train had stopped. They still had a car to go, and it seemed like they were swimming upriver against a stream of departing travelers.

"Can't you ride with me to Grand Central Station?"

"I'm afraid not," Rosie replied breathlessly. She had arrived back at her seat and now stood on her tiptoes and started yanking at the handle of her suitcase.

"Let me get that for you," offered Cooper, who was a foot closer to the luggage than Rosie. He held on to the handle as he made one final plea. "I love you, Rosie. I want to marry you. We can work things out."

Rosie stood on her toes as she kissed Cooper on the cheek and twisted her suitcase out of his hand. "I love you, too, Cooper, but there's more that separates the Bronx from Manhasset than the Long Island Sound." She turned and dashed down the aisle, off the train, and onto the platform. Cooper followed, but she did not look back as she disappeared down the stairwell at the center of the platform.

"You'd better get back on the train, son," the conductor gently advised, "unless you want your luggage to end up in the lost and found."

Cooper stepped back onto the train and walked slowly down the aisle. He slumped into his seat as the conductor announced, "All aboard! All aboard! Next stop Grand Central Station."

CHAPTER EIGHTEEN
HOME FOR LABOR DAY

Dead in a family tomb. That's where Romeo and Juliet ended up—dead in a family tomb. The thought turned over and over in his mind as Cooper put a pillow against the window, wrapped himself in the blanket, pulled his knees up to his chin, and stared out the window as his train glided into the tunnel under Park Avenue. From the bright morning light that had highlighted Rosie's hair just minutes ago, there was now almost complete darkness. The train was headed for its final destination.

The family tomb. That's where Cooper was headed right now; the family tomb! He felt tightness in his chest, his mouth was dry, and he had trouble swallowing. This was all a bad dream, but he couldn't wake up. It was all darkness out there, except for an occasional light bulb that streaked by. Is that what Rosie had been? A little light bulb streaking by in a dark tunnel? And where was he going? He was headed for the cemetery. Today, he'd said good-bye to Rosie, and tomorrow, he would say goodbye to Guts.

The train had been at Grand Central Station for at least five minutes when the conductor came through and noticed Cooper curled up under the blanket. "Wake up, kid," he called out as he gently shook Cooper's shoulder. "The train is at the terminal. It's the end of the line. Time to get up." Cooper turned and stared blankly at the conductor as he gathered his things and shuffled off the train. Indeed, the conductor was right. This was the end of the line.

He placed his luggage on the platform. He decided that it was too warm for his raincoat, so he folded it over his left arm, picked up the suitcase, and headed out through the gate into the main terminal. There was a river of commuters heading for the exits to the street or stairways to the subway system. He paused for a minute to stare at the great ceiling of the Grand Central Terminal and then mentally tried to calculate the best way home. He could take the shuttle into Times Square, and then change to the Seventh Avenue Line and ride one stop down to Penn Station, and then go down the back stairs to the Long Island Railroad platforms. As he remembered it, the Port Washington Line usually left from Track 17. But, he looked at the mass of commuters and decided that it would be simpler to take the Flushing Line from Grand Central out to Woodside and pick up his train for Manhasset there. Having settled that, he fumbled through the change in his pocket and found a crumpled package of Camels with two barely usable cigarettes left. He headed for the nearest newsstand and started to order a pack of Camels but changed his mind. Instead he handed the vendor a quarter and asked, "Could I have a pack of Chesterfields, please?" As he waited for his change, he scanned the morning papers. The headline on the *Daily News* jumped out at him: "POW Captured in New Jersey." Cooper picked up a copy, handed the clerk a nickel, and didn't wait for his change. There was Rudy's picture, big as life. He had a lump the size of an egg on the right side of his head and a black eye to go with it. Cooper smiled as he realized that he was responsible for Rudy's battered face. He was reading the caption under the picture when he heard someone call his name.

"Cooper! Cooper Dawkins! Are you Cooper Dawkins?" Cooper turned in the direction of the voice. A heavy set middle-aged man with a smile on his face was heading his way. He looked vaguely familiar, but Cooper couldn't place him. The man stopped about three feet away and repeated one more time, "Are you Cooper Dawkins?"

"Yes, I am."

"I'm Matt Goetz, your mother's cousin from Detroit."

"Uncle Matthew?"

"Yeah, that's who I am."

"You're the one who's the architect?"

"That's correct. My wife—I guess you'd call her Aunt Lilly—and I are just back from Europe. We're here for the Labor Day weekend. I was hoping to see you but not under these circumstances." The two males looked at each other.

Cooper studied Matthew Goetz's face. He could see the family resemblance. He looked a little like Pops. Same nose. Same smile. "How'd you know I was coming into Grand Central this morning?"

"After your mother called you with the sad news, I tried to call back and let you know that Aunt Lilly and I were here with your mother and that we would help in any way we could, but the lines to Vermont were tied up and then when the operator got through to Middlebury, the hotel phone was busy. I was about to give up, when a Dr. Martin called and said that you were on your way over to Ticonderoga to get the night train from Montreal. When your train came in, I stood at the gate until everybody was off the platform. I was looking for a phone booth to call your mother—and then I saw your Michigan sweater from across the terminal." Uncle Matthew studied Cooper. "You certainly have grown since I last saw you. That was…that was back before the war. You were just a little kid when we all went to the World's Fair together. How old are you now?"

"I'll be seventeen in November."

"I thought you were born on Halloween?"

"I missed it by thirty minutes. At least, that's what the birth certificate says. The first of November is All Saints Day. Pops—Grandpa Goetz—used to take me to church on my birthday. He said it was a very special day and that I should be proud to be born on All Saints. My sisters used to tease me and say that I wasn't a saint but a leftover from Halloween."

"If you hadn't been wearing that Michigan sweater, I wouldn't have recognized you," said Uncle Matthew. "You look much older than sixteen." Cooper smiled for the first time since the train left 125th Street. Then Uncle Matthew asked, "Have you had any breakfast?"

"Not really, just a cup of coffee and half a doughnut."

"Let's take care of that right now."

❖ ❖ ❖

Once in the booth at the coffee shop, Cooper showed Uncle Matt the front page of the *News*. Pointing to Rudy's picture, he declared, "That man used to be my boss."

"How did he end up on the front page of the paper?" queried Uncle Matt.

"It says that the story is on page four. Let me see what it says." Much to Cooper's surprise there was not only a picture of Rudy and Gretchen but one of the Lake Bradford Hotel—and two small pictures of Rosie and Cooper, taken from their school yearbooks. Cooper turned back to the front page and pointed to Rudy's very unflattering photograph. "This is the guy I worked for at the hotel in Vermont. He was actually an escaped German prisoner of war."

"Let me see," Uncle Matt said as he examined Rudy's picture and then turned to page four. "Is this a picture of you?"

"Yeah. I mean, yes, sir."

"You've done a lot of growing up since last fall." Then he returned to the paper. "What did you have to do with the capture of an escaped prisoner?"

"Go ahead and read the story."

GERMAN POW CAPTURED (continued from page 1)
Atlantic City: Carl Schumacher alias Rudolph Hoffman, an escaped German prisoner of war, was taken into custody by the New Jersey State Police last night at a truck stop on Route 9 near Atlantic City.

Schumacher is believed to have been a prisoner at Camp Blanding, near Jacksonville, Florida. It is also alleged that he is responsible for the murder of Rudolph Hoffman, who delivered bread to the camp. Schumacher cut his throat and assumed Hoffman's identity.

Most recently the POW worked at the Lake Bradford Hotel in Vermont, where he was the chef. His true identity

was uncovered after he was arrested for threatening to cut the throat of a Jewish waitress, Rosalyn Morris, of the Bronx.

The second murder was thwarted by the quick action of Dr. Aaron Martin, head of the history department at Manhasset High School, and one of his students, Cooper Dawkins, also from Manhasset on Long Island's North Shore.

Dr. Martin distracted Schumacher's attention by yelling at him in German, and Dawkins knocked him unconscious with a frying pan.

At first, the hotel owner and Miss Morris declined to press charges and were satisfied when the man and his wife, Gretchen, were discharged and escorted to the New York State line by the Addison County Sheriff. He was driving a pre-war Packard with Florida license plates.

"Good grief, Cooper, this article makes you out to be a something of a hero."

Cooper shrugged and busied himself with what was left of his scrambled eggs.

When the waitress brought the check, Uncle Matt, conditioned by the customs of Detroit's Downtown Athletic Club, asked, "Has the gratuity been added?"

The waitress gave him a quizzical look.

"I mean, has the tip been added to the bill?"

"Not yet, sweetheart!" she answered.

✤ ✤ ✤

HOME FOR LABOR DAY

A taxi dropped them off on Thirty-Fourth Street at the entrance to the Long Island Railroad. There was a short four-car train loading on Track 17 when they arrived.

"Can we sit in a smoking car?" asked Cooper.

"OK, if we can sit on the right-hand side, so that we can see what's left of the old World's Fair when we go through Flushing Meadow."

"I think we can do that," replied Cooper. He was definitely warming up to his Detroit relative, uncle, cousin, second cousin, or whatever. Cooper remembered that before the war, the whole family—Pops and Grandmother Goetz, Grandmother Dawkins, his mother and father, two sisters, Guts, and his parents, along with Uncle Matthew and Aunt Lilly—had spent the day at the World's Fair. Gamma Dawkins insisted that everybody attend the British Empire exhibit and then they all stood in line for more than an hour to get into the General Motors Futurama, where they got into little cars and were glided into the "World of Tomorrow." Cooper had been fascinated with the beautiful new cities, some of them built under plastic domes, with great superhighways covered with cars shaped like teardrops. He returned to the Futurama several times before the fair shut down. In retrospect, he realized that his interest in architecture had begun in Flushing Meadow.

As the train emerged out of the tunnel on the Long Island side of the East River, Uncle Matthew broke into Cooper's dream world. "Do you remember when we went to the General Motors exhibit and took that ride into the World of Tomorrow?"

Good Lord, thought Cooper. Can everybody read my mind? Where does a guy find any privacy?

"You know," stated Uncle Matthew, "that World of Tomorrow was supposed to be in 1960. That's only thirteen years away." He went on to describe his summer at the Sorbonne in

Paris, where top architects from all over Europe had gathered to share their vision for rebuilding the great cities of the continent. "It's an exciting time to be an architect."

"There she is!" shouted Cooper, as the train broke away from the apartment house canyons of Jackson Heights and Corona and into the open spaces of Flushing Meadow. "There's what's left of the fairgrounds. Too bad they tore down the Trilon and Perisphere. See that building over there? It's the New York City Building. They turned it into an ice skating rink, and now it's the temporary home of the General Assembly of the United Nations."

Uncle Matthew was glued to the window until the train pulled into the Flushing Station. They stopped at Broadway Flushing, where the tracks, now elevated, crossed over Northern Boulevard, Route 25A, which in the old days had been known as Long Island's Broadway.

For a few brief minutes, Cooper had been so drawn into his memories of the World's Fair and his fascination with modern architecture that he had forgotten why he was on a train with Uncle Matt heading for Manhasset. The sight of an ambulance on Northern Boulevard brought him back to reality, and he turned to Uncle Matt. "Tell me about Guts. I know that he was killed in a wreck. Did he suffer much? Could the doctors do anything to save him?"

Matthew Goetz, looking pained, took a deep breath. "You know the steep hill that goes from Belle Terre down to the Harbor in Port Jefferson? Well, Jack Jr.—I mean, Guts—had been playing golf that afternoon with your grandfather, Pops. When they finished up, they went into the clubhouse to celebrate. It seems that Guts had shot an 80. It was the best game of his life. He had birdied three holes. One of the birdies on a par three missed being a hole in one by less than six inches. Actually, it was an eagle. Your grandfather told everybody that with a little training and a lot of practice, his grandson could be another Bobby Jones.

"When they parted company, your grandfather headed back to the beach cottage, and your cousin said he was going into Hicksville. About that time, an afternoon thunderstorm moved in off the Sound. From what we know from the police reports, when his car—he called it the Humpmobile—headed down the hill into Port Jeff Harbor, it hit an oil slick and started to skid. The skid turned into a roll. The car must have turned over a dozen times before it came to rest about a hundred feet from the Bayless Dock and the entrance to the Bridgeport Ferry parking lot. As you can imagine, the roof was crushed. They had to get a welder from the nearby body shop to cut the car up before they could get Guts out of the car. Miraculously, he was still alive, and the ambulance took him up the hill to the Port Jefferson Hospital. The doctors did what they could, but his skull was fractured in a dozen places and his brain was swelling. It was not a pretty sight. He was in a deep coma, which, thank God, meant that he knew nothing and felt nothing. There was talk of taking him by ambulance into the city, where a neurosurgeon might be able to help him. The family gathered. The minister from the Episcopal church in Port Jeff came to the hospital. He prayed with the family and anointed your cousin with oil and stayed until your Uncle Jack and Aunt Ellen arrived with the Lutheran minister from Hempstead. When the nurses changed shifts in the morning, the head nurse went into the room to wake everybody up. Your cousin didn't wake up that morning." Matthew's voice cracked, and he gulped for air.

Cooper moved across the aisle to the left side and stared out the window at the early morning sailboats on Little Neck Bay.

Matthew Goetz slipped into the seat beside Cooper, resting his hand on the young man's shoulder. They rode on in silence until the train left the Great Neck Station and clanked onto the single track that would take them into Manhasset.

"The doctors said that once the car started to roll, Guts was unconscious," Uncle Matthew explained, "and with the exception of his initial fright when the car went out of control, Guts felt no pain. He didn't suffer."

"Will I have to look at his body?" Cooper asked. When Grandma Goetz had died they brought her coffin to her home, and she lay there in the front parlor for two days and two nights until all the relatives and all the neighbors had come in and stared at her and made statements like "Doesn't she look natural," or "Didn't they do a beautiful job with her hair," or "She just looks like she's sleeping." Cooper shuddered when he thought he would have to go through all that again and not with an old lady who, they said, "had had a full life" but for a young guy whose life was just beginning—who had just fallen in love.

"No," stated Uncle Matthew. "Your cousin's body has been taken to Fairchild's Funeral Home. The family will be there from seven until ten tonight, so that people can come by to pay their respects. The casket will be closed." He wanted to add that there was no way that a mortician could cover up the damage to that broken head, but he knew that he had said all that was required. Cooper understood.

The train rattled and swayed across the trestle that crossed the deep ravine at Spinny Hill between Great Neck and Manhasset.

"Manhasset! Manhasset!" cried out the conductor. "Passengers getting off at Manhasset, please use the rear door."

HOME FOR LABOR DAY

※ ※ ※

The taxi pulled up in front of Pops' house. Aunt Lilly came out on the porch to greet them. She said all of the expected things about how Cooper had grown and how sad it was to meet again under these circumstances and asked if he'd like something to eat. Cooper managed to decline politely and asked to be excused. He had gotten very little sleep. As he was heading up the stairs, Aunt Lilly added, "Your father called to see if you had arrived. He's down at Cape May, New Jersey, and will be here in time for the services tomorrow. And your mother called a while ago. She's over in Hempstead with her brother and his wife. She says that your Uncle Jack and Aunt Ellen are pretty upset. She promised she would help them go through your cousin's clothes and pick out a suit to take to the funeral parlor. I don't know why they're worrying about the proper clothes. They're not going to open the casket anyway."

Uncle Matthew shot a look at his wife, which she understood meant "Please be quiet; you've said quite enough." Then he picked up the boy's suitcase and headed up to Cooper's room on the third floor. Cooper noted that the house had the familiar smell of his grandfather's cigars and a faint hint of the lavender, which had been grandmother's favorite fragrance. Cooper thanked Uncle Matthew for meeting him in New York, entered his room, closed the door, and fell on his bed.

It was early afternoon when he woke up. He tiptoed down the hall to the bathroom and then quietly listened for sounds of his aunt and uncle. Somewhere down on the first floor there was the sound of classical music. *They must be tuned to WQXR*, Cooper thought, but he had no intention of listening to the concert. He had other plans.

Cooper slipped down the narrow back staircase that had once led from the servants' quarters to the kitchen. He quietly slipped out the kitchen door and through the hedge at the back of the garden. He made his way through side streets to the railroad station and waited patiently for the next eastbound train. It would only be ten cents, ten minutes, and two stops to the end of the line at Port Washington. This was the route that he and Guts had taken when they were little kids, back before the beginning of the war. They would tell everybody that they were going hiking in the woods and would get Grandmother Goetz to make them some peanut butter and jelly sandwiches, which they liked to call "PB&Js." Once in Port Washington, they would head for the sand pits, where all of the dump trucks and concrete mixers picked up their sand and gravel during the week.

After a few minutes a four-car train arrived. Cooper climbed aboard and was soon stepping off at the Port Washington platform. As he walked out of the terminal, he figured that by three o'clock on this Friday before the Labor Day weekend, all the trucks would be gone and the gate would be locked. When he arrived at the sand pit, the gate was closed. So he carefully climbed up the hill at the side of the quarry and found his old secret opening in the fence, now overgrown with weeds.

Cooper slipped through the gap and sat down to survey the great yellow cut in the hillside. It had been several years since he and Guts had been there. There hadn't been that much sand removed during the war, but it was obvious that the postwar building boom was cutting deeply into the west side of the hill.

Cooper took off his shoes and socks, rolled up his trousers, and took off his Michigan sweater and T-shirt. He walked along the edge of the pit and looked out over the great gash in the hillside. For a brief second it became the granite quarry from the opening page of *The Fountainhead.* He was Howard Roark standing "naked at the edge of a cliff." He saw the lake that was "far below him. A frozen explosion of granite burst in flight over motionless water." Then it was almost as though a small hand reached out, and the two boys jumped off the edge into the sand and slid and rolled to the bottom, just like he and Guts had done so many times in earlier years. He repeated this ritual over and over, imagining that he was a kid again and that Guts was there with him, jumping and rolling and laughing as they tumbled through the sand. How long this went on, Cooper had no idea. He had no sense of time, but then all of a sudden, when he was out of breath, it seemed that Guts waved and smiled at his cousin and said, "Enough! It's time to go home."

❦ ❦ ❦

Grace Lutheran Church on Jericho Turnpike was packed. Guts' mother, Cooper's aunt Ellen, was a member and had taken Guts to Sunday school there. The altar was banked with flowers that overflowed into the side aisles. Guts' Hempstead High School baseball team, in uniform, was seated up front near the family. Uncle Jack's close friends, including Cooper's father and Uncle Matthew, served as the pall bearers. Pops' glee club, in white tie, gloves, and tails, filled the choir stalls and sang, "A Mighty Fortress Is our God" and "Eternal Father." The extended family occupied five pews.

The procession of cars, all with their lights on, tied up traffic for forty minutes along the narrow roads that took them from the center of Long Island to the North Shore and the old pre-Revolutionary War cemetery that surrounded St. Phil's-on-the-Hill. Cooper wanted to ride in the car with his grandfather, but at Pops's and Uncle Jack's insistence, he rode in the lead limousine. When it stopped at the entrance to the graveyard, Cooper jumped out, ran into the church, and emerged three minutes later in black cassock and white cotta, carrying the brass processional cross Pops had donated to the church just two years before in memory of his wife. Cooper took his post at the rear of the hearse where the pallbearers were gathered. The stoic Dawkinses and the demonstrative Goetzes, who had spent so many holidays together before the separation, at first formed two separate clusters but were soon reunited in grief. Grandmother Dawkins was the first to break ranks and approach John Goetz Sr. She seemed to want simply to extend an ungloved hand of condolence, but her British reserve crumbled, her tears began to flow, and by the time she reached John, she grabbed his arms for support and sobbed on his shoulder.

Canon Mathiesen, the rector of St. Philips, motioned to Cooper that it was time to lead the procession to the grave. He lifted the cross, as he had done on a hundred Sunday mornings. But this time there was no music and no singing, just the sound of gravel underfoot and the muffled sobs and sniffles of those who followed. Cooper recalled the question posed by the Lutheran pastor less than an hour before: "Where was God when the only son of this family was killed?" The pastor tried to explain that God was present, even as he had been there when his only son was killed and that from the standpoint of the Heavenly Father, "It is not the end but the beginning." Cooper wished he could believe that.

He stood at the head of the casket with Canon Mathiesen. The Goetz name was engraved in bold letters on the polished marble, which marked the spot where Grandma Goetz had been buried just before the war in Europe ended, in the spring of

1945. The bronze casket rested on leather straps that crossed the opening of the grave. Pops, Uncle Jack and Aunt Ellen, Aunt Ellen's parents, and Cooper's mother and his sisters were seated in metal folding chairs under a canopy.

Canon Mathiesen recited, "In sure and certain hope of the Resurrection to eternal life through our Lord Jesus Christ, we commend to Almighty God our brother John Charles Goetz the third, and we commit his body to the ground; earth to earth, ashes to ashes, dust to dust. The Lord bless him and keep him."

When he had finished, Canon Mathiesen took off his white stole, kissed the cross at the neck band, and approached the family. Pops stood up and placed a fishing pole on the coffin. Uncle Jack followed with a putter, and the captain of the ball team added a baseball mitt. Then a young woman with curly red hair, who no one seemed to know, wedged her way through the crowd from the back and placed a rose on Guts' coffin.

Part of Cooper had detached himself and was sitting in a tree, watching what was going on, but the part that was on the ground clutched at the cross and convulsed in tears.

THE END

OTHER BOOKS BY BOB LIBBY

The Forgivenew Book

Grace Happens

Coming to Faith